BROKEN LIES

BOOKS BY RACHEL BRANTON

Finding Home Series
Take Me Home
All That I Love
Then I Found You

Lily's House Series
House Without Lies
Tell Me No Lies
Your Eyes Don't Lie
Hearts Never Lie
Broken Lies
Cowboys Can't Lie

Noble Hearts
Royal Quest
Royal Dance

Picture Books
I Don't Want To Eat
Bugs
I Don't Want to Have
Hot Toes

UNDER THE NAME TEYLA BRANTON

Unbounded Series
The Change
The Cure
The Escape
The Reckoning
The Takeover

Unbounded Novellas
Ava's Revenge
Mortal Brother
Lethal Engagement
Set Ablaze

Imprints Series
Touch of Rain
On The Hunt
Upstaged
Under Fire
Blinded

Colony Six Series
Sketches

Other
Times Nine

BROKEN LIES

RACHEL BRANTON

WHITE
STAR
PRESS

This is a work of fiction, and the views expressed herein are the sole responsibility of the author. Likewise, certain characters, places, and incidents are the product of the author's imagination, and any resemblance to actual persons, living or dead, or actual events or locales, is entirely coincidental.

Broken Lies (Lily's House Book 5)

Published by White Star Press
P.O. Box 353
American Fork, Utah 84003

Printed in the United States of America
ISBN: 978-1-939203-81-6
Year of first printing: 2017

For my new little granddaughter, Rachel.

I nviting Vaughn Abrams to the wedding probably wasn't one of Saffron Brenwood's best ideas. He'd been looking at her with *that* expression all evening, the one that hinted at an impending conversation about their future, a conversation she knew she wouldn't enjoy. She hoped it was only her imagination because he was a lot of fun, and everyone said they made a striking couple with their fair skin and matching blond hair. Breaking up with him would be harder than it had been with most of her boyfriends.

She sat at the bridesmaids table with two of her foster sisters, Halla and Elsie, their dates having gone for drinks. Saffron's feet were a little sore from dancing, and the floor was a bit too crowded now for real fun, but she'd get in a few more songs before the night was over.

"So," Halla said to Saffron, "how long have you been dating Vaughn?" Halla's blue eyes looked huge and eager in her narrow face.

Saffron lifted one shoulder in a half shrug. "Three months."

Halla gaped. "That's got to be some kind of record, right?"

"Maybe." It was exactly a month longer than Saffron had dated anyone in over eight and a half years since leaving her parents' home. She'd known Vaughn for a year before they started dating, though, and that was also different and maybe why he'd lasted so long. It helped that they shared a lot of the same interests, like hiking, river rafting, visiting second-hand stores, and hanging out with her foster sisters.

"Does this mean . . ." Elsie began, pushing back a dark lock that had escaped her carefully upswept hairdo.

Saffron glanced over to where Vaughn stood in line at the bar, getting drinks with Elsie's date. He met her gaze at that moment and shot her a smile before turning back to his conversation.

"Of course not," Halla answered for Saffron. "I knew the minute they started dating that he wouldn't last. Just like all the others. It's too bad, though. I like him."

Something inside Saffron's chest shifted, but she forced a convincing smile. "You do know me." Even back when they had all still lived at Lily's House as foster sisters, Saffron had been changing boyfriends as often as she bought a new pair of jeans.

"Oh, man," Elsie said. "I really thought this one would stick."

Halla gave an unladylike snort, which seemed out of place with the elegant blue bridesmaid dresses they were wearing. "Not a chance."

Saffron looked away from the table to the dance floor, where two more of their foster sisters, Ruth and Bianca, were dancing with their fiancés. She suddenly wished she were with them, sore feet or no. Zoey and her new husband, Declan, were also dancing, staring into each other's eyes as if no one else existed. Saffron was happy for them, but why did seeing them that way suddenly make her feel alone?

"Oh, no," Halla moaned, bringing Saffron's attention back to the table. "He got the wrong drink. Again."

Saffron's gaze shifted to Halla's tall, too-thin date, who was approaching the table. Halla was a good two feet shorter than he was, even in heels and with her short hair spiked an inch. The difference had made dancing all night a challenge, but the real problem for Halla was his lack of memory. He'd left for drinks long before the other men, but Halla had already sent him back once.

"I'd better go with him this time, even if that line is long. It's better than trying to dance." She rolled her eyes and jumped up to meet him, striding as if she were wearing her normal camouflage pants and boots instead of a bridesmaid's dress and heels. There had been some doubt that she'd wear the dress at all. But Zoey was the first of the original six Lily's House foster girls to be married, and they were sisters at heart, if not by blood, and not even Halla could let Zoey down.

"So are you going to break up with him?" Elsie asked, bringing Saffron's attention back to her. "I hope not. You seem so happy lately, and you deserve to be happy."

Saffron's smile came easier this time. "There's really nothing to break up. We're just dating. Besides, I have time. I'm only twenty-five."

Elsie nodded and kindly didn't point out that Zoey was younger than she was, and so were Ruth and Bianca, who had both become engaged this week. But Saffron saw the thoughts in her face and put her hand over Elsie's where it lay on the table. At nineteen, Elsie was the youngest and most romantic of the six sisters. "Don't worry about it. I'm fine."

"But why?" Elsie asked. "What happened to you before you came to live with Lily? You never talk about it. Is that why you always dump even the good guys?"

For an instant, Saffron couldn't breathe. Pressure started in her chest, splitting into a deep chasm of nothingness. Only Lily knew the secret of her past. Saffron had been the first underage girl Lily had helped after finding her passed out on a bench, and by the time Lily had taken in the other girls, Saffron had become good at denial. Lily had saved her life, and Saffron had gone on from her mistakes, but in some very real ways, Saffron felt as if her life hadn't moved on since that day, as if her emotions were forever frozen by what had happened to bring her to that point.

"I'm sorry," Elsie said. "You don't have to tell me."

Movements in Saffron's peripheral vision sent relief flooding through her. "Oh, look, here come our dates."

Vaughn was in the lead, a smile on his face. "Sorry we took so long. There was a line."

A slow song began as he set her drink in front of her. "Hey, let's dance," she said, popping up from her chair. Dancing would drive the memories away.

Vaughn sipped his drink before placing it on the table. "Sure."

"We'll see you in a minute," Saffron said to the others. She felt Elsie's eyes on her as she escaped to the dance floor.

Vaughn put his arms around her, and she leaned closer, loving the feel of his body so close to hers. She'd loved the attraction between them from the first moment they'd met at the end of last summer when he'd been the guide on a river rafting trip she'd gone on with friends.

They'd flirted probably more than they should have, and he'd asked for her phone number after the river trip. But she was a week into a new relationship, and she'd had to turn him down. Even after she'd said no, he'd helped her get a job at his cousin's sports store, where he was managing their rafting business on the side. She learned he had recently left his job of five years as an animator at Datatoon Studios in California and was now in Phoenix preparing to teach animation at a local university.

During the months that followed, they'd often run into each other at the store, gone out with the same group of friends, or talked on Facebook. Yet it wasn't until this summer, when they were both between relationships, that they'd gone on another river run together. He'd kissed her afterward, and that was all it had taken.

She almost wished she didn't like him as well as she did, but he hadn't pushed for commitment as hard as her past dates, so maybe they could go out another month or two before it had to end.

She snuggled her face into his neck. "Hmm," she murmured, breathing in his aftershave.

He drew back. "What?"

"You smell good."

He laughed, a contented sound that made her smile. "You say that every time I wear this aftershave."

"Ah, that explains why you wear it so much."

He laughed again, his arms tightening around her as the slow dance wound to an end. His face bent toward her, and his lips brushed hers with a kiss that was more promise than substance. Even so, it sent her heartbeat racing. When they stepped apart, his hands enfolded hers. "Can you come out on the balcony with me for a moment? We need to talk."

A sinking feeling in Saffron's chest warned her to say no. "I need to see Zoey off with the others."

"I don't think they're leaving yet. Look, Declan's talking with the DJ now. He must be asking for another song."

"Oh. All right then."

Vaughn pulled her gently in the direction of the deserted balcony. The late September evening felt too hot to Saffron, even in her short-sleeved dress, but that was probably due to the erratic pounding of her heart.

"Look," he started. "This might not be the best time, but I've been trying for—"

She stretched up to kiss him under the moonlight. He kissed her back, and for a moment she forgot her worry. This was something they did really well. In fact, making out with him was better than it had been with anyone else. She might be able to avoid this talk altogether if they kissed long enough.

Too soon, Vaughn pulled away. He was probably frustrated, like the others before him had been, at the slowness of their physical progress. Saffron always broke up with men before hitting the bedroom. Always. Before any real commitment. It was what she had to do to survive the losses that still haunted her.

"Saffron," he said, "these past three months—no really, this past year that we've been friends—I want you to know it's been good. Especially all the time we spent together this summer."

Oh, no, here it comes, she thought. A proclamation of love, after which he'd ask her to be his exclusive girlfriend, or even to marry him.

"It's been fun," she agreed, keeping her voice light. She didn't want to hurt him.

He fell silent for a moment, his blue eyes searching hers. "You are an amazing woman. Beautiful, smart, fun, sexy." He paused, swallowing hard. "I love being with you. And if I thought I had any chance with you, I'd follow you to the ends of the earth."

This was different from the normal approach. "Uh, thank you?"

He gave a soft laugh that held no real mirth. "I mean it. But I'd be blind not to see that you aren't as invested in me as I am in you."

"I love being with you," she protested. "I'm just not ready—"

"For anything more. I know." He nodded, giving her a gentle smile. "You've been up front about that from the beginning. But I do want more. I'm ready to move on to the next part of my life. That includes a family, children. I've loved teaching, and I plan to finish out this second year, but after that I might be going back into animation full time. Last week, Datatoon made me a substantial offer to head up one of their game design teams, and I'm considering it."

"That's great," she said. It didn't feel great, though. It felt horrible. "Why didn't you tell me?"

"You've had a lot on your mind, and I wasn't even sure I was going to consider it. I know how you love being close to—" He shook his head. "It doesn't matter. Like I said, I'm not sure what this year will bring, and I don't have to give them an answer right away. But in the end, that has nothing to do with what's going on between us."

"And what is that?" Saffron barely choked out the words.

"Nothing." As her eyes widened, he hurried to add, "Not that I don't want it to, but there's a part of you I can't reach, and I don't know how to." His forehead furrowed, and his eyes held a deep sadness that echoed in her stomach.

"Are you breaking up with me because I won't sleep with you?" She felt more hurt than angry at the idea. It was something she understood at least.

"Of course not." He ran a hand through his hair, pacing two steps away and then back again. "Before we got together, I watched you go through six boyfriends in less than a year. I'm happy you weren't sleeping with them. Believe me. I also know that though you didn't agree to see them exclusively, you didn't date others at the same time. One proposed, one invited you to meet his parents, and one asked you to move in with him—and in each case, less than a week later, you were dating someone else."

What could she say? He was right about all of it, except that there had been another proposal and two of her dates had called her frigid for refusing to sleep with them.

"And every time," he continued, "I could always tell when you were getting ready to cut them loose." He paused, holding her gaze as he finished. "Well, you don't have to cut me loose, because I already know."

"But . . ." She'd known it was ending too, so why did Vaughn's dumping her hurt this much?

"Saffron." He took her hands. "I don't know what happened to you. I wish I did. I thought I could be the one you would trust enough to let through."

Moisture glittered in his eyes, and she should feel some satisfaction that he was hurting too, but she didn't. Not even a tiny bit. She only felt exposed, vulnerable. He'd discovered the truth—that something was broken inside her. Something that made it so she could never love anyone the way she had once loved a boy named Tyson.

"Am I wrong?" he asked.

It took every bit of strength inside her to say, "No."

Vaughn squeezed her hands before bringing them to his lips to kiss. "If that ever changes, I'd love to know. Because I think we could have something great here."

Slowly, he released her, his eyes roaming her face as he backed toward the door. Waiting? If she flung herself at him, would he stay? She suspected he would, because he was that kind of man. But it would only delay the inevitable, and she cared about him enough not to lead him on. She wished she could give him what he wanted. She'd wished that more than once with other men over the past eight years, but tonight the feeling was different, as if a piece of the wall around her heart were breaking.

"I'll take off now," he said, thumbing over his shoulder. "Unless you want me to stay."

She'd had to be here earlier for photographs, so they had separate cars, which worked out well for this moment. Maybe that's why he'd planned their breakup in a public place where there wouldn't be a scene. As if she'd allow herself any kind of a scene.

"Goodbye, Vaughn," she said quietly.

He nodded, his face tightening momentarily in the way it always did when he tried to hide any emotion. "Goodbye, Saffron."

Only when he was gone did she turn to the railing and let a few tears escape. Maybe if she hadn't brought him here tonight as her date, he wouldn't have realized what they were missing. It was hard not to see the love in Zoey and Declan's eyes as they'd exchanged their vows.

"Saffron!" Halla called from behind her. "Hurry! Zoey's gathering her things to leave. We have to get things ready."

Saffron hastily wiped the tears from her cheeks, took a deep breath, and forced a smile as she turned to her foster sister. "Great. This'll be fun."

Halla stared at her. "What happened? Wait, did you just break up with him? Here? It couldn't wait one night? Seriously?"

"No, *he* broke up with me." Despite her control, her voice wavered. Saffron bit her lip to stop herself from saying any more.

"Oh, that jerk!" Halla rushed to her and gave her a hug.

"Not a jerk. He just knew it wasn't going anywhere." Instead of feeling better at Halla's support, Saffron felt worse. "What's wrong with me? Why can't I forget him and go on?"

Halla drew back. "Forget who? Because I know you don't mean Vaughn." Her eyes invited more.

"It doesn't matter," Saffron mumbled. "Maybe I'm always going to be alone." If anyone but Halla had come to get her, she would have bitten back the words. The other girls still had romantic dreams, but Halla was down to earth. She wouldn't try to convince Saffron that it was all in her imagination, or that real love was just around the corner.

"Because even when I'm with someone," Saffron added,

"I'm really still alone." A familiar numbness was spreading inside her, and Saffron welcomed the feeling. At least there would be no more tears.

"Maybe it's time to find out why," Halla said. "Maybe you need to face this head on like Zoey did when she testified against her uncle in court. Whatever it is that's bothering you might look different if you face it down. And if you need a listening ear, you know I'm always here."

Saffron nodded, tempted for the first time to confide in someone besides Lily. Halla, who'd had to escape her house through an upstairs window to get away from an abusive and controlling father, had a clear grasp on how some parents didn't do what was right for their children. She'd understand.

Elsie appeared in the doorway. "Hurry, you guys! You're missing it."

Saffron and Halla followed her back into the reception center and out to the front, where people were forming two lines. As Zoey and Declan, the new Mr. and Mrs. Walker, ran past them in a deluge of dried flower petals, Saffron cheered with the others. At least on the outside.

On the inside, her mind was churning. She'd assumed that one day she'd meet someone who would make her past disappear, but maybe she'd been going about this all wrong. Halla might be right that she needed to face the past, go back to where it all began. The idea of returning to Temecula was like a dead space inside her, but she needed to know. She'd recently connected with her younger sister on Facebook, and she did want to see her. Not so much her parents, and especially their mother.

And Tyson. The black hole growing inside seemed big

enough to consume her now. Maybe confronting him—wherever he was—would be cathartic. If she could find him. Eight and a half years had passed after all.

She watched Zoey climb into Declan's truck, which was decorated with balloons and streamers. She looked so happy, nothing like the terror-stricken young woman who'd been called to testify in court a few years ago.

"Okay," Lily shouted. "Let's pack up their gifts and get out of here."

Dutifully, Saffron helped load gifts into the waiting cars. Then she drove her blue Hyundai Elantra to help unload the gifts at Lily's House where they would be stored until Zoey and Declan returned from their honeymoon.

Saffron always loved coming to Lily's House. It was home, the place where she and her fosters sisters had all finished growing up after running away or having been abandoned by their own families. Even as adults, Saffron and the others turned to Lily like a mother, though she was only four years older than Saffron.

One by one, Saffron's foster sisters left with their dates, and Lily's current foster girls went to bed. Mario, Lily's husband, took their sleepy boys upstairs to tuck in. When they were all gone, Lily, with her ten-month-old asleep in her arms, pinned Saffron with her knowing stare. "Stay for some herbal tea?"

"Yeah, thanks." Saffron didn't want to go home to the apartment she'd finally been able to afford on her own. She would have to gather up everything that reminded her of Vaughn and either send it to him or throw it away. Facing that right now made her want to give in to the tears pressing at her eyes.

In the kitchen, Lily laid baby Cherie in Saffron's arms. "If you'll just hold her while I make the tea."

How did Lily always seem to know what she needed? Saffron willingly held Cherie to her chest, feeling the little body settle into hers, hearing her tiny breaths. Holding Cherie, and Lily's boys before her, had always been a balm to Saffron's soul. But it also hurt as her mind invariably wandered to what might have been.

Lily hummed as she put cups of water into the microwave. Two minutes later, she brought the water over with several boxes of herbal tea on a tray. Saffron wasn't ready to give up the baby yet, so she just pointed to the apple spice tea and let Lily put a bag into her cup.

"So," Lily began as the tea steeped. "Do you want to talk about it?"

"It's just . . . all of the girls are going on with their lives, but I only pretend. You know what I mean, right? I've dated a lot of wonderful guys, but the minute they want more commitment than a few kisses or a fun date, I end things."

Lily nodded. "It's something I've worried about the past few years. Why do you think you do that?"

Saffron let out a long sigh. "I don't know. No, that's not quite true. I think I'm still in love with Tyson." She paused, grateful that Lily didn't rush in with any words. "I've tried not to love him. I mean I was only a kid when it all happened. How could love at that age be real? And yet when I think about a future, about a family, it's only him I see." Now her tears came, tears for herself, tears for Tyson, tears even for Vaughn, who'd never had a chance.

"And I'm still so angry at my mother for throwing me out," she continued. "Abandoning me when I needed her most. If she'd only stood by me, maybe . . ." Maybe things would be different. She and Tyson might be together. She might be in a house where their sons slept upstairs and it might be their baby lying in her arms right now.

"The maybes are the hardest part," Lily agreed. She began removing the bobby pins that held her blond hair up in a twist.

The fact that Lily didn't come right out with a list of options told Saffron Lily knew exactly what she should do, but it was something hard, something that needed to be her choice. She'd seen Lily, who was a fountain of wisdom, counsel dozens of foster girls who had gone through her house in exactly the same way.

"Are you managing me?" Saffron asked, attempting a smile.

Lily laid another bobby pin on her growing pile and chuckled softly. "I was only twenty-one when you came to live with me. Remember how we hid you in my room at college?"

"Oh, yeah." In the beginning, Saffron had done nothing but lie in Lily's bed, trying to recover from severe malnutrition and the endless heartbreak.

"The point is that we've been friends a long time," Lily said. "It's not managing. It's trying to help a friend decide what she should do. But I think you're right that you're stalled emotionally, and it breaks my heart." Lily teared up and it took a moment for her to recover and begin speaking again. "Remember when we moved in here, and we told you that even if you helped out with the house payment, you couldn't have boys sleep over? And you said—"

"If I ever find a boy worthy of sleeping over, I'd probably

marry him. But don't hold your breath because I was sure he didn't exist." Saffron sighed. "Oh, yeah. I remember. The girls still tease me about it."

"At first I thought you wanted to avoid getting hurt again, but for a long time now, I've known it's something more. Because there have been a few guys I thought you might fall for, and Vaughn is probably the best of them all."

Saffron blinked and another tear escaped her eye. "What I felt for Tyson . . . I thought it would go away. That I'd wake up one day and it would be gone, but it hasn't changed at all." She took a deep, shuddering breath. "I think . . . I think it's time. I think I have to go back. I need to find him. I want to know why he never looked for me."

"Maybe he didn't know where to look."

Saffron had told herself this over the years, but it still hurt that Tyson hadn't come after her. He had to know something was up when she disappeared. Instead, he'd left her all alone to deal with the consequences of their love. The horrible, heartrending consequences that still made her cry when she was alone.

"Maybe," Saffron allowed. She could at least listen to his reasons—if he cared enough to share them.

"It'll be good to see your sister," Lily added.

"It will." Kendall had only been ten when Saffron had to leave. That day, as she'd thrown a few things into her backpack, Kendall had begged her not to go, and their mother had come in and ordered Kendall away. Saffron hadn't been allowed to say goodbye.

For years, the idea of Saffron's old life in Temecula had felt more like a vivid dream than reality. Kendall was certainly less a sister than the foster sisters who had been her family over the past eight years since Lily had found her. Even her days with Tyson and how much they'd been in love was like a life lived by someone else.

Only the way it had ended, that night with blood everywhere, stayed with her as if it had been yesterday.

This summer after she'd started dating Vaughn, for reasons she couldn't pinpoint, her thoughts had been continually drawn to her sister. Maybe because Vaughn was always talking about his younger sister, or maybe because Saffron was seeing less of her foster sisters. She'd looked for Kendall, found her on Facebook, and sent her a message, letting her know the name she was using now and telling her she was in Phoenix. Almost immediately, Kendall had begun asking to see her. Saffron had avoided the request so far, partly because Kendall was still living with their parents in Temecula, but also partly because the memories were too painful.

"Actually, I've been meaning to talk to you about Kendall," Saffron said. "I think something is wrong with her. But she won't say what."

Lily set down her tea. "Well, she is living in the same house you haven't been able to return to in eight and a half years. I mean, people can change, but maybe it's not easy for her there. She might see you as a way out."

Saffron sniffed hard, fighting more tears. "I know. And if she needs help, I should give it to her. I'm definitely going back. Even if it ends up being just for her and I don't find Tyson at all."

Lily's smile was gentle. "Then maybe it's time I returned something to you." She rose and leaned down to take the baby from her arms. "And this one, I'll go tuck in with her daddy."

Reluctantly, Saffron relinquished the warm bundle to Lily. The baby had steadied her, had given her the human connection she'd so desperately needed after this terrible evening.

Lily returned in minutes with a small white jewelry box that Saffron recognized immediately. Her heartbeat thundered inside her chest. She knew too well what was inside, and she accepted the box without opening it. As she did, Lily's hands closed around hers, holding her fast and staring into her eyes.

"Saffron, you can do this. But if you need anything from me, I'm here." Lily released her and stepped back.

"You always have been." Saffron stood, clutching the little box. "I'd better get home."

Lily nodded and walked with her to the door. She stood there, framed by the light until Saffron placed the little jewelry box next to her purse on the passenger seat and drove away.

Was she really going back to California? Yes, she needed to or nights like this one would forever be in her future, with good men like Vaughn walking away because she couldn't love them. Or breaking up with a man she liked because she couldn't commit. Another tear skidded down her cheek.

In her room at her apartment, she sat on the bed to slip off her heels and automatically checked her phone, which she'd silenced during the wedding ceremony and had neglected to turn back on. There had been two calls from Vaughn. Her heart leapt. Maybe he'd reconsidered.

But the text message he'd also sent destroyed the hope: *Just checking to make sure you're okay. I understand if you don't want to talk to me. I'm really sorry. I wish things could be different, but I hope we're still friends.*

Maybe he would have been the one to finally heal her heart, but now she would never know. *He* would never know. "You tried only three months," she whispered, deleting the text. "Your loss." But the words were a waste because she didn't know if even three *years* would have been enough time.

Beside her on the bed, the jewelry box beckoned with a temptation she'd never been able to resist. That was why she'd placed it in Lily's safe-keeping soon after she'd gone to live with her. Lily kept two locked boxes in her closet for that explicit purpose—to store the girls' special treasures or important documents. Unlike the others who'd gone through Lily's House, Saffron had never asked for it back.

Inside was a folded piece of paper, a small, pale blue shirt, and two pictures of the sweetest angel in the world. She held the shirt to her face, breathing in the smell that wasn't there any longer but that her memory filled in. One of the pictures was a close-up of a baby wearing the shirt, his eyes shut, as if asleep. The other picture was of her holding his tiny form, gazing down on him with bewildered tears in her eyes.

Next, she unfolded the paper, though she already knew what the birth certificate said: Tyson Dekker Junior, son of Rosalyn Brenwood and Tyson Dekker.

Rosalyn. A name she hadn't answered to in so long that she felt it belonged to someone else. For endless moments, she sat there, holding her treasures, eyes tightly shut.

When at long last the brutal ache began to ebb, she replaced the items inside the jewelry box, set it in the top drawer of her nightstand, and pulled out her suitcase.

She was going to find Tyson—and face her family. It was the only way.

2

When Vaughn fell out of bed Saturday morning, he felt as if he hadn't slept at all. His eyes were gritty and his stomach was sour. Worse, all he wanted to do was throw himself into his car and drive to Saffron's apartment. He couldn't get those last minutes with her out of his mind. The quiet way she'd said goodbye—all the while looking as if he'd betrayed her.

Maybe he had.

But was he supposed to just wait around until she dumped him? All the signs were there. The change of subject when he wanted to make plans for next year, her refusal to go to his parents' house or to attend family events, the way she went quiet when he mentioned children or asked about her family. It was insane. Women were supposed to want commitment, weren't they? They were supposed to want to get married. His sister had talked about nothing else before she found her husband, and all of Saffron's sisters—her fosters sisters—talked about getting married. Saffron was the only one who never joined in those conversations.

Often when Vaughn and Saffron were together with her sisters, she'd stare off into the distance, tuning everyone out when the conversations took a serious note. Every time it happened, her sisters had cast him pitying looks. Maybe if he didn't love her so much, he could have stayed until she broke up with him. Instead, he'd hoped to shake things up, to give them a chance to become a real couple. Maybe the wedding reception hadn't been the best place to break up, but he'd wanted to make sure she had people around her. Support. In case she did care about him the way he wanted her to.

Running a hand through his hair, he paced the kitchen in his apartment. He stubbed his toe against the island and welcomed the pain. What had happened to Saffron? On the surface, she was everything he'd ever dreamed of in a woman—competent, loving, creative, well-read, and smart. He was so attracted to her that he often planned dates with other couples so he wouldn't push her for a deeper relationship she apparently wasn't ready for. He could tell she cared about people, and she worked hard. He could imagine a future with her.

Yet there was a point he couldn't pass in their relationship. That no one could. He'd watched her with guy after guy, and he'd told himself when each relationship ended that it happened because they weren't right for her. And he *was* right—he'd known it since the day they'd first met. But she'd been dating someone else, and then when she was free, he'd been dating a woman, and by the time he'd even heard about her breakup, he was too late and she'd met someone new. There had been no time for them—until this summer.

For him, the past three months had been magic—except for the realization that Saffron wasn't going to let him in, not unless he did something drastic. So he had. And now he might have lost her forever.

Everywhere in his apartment he saw things that reminded him of Saffron. The picture of them he'd added to his river rafting memory wall, the new sofa she'd helped pick out, the blinds he'd bought to protect the rare moments they spent here alone. The little ceramic turtles and the plant she'd bought to brighten his apartment.

He just wanted her back.

Finally, he sat at his table, checking his phone again, though he knew there would be nothing there. *I hope we're still friends,* he'd texted last night. When he really wanted to say, *I don't know how I'll ever live without you.* Had he made his interest in her clear enough during their talk? She had hardly spoken.

Maybe he'd acted too soon. Maybe all she'd needed was time.

That's probably what all her other hundreds of boyfriends thought.

Near the beginning of their relationship, he'd attended a barbeque at Lily's House to welcome a new foster girl into their ever-growing family. At Lily's request, he'd gone inside the house for a kettle of freshly cooked corn on the cob and had heard a conversation between Saffron's foster sisters in the sitting room before he'd had a chance to make his presence known.

"How long do you think this one's going to last?" Halla had asked. "I think he's number fifty-two, or did I lose count?" The others laughed and called out anything from a few days to two months. Nothing beyond that.

"It's too bad," the curly-haired Elsie said. "I think he's perfect for Saffron."

A girl who was too young for Saffron to have ever lived with asked, "What's her story anyway? I haven't heard."

Knowing he shouldn't be listening but feeling compelled, Vaughn had walked closer to the doorway leading from the kitchen into the sitting room, hoping to learn more about Saffron. All the girls at Lily's House were there for a reason, both the girls placed by the state and the girls who simply showed up on Lily's porch. Abuse and neglect were the main reasons, but some had been orphaned, and maybe Saffron was one of these and that was why she never wanted to discuss family.

"The only thing we know," Halla said quietly, "is that her mother kicked her out. That's all she's ever said."

"I think her heart was broken." This from Elsie. "And it won't heal because she doesn't talk about it."

The moment had stayed with him, but at the time, he still believed he was different, that Saffron would open up to him. She hadn't, though, and maybe it was because of what he'd overheard that made him decide he couldn't be another notch on Saffron's belt. But already he missed her. He let his forehead drop to the table, bumping it a few times, as if to somehow numb the pain.

Maybe he should stop by her house this morning to see how she was doing. Her car had been emitting a whistling noise from the engine, and it definitely needed new brakes. Two days ago, she'd accepted his offer to help drop off her car at a repair shop, so he could at least let her know he was still willing to help. Besides, the plan wasn't to disappear out of her life completely. It was ultimately to fight for what he believed they could create together.

That meant he wasn't giving up. Not yet.

A banging on her door pulled Saffron from a restless sleep. She sat up, looking around her in confusion. Why was her nearly full suitcase on the floor? And why was she still in her bridesmaid dress?

Slowly, memory returned. That's right, she was going home. No, not home, but back *there*. Back to the place she'd sworn never to return. She was going to find answers. Maybe she'd find a miracle.

She stumbled over the heels she'd worn last night on her way to answer the door. Her mouth felt gummy and her nose clogged, though she didn't remember crying after leaving Lily's. Long strands of blond hair fell down one side of her face, and more was coming loose by the second. She didn't want to know what her eyes must look like.

Well, it would only be one of her sisters that Lily had sent to check up on her, or Lily herself. How many times had she appeared on one of her sister's doorsteps after a call from Lily? She couldn't remember how many times, but more than she could count on both hands.

More banging. "Just a minute," she called, darting into the bathroom. She had marks on her face from sleeping weird, mascara ringed her eyes, and her hair was a disaster. It didn't matter. She splashed a little water on her face to help her wake up. Then, yanking bobby pins out as she walked, Saffron hurried to the door and pulled it open. Halla and Elsie stood there.

"Good. I thought we'd have to use our backup key." Halla's eyes fell down her body. "You're still in that dress? How late did you stay at Lily's?"

"I was tired." Saffron moved back from the door and let them in.

"We brought treats." Elsie lifted a cloth bag. "They're from Ruth. She made them especially for you this morning when we told her what happened."

Saffron's mouth watered. She'd helped out enough at their sister's cafe to appreciate everything Ruth made. "What happened exactly?"

"You know, you getting dumped." Halla sauntered across the living room to the tiny counter that fit only two barstools. "It's a first for you."

Vaughn, Saffron thought, and sorrow hit her in the gut. Halla was wrong. She'd been left by a man before. Yes, she'd been the one to leave Temecula, but she'd given Tyson the opportunity to find her. She'd waited at a pay phone for two hours each day for a week before realizing he was never going to call.

Some of her expression must have shown on her face because Elsie hugged her. "I'm so sorry."

"The least he could have done was wait for you to break up with him," Halla said with a snort. "The jerk."

Elsie scowled in Halla's direction.

"What?" Halla said. "We all know where it was heading. Ask Saffron if you don't believe me."

Elsie ignored her. "Ruth would have come with us, but

she has to work, and Bianca's gone with Stephen to move her stuff back to Phoenix now that Zoey's married."

Saffron somehow managed to smile past the grief she was feeling. All these years, she'd believed she was over Tyson, and now she felt desperate to see him. As if the haze that had protected her from memories of him were peeling away.

"I'll just get changed," Saffron said. "Can you un-zip me?"

"Is that why you didn't change?" Halla said. "You really should move back in with us when Ruth gets married."

"I can reach it fine." Saffron said. "But it's easier if you do it. I'll be right back."

She'd wanted an apartment alone because she had all her jewelry equipment spread out on two long folding tables in her living room. The apartment doubled as her factory and store. Between her online income and the boutiques that bought from her, she could finally, after four years, pay all her bills with her jewelry income. She still worked at the sports store only because she liked the social aspect and the extra income. It was also a great place to meet guys.

Again the wave of grief. She didn't care if she ever dated again. She wanted to find Tyson. But find him to . . . what? Confront him? To see if he still had feelings for her? To tell him about the horrors she'd endured alone? Even thinking about it made her want to stay in her safe apartment, but if she didn't face the past—face him—she would never understand what happened, and maybe she'd never be able to move forward.

Last night Vaughn said he wanted children. Did she?

She didn't even know because it hurt too much to think about her son.

She dressed in black jean shorts and the first black T-shirt that came to hand. It was too big for her, and might not even be clean, but it fit her mood. In the bathroom, she put lotion on a cotton swab and cleaned up most of the black under her eyes. That would have to do.

When she returned to her kitchen, the girls had set out a nice spread of pastries, coffee, and hot chocolate. They'd also taken the third stool she kept in the closet and placed it on the other side of the counter. Halla already perched there, sitting sideways on the stool because her knees hit the cupboards.

"Hmm, looks great." Saffron sat next to Elsie and grabbed an eclair, sinking her teeth into it, and then taking another bite before swallowing the first. "You brought so many."

"Because it's a pity-party," Halla said. "You know the rules. Even if we never held one for you, you've participated in at least a few."

"Oh, yeah. Where we eat ourselves sick and then spend the next two weeks regretting it."

"Yep, that." Halla bit down on a blueberry turnover. "But you sure feel good while you're doing it."

Saffron grabbed a raspberry cheese pocket and a Portuguese mil-folhas that was Ruth's specialty and put them on her plate. She was feeling better already. "So you didn't come because Lily called?"

Halla and Elsie shared a look. "Well, that too," Halla answered. "But we were coming anyway. You should taste this." She broke off a piece of her turnover and handed it to Saffron.

"Mmm, good." Saffron chewed, reveling at the sweet taste. What a great idea. A pity party was exactly what she needed.

"Lily said you were going somewhere," Elsie said. "Where?"

"Home." Saffron said, the words muffled with her next mouthful.

Halla set down her pastry. "Home?"

"Well, not really home, but to Temecula. I'm going to see my sister." Saffron's fingers dug into her pastry as she clutched it a little too tightly.

"You have a sister?" Elsie asked as Halla just stared.

"Yes, her name's Kendall." The words were difficult to get out. "She was ten, I think, when my mother kicked me out."

Elsie's brown eyes grew wider. "But you were only sixteen. What happened?"

Saffron dropped her pastry and wiped her fingers with a napkin. It would be so easy to say nothing, to decide to stay here and not face the past. But the memory of Vaughn's eyes as he asked her if he was wrong about them forced her to be truthful.

"I fell in love and got pregnant. I think I still love him, and that's why I'm broken inside. So I've decided to go find him."

Halla shoved another pastry her way. "Eat that and then tell us everything."

The first time Saffron met Tyson Dekker had been in kindergarten when she accidentally butted in line without realizing it. One of the kids complained, but Tyson just rolled his eyes and said, "Who cares? What's it matter? Just ignore her."

At first she'd been offended, until a few days later it happened again, and she realized it was his way of telling the other kids it wasn't important who lined up when and to forget it. A week later, she was late to get in line again, and he said, "You can get in front of me."

From that moment, she was in love.

As far as crushes went, it wasn't epic. From kindergarten through third grade, she'd occasionally share her treats with him, and he'd stick up for her if anyone teased. They were in different classes in fourth and fifth grades, and they attended separate middle schools, but in the ninth grade they ran into each other again. His carefully combed dark hair had become artfully messy, and they were no longer the same height. He took one look at her and left his group of friends.

"Hey, want to butt in line?" he'd asked. His eyes seemed to drink her in.

"Absolutely."

And just like that, they fell in love. They met at school events, held hands in the hallways, and kissed in the bleachers at football games. The only thing they didn't do was go to each other's houses because Saffron's mother didn't approve of her dating so young, and especially dating a boy whose family didn't have their economic advantages. Tyson's family was equally unwelcoming. He came from a military family—or had been before his dad was injured in a mine explosion—and they had plans for their only son that didn't include a woman until much later in his life.

Maybe because they were welcome at neither house they'd clung to each other that much more tightly. By sixteen at the beginning of their junior year, they were planning to marry. Three months before the end of their junior year, she found out she was pregnant.

Her world exploded.

"So you never got to tell him about the baby?" Elsie asked. Tears wet her cheeks, though Saffron herself was dry-eyed after her story, as if the numbness had returned right when she needed it.

"Not after I took the test," Saffron said, "but he was with me when I bought it. He knew my period was late."

"He doesn't seem to be on social media," Halla said, looking at her phone. "Unless this guy is him?" She turned it around to show the Facebook image of a man who looked at least ten years older than Saffron.

Saffron shook her head. "No. But that doesn't surprise me. He was more the type to call up friends instead of interacting online." Saffron used social media herself mostly to interact with her jewelry group where she posted her latest creations for her regular customers. "I know where he lived in Temecula," she said. "I'll just start there."

"Ooh, it's so romantic," Elsie said with a little sigh. "You going to look for him, I mean. I bet you'll fall head over heels in love again."

Halla scowled. "But he didn't come after you, right? So

maybe he's a jerk. And what are you going to tell him about the baby?"

Saffron stuffed another bite of pastry into her mouth to avoid answering. She'd told them the truth about Tyson Junior, but she didn't want to think about what to tell his father.

Elsie shot Halla an evil stare across the countertop. "This is a good thing. No matter what happens." She put an arm around Saffron. "Don't listen to her. Love like that doesn't die."

Which was exactly why Saffron had to look for him.

"I don't suppose he has the same number after all these years," Halla said.

"No. I called it back then and it had been disconnected." Saffron didn't have the same number either, but that was only because her mother had confiscated it when she'd found her heaving into the bathroom toilet.

"Something must have happened to him," Elsie mused.

Saffron's mind had played all too often with that scenario. She'd left him the message to call her at the payphone before his phone was disconnected, but maybe he'd become deathly ill and hadn't been able to return her call. Maybe he'd lost the phone and had to get a new one so he never got the message at all. But her more practical side said her mother was somehow involved in turning him against her. What had Veronica Brenwood been able to say to make him stop loving her? It wasn't pleasant to think about.

"Saffron, the *door!*" Halla's aggrieved tone told her it wasn't the first time she'd said the words.

"I'll get it." Elsie slipped off her chair.

"You expecting someone?" Halla asked.

"No." If it had been any other Saturday when she didn't work at the sports store, she'd have expected Vaughn. Today would have been a lazy movie-streaming kind of day together if they hadn't broken up.

"If it's a salesman," Halla called after Elsie, who was almost to the door, "tell him to get lost. The same if it's one of Saffron's many admirers. Men aren't allowed at pity parties, not when they're the reason they exist in the first place."

Elsie snorted a laugh. "Will do."

What would she and Vaughn have watched? Saffron wondered, her thoughts still on the day she might have had. Of course now she'd have to start avoiding him. Her job at the sports store was going to be awful, but maybe she could make sure to work on weekdays, when he was teaching classes and wouldn't run into her.

"Are you okay?" With a concerned face, Halla pushed another pastry across the counter.

Saffron looked down at her full plate. "I was just thinking I need to take off work at the store if I'm going to California. I hope I can get someone to work for me. It's late notice."

"You will, or you'll quit." Halla looked determined. "It's not that great of a job. They don't pay well, and this is your life we're talking about."

"I would hate leaving them short-handed."

The idea of quitting, however, was appealing. No chance of running into Vaughn. After her obligations there were through, quitting would also give her time to expand her business. If she started working at a boutique instead, she might have more sales in the long run. She'd find plenty of ways to meet new guys besides the sports store. Or better yet, she'd give up men altogether. She stuffed a bit of rasp-berry cheese pocket into her mouth.

"I can't believe you have a sister," Halla murmured. "How do you feel about that? I mean, I totally understand why you haven't been in contact, but now that she's an adult, it's the right thing to do."

"I'm not sure how I feel about her yet, but I hope she's okay."

Halla made a face. "It was probably better for your sister than for you. She was all they had left. They might have even looked for you."

"I doubt that." Saffron hoped life hadn't been unbear-able for her sister, that her mother had loosened up instead of cracking down, but Saffron was terrified that her leaving had made things worse. "The funny thing is that, yes, I know I wasn't the perfect kid, but I never did drugs, I didn't get drunk, and my grades were good. My room was even clean."

Halla folded her arms and studied her. "You are a bit of a neat freak, even with your jewelry parts."

"Probably thanks to my mother. But she didn't care about all the good things I was doing. She only cared about me going to the college she wanted and impressing her friends. At least that's the way it seemed to me. I mean, who points to the door and sends their pregnant sixteen-year-old out into the world alone?" Her voice hitched on the last words.

"No one," Halla agreed. "You know what? I should have brought more pastries. We don't need a pity party, we need a pity week. You've been through a lot."

Saffron managed a smile at that, though there was more

she hadn't told them. Talking about losing Tyson and her baby had been tough enough.

"What is taking Elsie so long?" Saffron glanced over to the door, where Elsie was talking to someone they couldn't see.

"More for us."

Saffron took another huge bite. "This was a good idea," she said, a bit of pastry falling to the countertop. "Oops."

Halla laughed and stuffed the rest of her pastry into her mouth. "New pity party rules," she said, her voice garbled. "You can only talk if your mouth is full."

"I like that idea," Saffron said. Only it came out more like "Oi wike dat idee." They both laughed.

"Uh Saffron?" Elsie called from the door. "Someone's here to see you."

Saffron crammed in more pastry. "Well, invite 'em in. We've got plenty, and what's a party without more people?"

"Huh?" Elsie said. "I can't understand you. Your mouth is full."

Saffron was about to explain when someone pushed past Elsie and came into the apartment. "She said for me to come in."

Saffron's smile vanished. It was Vaughn, looking as great as ever with his blond hair a bit tousled. His eyes riveted on Saffron. Hope flared through her, but anger followed just as quickly. He'd dumped her, and showing up here now took a lot of nerve.

Besides, she didn't want him anymore. She was going to find Tyson, the father of her baby, the love of her life, and whatever came of that had nothing to do with Vaughn. If he was here to ask for forgiveness, he was too late. It was over between them as she'd always known it would be.

3

Vaughn probably shouldn't have given in to his urge to see Saffron this soon, but he had to make sure she was all right. Apparently she was—and having some kind of party. Through the crack in the door, he could see she looked good, if paler than usual, though maybe that was because of her black clothing. Was that a man's shirt she was wearing? It certainly wasn't one of his. Her hair was down in the way he loved it, glinting with golden highlights. He'd be lying if he didn't admit to himself that he was a little hurt at seeing her smiling when it felt to him as if his world had ended. But it also meant his decision to break up with her had been the right one.

"Well, come in, I guess," Elsie said, shutting the door behind him. "Even though you're already in, so inviting you is pointless."

With an apologetic smile in her direction, Vaughn walked across the carpet, feeling awkward. He hadn't expected her sisters to be here, though maybe that meant something he hadn't considered.

Some part of his mind registered the pastry-littered

countertop, but mostly he was looking at Saffron. Up closer, he could see that her cheeks were stained with tears and the slightest bit of dark makeup. Maybe she wasn't as okay with their breakup as he thought. Only her eyes weren't sad, they were angry and challenging. Her passion was one of the things he loved about her, but he was beginning to suspect he wouldn't like being on this end of it.

"What's this?" He gestured to the treats.

"It's called a pity party," Saffron said. "We do it whenever one of us is dumped."

A slight gasp from Elsie told him Saffron's admission was unexpected.

"So, have a pastry," Saffron went on. "They're from Ruth, and you know what that means. I've only eaten two so far, but I plan to eat at least four more in the next hour." Forced amusement punctuated the words. "After eating so much, I'll be over you."

Over him. Like he was a toothache or a bad haircut. But what else had he expected? "I stopped by to make sure you got home okay, and that you're all right." *And have you changed your mind?* He was a fool to expect that turnabout, given her track record, but he couldn't help hoping.

"I'm fine," Saffron said, her voice and gaze both deceptively calm. Too calm. "But if you'll excuse me, I need to pack and find someone to work for me next week."

"Are you going somewhere?"

Saffron stood, a pastry in her hand and tasty-looking crumbs sticking to her lips. "I think you lost the right to ask that, but if you must know, I'm going to California to see my sister, my *biological* sister, and the boy I loved in kindergarten."

Something glittered in her eyes before she turned gracefully and strode toward her bedroom, slipping inside and shutting the door with a soft click.

"I didn't even know she had a sister," he murmured, his chest so tight he could scarcely breathe.

"Neither did we until an hour ago," Halla said from her stool on the other side of the counter. "Anyway, things weren't good for her at home. Obviously, I guess, or she wouldn't have ended up at Lily's House."

"She never talked about any of it to me," he said. That was one of the reasons he'd known something wasn't right between them.

Halla and Elsie exchanged a look, as if silently asking the other how much they should tell him. In the end, Halla said, "Well, maybe going back home will help. I just hope it doesn't break her heart again."

"There's someone else, isn't there?" he asked, remembering the conversation he'd heard months ago at Lily's House. "This isn't just about her sister, is it? Is there someone in her past? A man?"

Elsie nodded, and Halla added, "It's complicated. But you'll have to ask her."

"If she'd tell me, we wouldn't be here right now." He knew his eyes were going red by the pity in Halla's eyes.

"You still love her." Halla spoke the words like an accusation.

So what if they knew his heart was breaking? He didn't care. "Yes."

Elsie glared at him. "Then why did you break up with her?"

Because she wasn't really mine. No way could he say that and still retain any kind of dignity.

Thankfully, Elsie didn't give him time to answer but sighed and sank onto her stool, taking another pastry. "That is so sad."

"Pastry?" Halla offered.

Vaughn shook his head, the idea of eating anything turning his stomach. He glanced once more toward the door of Saffron's bedroom, wishing he could go inside and take her into his arms. He'd kiss her until her lips softened and her laughter returned. He'd promise to stay with her for as long as she wanted him, even if that was only another week.

Stop it, he thought. When he'd decided to let her go, he understood it wasn't going to be easy breaking through her walls and getting her back. He wasn't giving up now.

But what if she never let him in?

"Do you think she'll come back?" he asked Halla, who never sugar-coated anything.

"I don't know," Halla said. "I just don't know."

He felt ripped apart by her words. He nodded and turned toward the apartment door. "I'd better take off. I'll text her later."

At least seeing Saffron safe had calmed something inside him. The urge and worry was gone, replaced by a growing determination. He would have faced any dragon for her. He would have climbed any mountain or crossed any sea. He would have lived in any conditions with her by his side.

Yet how could he help her with this? And how could he compete? He had to find a way.

Elsie walked with him to the door. "For what it's worth," she said quietly, "I thought it would work out between you two."

"Thanks," he muttered.

She opened the door for him. "This is something she has to do. I think you helped her see that."

"Really?" He slapped his hand against the door frame. "Because it seems like I just sent her into someone else's arms."

Elsie's brow furrowed. "Maybe you did. Or maybe you're helping her get over him."

In all the really terrible scenarios he'd gone over in his mind when he decided to break up with Saffron, her going to find an old love hadn't been a part of them.

"Give her time," Elsie said. "Things might change."

He hesitated at the door. "Look, if you have the chance . . . will you tell her . . ." He sighed and shook his head. "It's up to her now. I can't force her to feel anything she doesn't."

Elsie met his stare. "You lasted three months, and I know she cried after you left the reception. That's something."

He gave Elsie the smile she expected, but it felt fake. Three months wasn't nearly enough to love Saffron, and he didn't want her to cry. He wanted to excise her hurt and make her whole again. Whole enough to return his love.

What if that meant he would ultimately lose her to another?

His hesitation at the door had turned into something bordering on rudeness, but Elsie watched him with kindness in her eyes. Making a quick decision, he turned and strode past Elsie and back through the living room to rap sharply on the door to Saffron's bedroom.

Halla jumped up and came toward him. "I don't think—"

"Come in," Saffron called.

He opened the door to find her kneeling by her suitcase, folding clothing. "Oh," she said with a little gasp, "it's you."

Of course. She'd expected her sisters to have gotten rid of him by now. Well, this was only the beginning of the surprises he would plan.

The sight of her suitcase made him want to pick it and her up and take them to his place where they belonged. Instead, he pulled out his set of keys, removed the key to his Prius and tossed it to her along with the key fob.

She put her hand up at the last moment to catch it. "What's this?" she asked, looking down at her hand with confusion.

"Your engine isn't running right, and weren't you getting new brakes? If you can't wait to fix your car, take mine. In the meantime, I can use yours here and get it fixed."

"No." She held up the key to throw back, but he put his hands in his pockets.

"Please," he said. "I'll worry if you don't."

"I can get it fixed there," Saffron said, coming to her feet. "It's not that far."

Halla and Elsie crowded in behind him. "It'll take five or six hours to get to Temecula," Halla commented. "You don't know any mechanics there, and you'll need a car to get around, so you really should get your brakes fixed first. Plus, you have no idea how long you'll be there."

Temecula. So that's where she was going—and with no time frame for return. That was a worry. Questions pushed to escape his mouth, but he kept them in. Saffron was a capable woman and almost always made good decisions.

"I can see you're anxious to get going," he said. "Look, why don't I bring your car to you after I get it fixed? Datatoon Studios wants me to go talk to them anyway. They're not far from Temecula. We can exchange cars then." Datatoon had been at him to tour the new facilities as an enticement to come back to work for them, and he might as well agree. He'd love seeing his old friends there.

"You don't have to take care of it," Saffron ground out. Despite his casual attitude, she was growing irritated. Or maybe it was because he wasn't pleading for her to stay that she was angry. Dare he hope?

"I know that, but won't it save you time?" He offered her his best smile. "I'd really like to help."

He loved the flush on her face and the way her blue eyes challenged him. "Well, I guess that's what *friends* do." The emphasis on "friends" told him she'd read his text and had not been pleased. Maybe another good sign. He was tempted to go to her, take her in his arms, and tell her he loved her, but doing so would set him back where he'd started, or worse. This wasn't some romance movie like the ones she and her sisters were always watching on their girls-only nights.

"I'll get her extra key," Halla said. "I think it's a perfect idea." When Saffron started to protest, Halla held up her hand. "Nope, don't say it. We'll all worry something will happen to you on the way, and if you don't agree, I swear I'll tell Lily about your car. Then you'll definitely get stuck.

She'll never let you drive it to California if it needs new brakes."

Vaughn almost laughed. Halla had pulled out the big guns. Lily wasn't all that tall or threatening, but these girls loved her so much they would go to great lengths to make sure she didn't worry.

"Fine," Saffron agreed, her eyes flashing. "But just so you know, I'm definitely going to open it up on the freeway. All the way."

"Feel free," he said. Saffron did like to drive a little fast, but she was one of the best drivers he knew, and he wasn't worried. Besides, he was fighting for a future with the woman he loved. "I'll need your address in Temecula."

"Not sure yet where I'll be. I'll let you know."

"Okay." So obviously she wouldn't be staying with her parents or sister. More questions threatened to spill from his lips. Like how long she'd be gone, how old was her sister, and was the "boy" she'd referred to also living in Temecula? But he'd won this skirmish and he didn't want to press his luck. "I'll let you know what I find out about your car."

Halla had returned with Saffron's key and pressed it into his hands. "Thanks," he said. With a nod at Saffron, he let himself out of the apartment, feeling as if he'd left the best part of himself behind.

And he absolutely didn't mean his car.

4

Vaughn hadn't seemed to care about anything but her stupid car. He'd broken up with her, and by rights he should leave her alone, right? She never called men that she broke up with, and she certainly didn't show up at their houses afterword.

He came because he doesn't want to be broken up, Saffron thought. There could be no other explanation. She felt a little satisfaction that he did still want to be with her, but at the same time she had to respect that he wasn't waiting around for her to dump him.

"He's totally in love with you," Elsie said from the bedroom doorway. "I don't understand why he even called it quits."

"Because I'm broken," Saffron said under her breath.

"What?" Halla and Elsie said together.

"Never mind. It doesn't matter." Saffron's gaze dropped to the key in her hand. His car was a silver Prius, a very nice one. Though her Elantra was only two years old and the bright blue made her happy, she loved his car, and she was going to enjoy driving it.

"You're not worried about him taking care of your car, are you?" Halla asked.

Saffron wasn't, not at all. "He's dependable, and I guess it will save me a headache. But now that he's gone, let's get back to our pity party. Better yet, I'll pack a few of these pastries and get on the road. I want to be in Temecula tonight before dark. I've found people to cover my shifts for most of next week, and I've left a few messages I hope will cover the others."

"Let's do it!" Halla said. "First we should stop and tell Lily we're going."

"We?" Saffron arched a brow.

Halla nodded. "I'm coming too."

"What about school?" Saffron asked. Halla had just started her senior year in college, and Saffron didn't want to be a reason for her to not to graduate this year. At twenty-three, she was already taking longer than most of Lily's girls to finish school. Or at least of the ones who'd opted for higher education. Lily was big on college, and had even convinced Saffron to take a few business classes.

"Most of my classes are projects," Halla said. "I'm bored with them, and I can afford to miss a couple days. I'll drive back for a test on Wednesday morning, though." She smirked. "Maybe I can even get a ride with Vaughn if he brings your car around before then. But I'm not letting you go alone. I'll run home and pack a bag and meet you at Lily's."

"I wish I could come too," Elsie said, making a face, "but I can't miss any of my classes." Her eyes turned pleading. "You are coming back, aren't you?"

"Of course I am. My life is here." Saffron felt like a liar.

Because there was a huge part of her that was still with Tyson and their baby.

The baby he had abandoned as surely as he'd abandoned her.

Lily was in action mode when Saffron arrived. "We've got a new girl," she said when Saffron found her in one of the upstairs rooms. She was making up a bottom bunk bed, while baby Cherie played with toys in the middle of the small room. "Emergency placement, even though we're already two girls over our allotted ten from the state. Her foster father hit one of the three kids placed with them, so they were all removed from the home. Good thing we finished the addition over the garage for the over eighteens, or we wouldn't have a bed for her."

"How long is she here for?" Saffron asked.

Lily straightened from the bed. "I told them if they put her with me, she's here to stay permanently. I don't want her juggled around."

This didn't surprise Saffron. Lily had only relinquished three underaged girls in the eight years they'd known her, and all of those had been to their biological parents. There had been another girl who'd repeatedly run away, but after four times, Lily won her over, and she'd finally stayed put.

"Hopefully, they'll honor that," Saffron said.

Lily gave her a smug grin. "Oh, they will. I made them sign a contract. They've been shuttling this sweet girl between homes since she was orphaned at six when her grandmother died."

That seemed impossible to Saffron. "Why wasn't she adopted?"

"Because until recently, her mother was thought to be alive."

A swell of bitterness filled Saffron's throat. Mothers were supposed to protect their children, not prevent them from being happy. Of course, Saffron hadn't done much of a job protecting her son.

"Her name's Tara, by the way," Lily said with a smile. "We'll have a welcome party tomorrow at dinner." She paused and looked past Saffron. "Well, look who's here. Good, now you can meet her. Hi, Tara. Did Mario finish already with the grand tour?"

Saffron turned to find a young teen clutching a worn backpack. She had straight black hair and a scowl on her face that did not look remotely sweet.

"I hope he took you out to see my sister's horses," Lily continued. "Because we all take turns helping feed them. Anyway, I got your bed all ready—it's this bottom bunk here. And if you have anything you'd like to give me for safe-keeping, I can lock it up for you. The girls here are mostly honest, but I don't like to leave temptation lying around. I think you'll find everyone here respects each other. You can even leave out money on the table, and it's still there in the morning."

Saffron knew this was Lily's way of telling Tara that stealing wouldn't be tolerated. Stealing meant extra chores, and Lily always discovered which of the girls took something that didn't belong to her.

Tara glared at Lily and silently went to sit on the freshly

made bed, hunching over the backpack in her arms as if protecting it from Lily.

"Oh, and this young woman is Saffron," Lily continued as if the girl hadn't been rude. "She used to live here. In fact, she was the very first girl to live with me. Now she comes back to chat or to help out when I need it." Lily smiled at Saffron and added, "So, why are you here? Have you decided for sure about California?"

"Yes. I'm leaving now," Saffron said. "Halla's coming with me, so we won't be here tomorrow for Sunday dinner, or at Tara's welcome party." Saffron shot a glance at Tara, but the teen lifted her shoulders in a gesture that said she didn't care.

Lily picked up Cherie. "I think you're doing the right thing, but let me go down and make you a lunch, okay? I have a small cooler you can take, and extra water."

Saffron gave her an embarrassed smile. "I didn't even think about that."

Lily waved the comment aside. "Oh, you would have stopped and bought something on the road, but this will be better for you. Mario picked fresh strawberries this morning. Are you taking some of your jewelry parts?"

"Of course." How well Lily knew her. "I have a few orders I need to fill. I'll work on them as I can."

"Good. Maybe you can visit a few boutiques while you're in California, see if they'll carry some pieces for you."

"Maybe." Saffron didn't know if there would be time. "Here, let me hold Cherie." Saffron took the baby from Lily's arms. "I'm going to miss this cutie."

"That makes it sound like you might be awhile." Lily

took a few steps toward the door, pausing to await her response.

Saffron shrugged. "As long as it takes. I have to know."

"I understand, and that's good. Just go into it with your eyes open. It's been eight years. There might be someone else to think about."

Meaning Tyson might have gone on with his life. That possibility was one of the reasons she'd never wanted to look him up. He hadn't come after her, and seeing him happy when she felt broken was a risk she'd never wanted to take—until now. "I know that. But I have to see him." Saffron blinked away threatening tears.

"Okay, give me a few minutes, and I'll have your lunch ready." Lily's gaze switched to Tara. "Come down to eat when you're ready. The kitchen is always open as long as you clean up after yourself." Lily looked at Saffron pointedly and then at the sullen girl on the bunk bed and back again, a clear indication that she wanted Saffron to say something to the child.

Saffron smiled as her urge to cry disappeared. Helping others, Lily always said, was the best way to solve your own problems. Saffron turned to Tara as Lily disappeared from the room. "So," she said. "You're going to love this place."

The girl gave a soft, unbelieving snort.

"No, really," Saffron said. "You don't know it yet, but this is the last foster home you'll ever go to. Lily's for real. I promise you that. In fact, I wasn't placed here by the state. Lily found me at a low time in my life and took me in. I loved it so much, I stayed until I was twenty."

Was that hope in the girl's eyes?

"But there's one thing you really need to know about

living here," Saffron said in the most serious tone she could muster. She set Cherie next to Tara on the bed. "Make sure she doesn't fall off, okay?"

After a hesitation, Tara nodded, placing an arm around Cherie, who promptly began playing with the keychains attached to Tara's backpack.

Saffron climbed up to the top bunk. "Once a month," she said, "they hold Lily's House bunkbed competitions, and you need to practice up."

Could she even still do it? Saffron moved to the middle of the bed and held onto the safety bar with her hands. "Don't worry about the beds. They are totally solid." She leaned over head first, still holding onto the bars, and flipped over, her feet landing solidly on the ground. Not bad for being out of practice. "You should have seen one of the girls who used to be here. Ruth. She could stop midway and move her feet in a little dance in the air before landing. Other girls flip back up too. It's quite a serious competition."

Tara's sneer was suspiciously close to a smile. "It's stupid."

"No, it's fun. Practice up. Because the winner has a week of no chores, and the competition is stiff." Leaning over, Saffron grabbed the baby. "And I meant what I said about Lily. It doesn't matter what you do, she's going to love you, so you might as well get used to it. Mario, too. Once you're here, you're family. Everyone else in your life might have betrayed you, but not Lily and not Mario. Not us."

Tara rolled her eyes. "And I guess she always brings you over to say that."

"Don't be silly. I had no idea you'd be here. I just stopped by on my way to California." Saffron's voice hardened. "Look, you're not the only one who's had a horrible life before you came here, but you're one of the lucky ones because all that is over now."

"If you like it here so much, why are you leaving?" Tara retorted.

Saffron probably shouldn't answer, not in her current mindset, but now that she'd started talking about her past, she couldn't seem to help herself. Besides, the sooner this child dumped that giant chip off her shoulder, the faster she could heal and contribute to the Lily's House family.

"Because I have to face the woman who's responsible for killing my baby." The words felt like sawdust in Saffron's mouth, but the expression in the girl's eyes showed they might have shaken her momentarily out of her self-pity. "But I'll see you when I get back."

Though I might not be back to stay, Saffron added silently. Anything was possible at this point, and she had to hold on to the idea that the feelings she still held for Tyson might mean something real.

5

Saffron and Halla made it to Temecula's Windsor Crest area in a breezy five hours that had Halla swearing she was going to buy a Prius after she got her first real job.

"You have to finish college first," Saffron reminded her.

"Yeah, I know, but I have fifty thousand followers on my blog already, and I'm thinking about monetizing it by adding advertising." Halla had always been a writer, even in high school, and after a year of delaying college, her choice of journalism for a major in addition to an editing minor hadn't surprised anyone except herself.

"You might as well." Saffron brought the Prius to a stop in front of a one-story house. "It would help you pay for college."

"So what now?" Halla asked.

Saffron had no idea. She stared up at the house that belonged to her parents. The place was smaller than she remembered, though still impressive. The immaculate lawn was very green and lacked any of the rock features that dotted many of the houses in California and Arizona.

Sweeping trees, three garages, and arched windows gave it an air of wealth and permanence.

It didn't look like a house owned by people who would throw their child away.

"It's kind of impressive," Halla said half apologetically.

"You haven't seen the rockwork on the covered deck or around the pool," Saffron said, trying to mask her urge to flee.

She remembered vividly her last day here, taking a taxi to the bus station and spending far too much of her small funds in the process. Her mother had stood in the doorway, hands on her hips and a determined expression on her face. That moment haunted Saffron's dreams almost as much as the day at the hospital.

"I can't do this," Saffron whispered. "I can't walk up there."

Halla studied her. "Yes, you can—but maybe not today. Let's go to our hotel. You've come a long way already, and I think your sister will agree to meet us there for at least the first visit. You can face your mother later."

"Good idea." With relief, Saffron put the car into gear and drove away from her mother's house. "Can you get my phone and text her?"

Halla grinned. "You text. I'll drive. Come on, stop the car and change places with me. You got all the fun on the way here."

"Okay, okay." Saffron edged over to the curb and traded places. She was tired of driving anyway—and hungry too. She was looking forward to digging deeper into the cooler of food Lily had sent with them and to maybe stretching out on a bed for a few minutes.

The thought of a bed brought an unbidden flash of memory to her mind. Of lying in her room with tears leaking down the sides of her face after her mother had told her to break up with Tyson. Before the baby. Before any of it.

"But I love him," she'd declared. "I know you think I'm too young, and it's not like I want to run off and get married. I want to go to college, and so does he. We just want to hang out. I'd like to bring him here."

"You need to concentrate on school," her mother said in her clipped, no-nonsense voice. "You need to marry someone like your father, who can take care of you."

Saffron didn't even know what her father did, except that he worked for a big company and was always gone. During their last vacation to Catalina Island, he'd appeared for only one day. "Tyson's father served in the military," she told her mother. "That's honorable."

Her mother's lips pursed. "My sources say he wasn't in active combat, but he's been collecting disability for ten years already. That's not the kind of life I want for you."

You mean for you, Saffron wanted to say.

"Promise me you won't see him anymore."

"We go to the same school. Of course I'm going to see him."

"You know what I mean." Her mother's stare pierced her. "Break up with him now. It's for your own good, Rosalyn. You may not understand that now, but you will one day." With that she'd left, shutting the door with a decisive click.

"Saffron?" Halla said, calling her back to the present. "Aren't you going to text your sister?"

Saffron banished the unhappy memory. "Oh, right. I think I'm a little tired. I didn't sleep much last night."

"Because of coming here or because of Vaughn?"

"Coming here," Saffron said, but honesty forced her to admit: "Okay, maybe Vaughn too. He was fun to be with, but it's not like we had a future or anything."

"Because you're still hung up on a guy you haven't seen for nearly nine years?"

"Well, it sounds stupid when you say it that way. But you don't know how it was between us. He was my other half."

Halla glanced at her and then turned her attention back to the road in front of them. "What if he's married now?"

Saffron's heart twisted. "At least I'll know." If she hadn't been able to move on, maybe he hadn't either. It was a big chance, but one she had to take.

She turned on her phone and began texting. Kendall must have been waiting for news because she answered back immediately. "She says she can come in an hour," Saffron said.

"That'll give us time to get to the hotel. Does she have the address?"

Saffron was already copying and pasting the address into her conversation. "She does now."

They'd chosen the Rodeway Inn because it cost less than most and was close to Saffron's family. They checked in, and Saffron couldn't help but see the hotel as her mother would see it: a place for those who couldn't afford better.

"What a nice place," Halla said as they entered the room, Lily's small cooler between them.

Saffron hugged her. "Thank you for saying that."

Halla gave her a confused look. "Are you okay?"

"Yeah. Let's eat."

They set their bags by the first twin bed and walked to the small table where they set the cooler. Halla dug through it. "I thought I saw some of Lily's chicken salad. Was I imagining it?"

She wasn't. There were also rolls, fruit, small bottles of juice, and a couple more of the turkey sandwiches they hadn't eaten on the way. The food comforted Saffron, somehow reminding her of safety and love.

All too soon—and not soon enough—there was a knock on the door.

Halla grabbed her purse that was just large enough for her cell phone and her tiny wallet. "I'll leave you two alone—after I meet her, of course."

"Are you sure?" Saffron was suddenly nervous.

Halla gave her a wry smile. "Believe me, she doesn't want me around, not after all these years of not seeing you."

She had a point. Saffron gathered her scattered courage. "Okay then."

"Text me if you need me," Halla added.

"I will." Saffron hurried to the door, pulling it open with a bit more force than necessary. Her eyes fell on a slender, pretty young woman she knew only from Facebook. Kendall had bleached hair that just reached her shoulders and she had grown taller than Saffron herself. There seemed to be no trace of the child she'd been.

"Hi," Saffron said a bit breathlessly.

Kendall nodded, her blue eyes large in her narrow face. "Hi, Rosalyn—I mean Saffron." A nervous hand tucked her hair behind her ear, revealing multiple piercings. Saffron leaned forward and hugged her, wanting to bridge the space between them. Her own sister, but she was a complete stranger. Saffron felt strangely disappointed, as if Kendall shouldn't have grown at all while she'd been gone. Kendall hugged her back.

Halla stuck out her hand as Saffron released Kendall. "Hi, I'm Halla."

The words jolted Saffron from her bad manners. "Oh, right. Halla's my si—" She stopped. She'd been going to say "sister," of course, as she always did, because Halla and the other girls were her family—but it felt wrong somehow to say now to her biological sister.

"Saffron and I are foster sisters," Halla filled in smoothly. "We both lived at a place called Lily's House. It's nice to meet you."

"You too." Kendall's voice was strained and tinged with anger as her eyes ran over Halla's clothes, taking in the black tank top and camouflage cargo shorts that were her customary summer attire.

"I can sure tell you're sisters," Halla added, her head swinging between them. "You look a lot alike."

Saffron supposed that was true. They had similar coloring and build, though Kendall was taller and thinner, and her hair whiter. Their eyes—inherited from their mother—were the same.

"Well, I'll just leave you two to catch up." With a smile, Halla slipped past Kendall and started down the hallway, humming softly.

"Come in," Saffron said to Kendall.

Kendall came inside, stalking rather than walking, then

paused and waited until Saffron passed her, heading to the table.

"We were just eating," Saffron said, settling into one of the two chairs. "You hungry?"

Kendall winced slightly before smoothing her features. "No, thank you."

"So . . . it's good to see you." The words felt lame compared to the emotions in Saffron's heart. She wanted to ask a billion questions, to touch her sister's face and smooth the strands of her hair as she had when they were younger.

Kendall didn't sit. "So she's your sister now? I guess I was pretty easy to replace."

Saffron stared up at Kendall's taut face. "Of course nothing could replace you. It's not like that."

"Then what's it like?"

"Please sit?" Saffron hadn't thought of the situation from her sister's point of view, but she was right to be upset.

Kendall's nostrils flared as she placed her phone and car keys on the table and dropped into a chair. "Okay, look, I need to get something out. I want to be clear. Why didn't you come back sooner?"

Saffron hesitated in her response. How to explain when she was asking herself the same question?

"I know you and Mom had problems," Kendall rushed on, "but that wasn't my fault. I looked up to you. I missed you! I keep wondering why you didn't contact me sooner, and . . . and I guess I'm a little hurt. It doesn't help when you show up with *her*." Kendall glanced toward the closed door. "You're close, aren't you? I can tell. It's not like you really need me, so why are you even here?"

"I'm sorry I stayed away so long. I should have come back sooner. And I really want to get to know you. It's just . . ." Saffron knew she should have gotten over losing her baby. Except she hadn't.

Grief swept through her in a rush, as if it were a new emotion, not one dimmed by time. The feeling was always present, but when it flared like this, she was always surprised at how overwhelmingly fresh and raw it felt.

Tears made it hard to see. "There's a reason," she said finally. "I just don't know if it will seem like enough to you."

Kendall jumped to her feet. "That's right, because I don't understand! I can't see what would be so awful that you would leave me. I waited and waited for you to come back. Even Mom thought you would come for dad's funeral, but you didn't. Not even a phone call."

"Funeral?" Shock waved through Saffron. She felt stupid, as if she couldn't quite understand the words. Her brain was struggling to keep up, and her mouth held the distinct flavor of ashes. "How did he—? When?" How could she not have known her father was dead? He'd never been around as she was growing up, but he'd been a constant in their lives, if only from a distance.

"You didn't know?" Kendall sat back down, more subdued now. "Well, he died of a heart attack in Japan when he was on a business trip. It was the August after you left."

August. The grief swelled again, and she couldn't help the tears. But they weren't for her father. She didn't know him well enough to cry for him.

"I'm sorry," Kendall said. "I didn't know that you hadn't heard." She placed her hand over Saffron's on the table, gazing at her with concern, her earlier anger gone. In that instant, Saffron saw the little girl Kendall had been, and the grief inside widened. She'd lost more than her son and the man she loved when she'd left here. She'd also lost Kendall, but only this minute did she glimpse how much she'd cheated both of them. She'd been too wrapped up in her private pain to care about anything else.

Kendall appeared to be waiting for more—and she deserved an explanation. "I had a baby," Saffron said, trying to blink back tears. "August was when he was born. The month after I turned seventeen."

"You have a son?" Kendall's eyes looked huge in her narrow face.

Saffron shook her head. "Not anymore," she whispered. The words sounded slow to her ears, and garbled as if she were under water. "I wasn't healthy, and he came three months early." She paused, knowing she had to say the rest. "He only lived a little while."

"Oh, no! I'm so sorry." Kendall sat back in her chair, folding her arms over her stomach. "But suddenly it all makes a little more sense. Why you left, I mean."

"It's why Mom made me leave." Saffron's vehemence was more pronounced than she intended, though it was only a fraction of her real feelings. "She suspected about the baby, and when she heard me throwing up, she confronted me. I had the pregnancy test right there in my hand, so not much chance of putting her off. I told her I planned to marry Tyson and keep the baby, and she said if I wanted to be an idiot, I'd have to do it alone. Then she took my phone and ordered me to leave the house before Dad got home."

"I remember you packing," Kendall said, frowning. "I was so upset. Then Mom made me go to my room."

"What happened when dad got home? What did he say?"

Kendall shrugged. "Nothing in front of me. But why didn't you marry Tyson?"

"He was at football practice when I left. I called him later but . . ." Saffron shook her head. "Wait, how did you know I didn't marry him?" Kendall had been too young to know anyone at the high school, and their families didn't move in the same social circles.

"Because I ran into him last month when my boyfriend applied to do some work for him. I didn't know who he was, but he recognized my name, and we pieced it together."

"He's still in town?" Saffron's heart beat in an uneven rhythm.

"Back in town, I think. His dad's sick, and he's helping take care of him. Tyson's done a complete remodeling of the house—that's what my boyfriend's been helping with. In fact, I think I'm the only reason he gave Joel the job. They're almost finished."

"I'm assuming Joel is your boyfriend, but does that mean Tyson's a contractor?"

Kendall laughed. "No. He's a doctor. But he's doing the house himself—or a lot of it. Joel's just helping out with the work."

A doctor. That seemed more like the Tyson she'd known. In high school he'd been fascinated with the biological sciences. Though he'd planned to enter the army like his dad, Saffron had told him more than once that he should go into the medical field. Her mother had predicted he'd go nowhere, and there was a distinct irony in how wrong she'd been.

"So how long have you been dating Joel?" she asked Kendall.

Kendall smiled and her eyes sparkled. "A year—all my senior year in high school. And he's absolutely perfect, but Mom . . ."

Saffron's stomach tensed. "Let me guess. She doesn't like him."

"Well that, and she wants me to finish college. But I hate college, or at least all the classes I'm taking. It's only been a month, but it's awful. Interior design isn't my thing. Joel says I should do what I want." Kendall leaned forward, turning on her phone. "See, this is him. Isn't he gorgeous?"

She thrust out the phone to show Saffron a picture of a thin young man with longish hair and a wispy goatee. Saffron wasn't sure if it was the look in the man's eyes or the possessive way he was holding onto Kendall, but something about him made her uneasy.

Saffron wasn't about to say that to Kendall, of course—at least not until she'd met Joel and gotten to know him a little better. Her experience with the abandoned or troubled girls at Lily's House had shown her that in many instances appearances were absolutely wrong. "So you really like him?"

"I *love* him," Kendall corrected. "And I can't wait to be with him, even if Mom hates the idea."

"Oh, yeah? What's the rush?" Saffron was *not* taking her mother's side on this. She was taking Lily's, who always urged her girls to get a good start on their education and have their plans in place before they became serious with anyone. Even the few pregnant teens who had come through Lily's House had received career counseling before they got married. She wanted them to live their dreams—not someone else's—and to find someone whose dreams complemented their own.

"Because I'm pregnant." Kendall paused after the announcement, her stare a little defiant. "That's why I'm so glad you're here. I need someone to be with me when I tell her about the baby. Someone who'll help me stand up for myself. And I'm pretty sure that once I tell Mom, she's going to kick me out."

A sense of déjà vu fell over Saffron, and she had to stifle the urge to cover her ears. *Pregnant. Pregnant. Pregnant.* The word reverberated inside her head as it had when Saffron had discovered her own expectant condition.

"You're shocked, aren't you?" Kendall lifted her chin, her jaw clenching.

"Yeah, a little," Saffron managed to say.

As the impact of the words wore off, Saffron felt a brief sliver of jealousy crawl up from some dark place inside her. If only she could go back to the day when she'd taken the test. She'd still leave home, but she'd go straight to Lily, who would help her get the care she needed to save her baby. Her mother may have deserted her. Tyson may have deserted her. But Lily was a constant, like the ocean or a mountain, and she would have saved Saffron's child.

Saffron pushed the yearning back inside its hole. "Wow, that's big," she murmured.

"I know, and I've been feeling so alone." Kendall's brow furrowed and her frown was back. "Then you told me you were coming down and I knew it was fate. You came back just in time—I really need you."

Did that redeem her then? Saffron wondered. She reached for her sister's hand. "I'm here for you," she said, answering the question underlying her sister's words. "I don't know how good I'll be with Mom, because quite frankly she still scares me, but I can be with you when you tell her." More hesitantly, she asked, "So what does Joel say?"

"That we'll get married." Kendall's smile was back. "He's excited for the baby. He just needs another month to get things together so we can figure out where we're going to live. Right now he's crashing at a friend's. Mom's got all that room, but there's no way . . ." She shrugged. "You know how she is."

Saffron didn't, not anymore, but she could guess. "How far along are you?"

"Three and a half months." Kendall sighed. "I didn't mean for it to happen, and I know I was stupid, but now that it has, I'm so excited. I can't wait to have a little baby to love."

Saffron remembered that feeling, and how excited she'd been to tell Tyson the test was positive. Like Kendall, she understood that she'd been stupid, but at the same time she'd been filled with hope for the life she'd make with Tyson.

Grief grew inside her again, and for a long minute, Saffron struggled with her emotions. Somehow she had to be able to think about the past—and the future—without the grief and longing taking over her like this. She would be an aunt to this baby, and someday she wanted to have her own, and that meant she needed to put the past behind her.

"Are you okay?" Kendall asked.

Saffron forced a nod. "I'm excited about your baby. It just brings up a lot of memories."

"I bet." Kendall was quiet a moment before adding, "I can't believe I never knew that's why you left. I think maybe I wouldn't have been so angry at you."

Saffron's tears fell then, dripping down both cheeks. It was safer to cry for what she and Kendall had lost than for her baby and for Tyson. "I'm here now, and we'll work things out, somehow."

"When will we tell her?" At that moment, Kendall again reminded Saffron of her child self. So young and vulnerable.

"Whenever you're ready. It's your decision."

Kendall nodded, but the crease in her forehead didn't smooth. She was about to speak when her phone lit up with a text. She stood as she read it, reaching for her car keys. "Look, do you think we could get together later tonight? I need to go pick up Joel from work. He was supposed to be off already, but they were trying to put in a wheelchair ramp."

"He doesn't have a car?"

"Yeah, but it's not running at the moment. Anyway, I can't wait for you to meet him. You're going to love him."

"I'm sure I will."

As they walked to the door, a thought occurred to Saffron. "You're picking him up at Tyson's. Is he going to be there?" The thought of seeing him both thrilled and terrified her.

"He should be. They mostly work on evenings or Fridays and Saturdays because that's when Tyson's off and can supervise." Kendall stopped at the door and cocked her head, a slight grimace marring her features. "I guess you'll want to see Tyson, huh? I forgot to tell you he has a girlfriend. According to his mother, the only thing really stopping him from proposing are the repairs and his dad's illness."

"I see." The news wasn't surprising after all these years, but it felt unfair. Almost as if Tyson had abandoned her yesterday instead of eight and a half years ago. What was this woman like who had won his heart?

Kendall hugged her. "Sorry for the way I acted when I got here. I am happy to see you but . . ."

"I know." Saffron held on tight. Now that she had Kendall back, she wasn't letting her go. She had Vaughn to thank that she was here right now, and even if she was still mad at him, she'd make a point to let him know.

Saturday evening, Vaughn was surprised to see a text from Saffron. He'd been wondering if she'd bother to let him know that she'd arrived safely in California, but he hadn't requested it, knowing she was upset with him. Besides, he knew her foster mother well enough to know she'd probably checked in with the girls several times during the trip. He hadn't even tracked the GPS location of his car, though he was considering doing so when the text came in.

So apparently my dad is dead, she wrote.

He nearly dropped his phone. That wasn't at all the text he'd expected. He hurried to answer: *What? How? When? I'm really sorry.*

I didn't really know him, she answered. *He died about six months after I left home. Heart attack.*

All this was more about her family than she'd shared with him in the year he'd known her. He shut his laptop, hiding the simple animations he was grading for a class. Stretching out on his couch, he hit the call icon for Saffron's number.

She answered immediately. "Hi."

Her voice didn't sound like she'd been crying, but there was a distant tone that reminded him of how she'd been last night when he'd ended things. Shock, he supposed, but at least she was talking to him. "So you met your sister? How'd she look?"

"She looked great, but she's eighteen and pregnant."

"Oh, wow."

"She says she's going to marry the father, but . . . well, I haven't met him yet, so I don't have an opinion, but eighteen is really young."

"For most people, maybe." His own parents had married out of high school and had his sister ten months later.

"Yeah, you're right." She sounded relieved. "It might work out. She seems really in love."

Silence. Was there more? Because she wasn't hanging up. "How was the drive?" he asked in an effort to keep her on the line.

"Good. The GPS took us right here. We had a bit of a delay because of a fender-bender in front of us, but we still made good time. I made up the lost time by driving really fast."

"I bet you did." He laughed to show her he didn't care. Well, not much anyway.

"Ha ha. Look, I wanted to thank you for lending me your car. Mine would have been fine, but it made Lily happy."

"Anything for Lily."

"You're grading programs again tonight, aren't you?"

"How did you know?"

"That's what you always do when you aren't taking people rafting or . . ." She trailed off.

Or spending time with her. He was glad she didn't say it. "Let me know if you need me to bring anything when I come down with your car."

"And when is that?"

"Well, fixing the car should only take a day or so, but I'm not sure when I can get away from work. Might not be until Friday. Would that work?"

"Not exactly. Halla has a test on Wednesday that she can't miss, but it doesn't look like you'll be coming down before then."

"She can use my car to drive back for the test, if she needs to. Not a big deal." That meant he'd have to figure out how to get himself back to Phoenix after dropping off Saffron's car, but he wouldn't worry about it now. He could always fly.

"That's nice of you."

"Have you seen your mother?" It was safer than asking what he really wanted to know—if she'd seen the man her sisters had talked about. The man he didn't know but wanted to kick into the past where he should have stayed.

"Not yet."

He didn't miss the slight tremble in her voice. The same emotion she'd displayed when she'd told him about the abuse her foster sisters had experienced as children. What had Saffron endured? He wanted to ask, but he didn't want to push her any further away. He had won a small victory just in the fact that she'd contacted him. "You want me to come down and see her with you? I will if you want."

She laughed. "Thanks for the offer, but I can handle her. I'm not looking forward to it, but I can do it."

"I know you can, but should you? I guess that's what

I'm saying. Think about it. Anyway, I'm glad Halla is there with you."

"Me too." A long pause. "Well, I'd better go. I'm meeting my sister again tonight for a late dinner. Oh, and Vaughn?"

"Yes."

"Thank you. For the car . . . and for everything."

For everything what? he wanted to say. *For pushing you away? For not telling you that I'd wait for as long as it took if there was even a slight chance?* "You're welcome. I'm here if you need me."

"Thanks. Talk to you later."

"Later."

She hung up and he stared up at the ceiling. She'd texted him with personal information. She'd reached out to him. He hoped that meant something because being away from her was already killing him.

Saffron hung up the phone, feeling oddly better after talking to Vaughn. Maybe this being friends thing wasn't such a bad idea. The pressure she used to feel when he talked about his family or the future no longer existed. Thanks to Halla and Elsie, he knew about her coming here to find a man from her past, and he hadn't challenged her on it. She'd told him about her sister and father. It was freeing.

She glanced over at Halla, who had already listened to her rundown on her talk with Kendall right before Saffron had decided to text Vaughn. Halla was staring at her from the table with a thoughtful expression. "What?" Saffron asked.

"I find it interesting that you talked to Vaughn when you were barely civil to him this morning. You talked to him before Lily, before Elsie or the others. In fact, you barely explained to me what happened before you called him."

"He called me."

Halla rolled her eyes. "You know what I mean. You texted him first."

She had a point. "Well, I hadn't told him we'd gotten here safely. Or gotten his car here safely."

"Uh-huh, right." Halla didn't look impressed.

"Besides, you heard me—I wanted to thank him. I wouldn't be here for Kendall if he hadn't . . ."

"Broken up with you and made you cry?"

There was that. Saffron scowled. "I wasn't crying for him. Anyway, at least now I don't have to worry about disappointing him like I always did when he'd ask me to go see his family."

"Only because he won't be asking you. But it's something, I suppose. So when are you going to see Tyson? If he's practically engaged, that changes things." Halla came to sit next to her on one of the queen beds.

Saffron wasn't sure. She still needed to talk to Tyson, but that seemed even more frightening than confronting her mother. She wished she didn't have to see her mother at all, but thoughts of Kendall stopped that idea as quickly as it formed. Kendall needed her. Saffron had abandoned her sister once when there hadn't been a choice, but now she had a choice.

I'm strong enough to face my mother, she told herself. She didn't feel as confident as she had when talking to Vaughn.

Aloud, she said to Halla, "Either way, I still have to see

Tyson. I need to know why he never called. Why he didn't look for me." It was possible she'd seen their relationship differently than he had. She'd witnessed that scenario repeatedly from the girls who'd gone through Lily's House. Watching those girls pine for guys who cared nothing for them had taught her as much as she'd learned from her own experience with Tyson. She never wanted to be that girl again.

Her thoughts drifted back to Vaughn. He was a good guy, and once she got over being mad at him completely, maybe they really could be friends. But if she was honest, she had to admit, if only to herself, that she sure missed kissing him already.

Tyson Dekker surveyed the new ramp leading into his parents' house with satisfaction. In the past six months, his father had gone from partial mobility to complete reliance on a wheelchair. Putting in ramps, reworking the counters to make them shorter, and updating the bathroom was part of a plan to give his father more independence and his mother a well-deserved break.

Not that his mother ever complained, but he could see exhaustion in the slump of her shoulders. She'd made the decision to retire early from the grocery store where she'd been working for the past twenty years to take care of his father, just as she had once shouldered the responsibility to make up the difference between his father's disability and what they owed in bills.

Tyson had been five years old when his father had come

home injured from some ultra-secret skirmish overseas. His father had been a broken man, in constant pain, but he'd slowly healed enough to take care of the house and yard. Anything more was out of the question.

Sometimes when Tyson had watched his friends playing football or some other sport with their fathers, he'd wish his dad could be like them instead of hobbling around embarrassingly on his cane.

Only after many years did he realize he was the lucky one. At least his father had come home—and had been injured early on in his time overseas, before anxiety or nightmares set in. He'd been there for Tyson on his first day of kindergarten, was waiting for him in the kitchen when he came home from school each day, and gave advice as he prepared for his first dance. He was gruff and sometimes pushy, but Tyson knew he wanted the best for him. The best back then had meant the army, though somewhere along the way, Tyson had found another path.

"Whoa," his father said, steering his motorized wheelchair down the ramp for the first time. "This is a nice piece of work, son. I think you outdid yourself."

Before this ramp, his father would leave the motorized wheelchair in the single garage and, after painfully walking up the two steps, transfer to a manual wheelchair inside the house. Tyson's mother wasn't strong enough to pull the motorized chair inside, and without the motorized wheelchair, his father had needed a lot more help in the house. Hefting the wheelchair inside was one of the main reasons Tyson came here each day after work.

"Soon you'll be having races up and down it with all your friends," said Joel, one of the men he'd hired to help with the remodeling. The kid wasn't the brightest of the lot, but he had good hands and an eye for design—which Tyson never would have realized if it hadn't been for Roz's sister.

Roz. He'd been thinking of her almost every day since coming back to Temecula, which had at first surprised him. It shouldn't have. Temecula had been their place, and even though his parents hadn't encouraged their relationship, and Roz's parents had forbidden it, memories of her filled almost everywhere he turned. Like the school bleachers where they'd shared their first kiss, the In-n-Out Burger where they'd hung out on colder evenings when school was closed, the tree in his back yard under which, unbeknownst to his parents, they'd watched the stars and planned for the future.

A future Roz had thrown away.

The memories had made coming home a tough decision, but in the end there hadn't been much choice. His parents didn't want to leave their home, and they didn't have anyone else. They needed him. So Tyson slept in his old room at home and commuted to Oceanside to his job or to see his girlfriend, Jana Reynolds. He'd hoped to move back to his condo in Oceanside once the renovations were complete, but he really didn't think his parents would be able to keep up everything without him. Jana had suggested a gardener and someone to come in to help with cleaning and baths. She was probably right.

His mother put her arms around him. "Thank you. This is really going to help." She lowered her voice. "Your father is already much happier."

"I'm glad." Because his dad was never going to leave the wheelchair.

An expensive red Audi A3 drove up to the curb, looking slightly out of place in this lower middle-class neighborhood—or it would have looked out of place if his Infiniti Q50 weren't parked in the driveway.

It was like turning back time as he watched the girl slip gracefully from the car. She was taller than her sister had been, and her hair was over bleached instead of a natural blond, but there were enough similarities that his heart tightened as he watched her run to Joel and start kissing him.

Standing next to Tyson, his mother clicked her tongue in disapproval. "Leave it alone, Mom," he murmured.

"He's not good enough for her—anyone can see that."

"That's what her mother said about me. And from what I remember, you didn't have such a high opinion of her sister."

A swift intake of breath. "That's Roz's sister?"

He nodded. "It's the only reason I hired him, but I'm glad I did. He's got steady hands."

"As long as you're standing over him." His mother shook her head back and forth. "Whenever you're not here, he's more inclined to be on his phone."

That was true, but there was nothing Tyson could do about it except schedule Joel when he was there too. He was hoping to help the boy develop better habits—for Kendall's sake.

"No wonder you look at her like that." His mother gave him a sympathetic look.

What was she talking about? "I'm just trying to help them out," he said, pulling his gaze away. "She's a smart girl. We've had a lot of conversations, and I think she'd make a good nurse."

He brought out his phone to check the time. Maybe he could drive back to Oceanside to take Jana to a late movie. Their Saturday nights had been shot since he'd come back to help his parents.

"It wasn't that I thought Roz wasn't good enough for you," his mother said. "But you were too young to be so serious."

As a result, they hadn't been welcomed anywhere. He wouldn't say that now—or how Roz had needed a loving woman's influence since her own mother couldn't fill that role. Maybe with support, she wouldn't have betrayed him like she had. But hearing all that would hurt his mother, so Tyson stared blankly at his phone, feigning preoccupation.

"Everything worked out for the best," his mother added. "Look at how things are between you and Jana."

Yes, things between him and Jana were going well. Really well. She was an anesthesiologist resident, and she worked at the Tri-City Medical Center in Oceanside where he was working on his residency in pediatric surgery. He'd known her for two years and dated her one. For the past six months they'd been exclusive, not by agreement, but because neither had wanted to go out with anyone else. His parents loved her, and her dad—her only living parent—loved him, and lately she'd begun talking about a future together. No, *they'd* been talking about it, and if he could figure out a way to overcome whatever was stopping him from proposing, he'd make it official. He was lucky to have her, and he knew it. He'd even bought a ring.

"So," his mother said, "about you and Jana . . ."

She asked almost every week, often hinting at her need for grandchildren, but it was no more than he'd been asking himself. What was holding him back? He trusted Jana more than he'd ever trusted any other person besides Roz.

Maybe that was the problem. He'd trusted Roz, and they'd planned a future together, but everything had changed in a single day. No, he didn't believe he was stuck because of that. Jana wasn't Roz, and he was no longer a sixteen-year-old kid head-over-heels in blind love.

"Tyson?" his mother asked.

"I'll bring her for dinner tomorrow," he said. That would satisfy his mother. She and Jana could talk for hours.

Across the lawn, Kendall came up for air long enough to shoot a pointed glance at Tyson. Joel said something and tried to kiss her again, but she pushed at his chest and said something, looking back at Tyson once more. What could she want?

Well, he was going to find out because he was giving everyone Sunday off, but he needed to make sure they'd all be back here Monday night to finish the back ramp. Once that was done and he figured out help for his father on a daily basis, he'd be able to direct a little more attention to his personal life.

As Tyson walked toward the young couple, Joel pulled Kendall to him. Her body seemed to conform to his in a way that screamed of intimacy and brought a sharp stab of pain to Tyson's chest, stealing away his breath. He and Roz had been like that those last few months.

"Hi, Kendall," Tyson called, closing the last few feet between them.

"Hey." She dipped her head in greeting.

"So, good job today," Tyson added to Joel. "We'll pick it back up Monday night, right? Finish the back ramp?"

"Sure." Joel hooked an arm possessively around Kendall.

"Sorry about the late night," Tyson added. "I know it's the weekend."

"That's okay," Kendall assured him. "I've been busy anyway. My sister's in town."

"Oh, that's good." When he'd first employed Joel, Kendall told him that she'd reconnected with her sister, though he wasn't clear on why they hadn't been in contact in the first place.

Kendall was still watching him, so Tyson forced a smile. "How is she?" He didn't know how much he wanted to know the answer until she hesitated in her response.

"Uh, she looks good," Kendall said finally.

The response alerted a warning in Tyson. "Good, huh?"

"Well, I think she's still sad about what happened, which is understandable. Now that I know, I'm furious at my mother for what she did."

"What she did?" There had been so many things their mother had done.

"Yeah. Poor Rosalyn—or Saffron, I should say. She changed her name, by the way. Anyway, being all alone like that and"—her voice lowered—"having a baby. She had it rough."

Having a baby, a baby, a baby. He could feel Joel and Kendall's stares like a weight. This didn't seem to coincide with what Tyson knew to be true. There was also a decided note of accusation in Kendall's voice, but why would she be upset at him? He hadn't been the one to leave and not tell him about the baby. He hadn't decided to get an abortion without asking her.

His anger boiled under the surface. He wanted to grab

Kendall's shoulders and shake her for more information. But this was between him and Roz. Over the years there was a lot he'd thought of saying to her if their paths ever crossed, and maybe it was time he did just that. "Is she staying at your house?"

"My house?" Kendall laughed. "Yeah, right. Even if my mom would let her, I don't think Saffron would ever willingly stay under the same roof as my mother. It'd be World War III, right under my nose. No, she's staying at the Rodeway Inn with one of her foster sisters."

Foster sisters? This was making less sense by the minute.

"Well, we should go," Joel said, nudging Kendall in the direction of her car.

Kendall took a few steps and then said over her shoulder, "You should go see her. For old time's sake."

The old times hadn't been all that great, not in the end, and Tyson suspected he should turn his back and not go down this path. But he *wanted* to see Roz. The need felt like the old ache that had been with him every day for three years after she'd left and he'd been sent away from home.

"What's her room number?" he called after Kendall.

"It's on my phone in the car. Joel has your number, right? I'll text it to you."

Tyson could think about nothing but Roz as he finished putting away his tools. He remembered their classes together, after school clubs, and sneaking away from football practice to be with her. He'd only been on the team because his father wanted him to try out, so he cut as much as he could. He remembered sneaking food for them out of his house when they couldn't bear to be apart, of swimming in her pool at night when her parents were out of town. It had all been quite innocent—until the middle of their junior year when her mother had forbidden him to attend her family's Christmas celebration, and his parents had used the excuse of visiting family to exclude Roz from their traditional dinner. He and Roz had been so angry, so helpless—and so much in love. He hadn't realized the extent of the risk until it was too late.

"So, did you invite Jana for dinner tomorrow?" He practically jumped as his mother spoke from behind him in the garage.

"Not yet, but she'll come." Though he hadn't given up his condo since coming back to help his parents, more often than not when he had early shifts at the hospital, he crashed at Jana's place. Before this past month, they'd usually spent Sundays at her apartment as well, just the two of them. She wouldn't mind coming to see his parents, though. The love his mother had for Jana was mutual.

"You seem distracted." His mother's dark eyebrows had a few streaks of gray in them like her hair. When had that happened?

He straightened from storing a box of tools under a workbench. "Roz is back in town."

Her eyes widened and her lips pursed. "Are you going to see her?"

He shrugged. "Maybe I want to know why she did what she did."

"It's been so long. Does it really matter?"

Maybe it shouldn't, but somehow it did.

Worry pinched his mother's face, and he wished he could take it away. "Does Dad need anything before I take off?"

"No, he's good. In fact, I came out to tell you he's already fallen asleep in bed in front of the television. Are you going back to Oceanside tonight?"

"Probably. But I'll be back tomorrow." Tyson bent over and kissed his mother's cheek.

Her arms went around him in a hug. "Thank you, son. Drive safely."

She said this every time he left, but tonight the request was more pleading, as if she knew what he intended to do. Because it was time to find out why Roz hadn't told him herself about the baby, and most of all why she'd chosen to end their child's life.

7

Saffron watched in amazement as Joel pushed back his shaggy hair with one hand and with his other hand slapped yet another slice of pizza onto his plate. She was glad they'd come here instead of going to a more expensive restaurant because her sister's boyfriend was apparently training for a Major League Eating competition. Saffron had invited them out to eat because it seemed the least awkward thing they could do, given that they didn't want to go to her mother's or to where Joel was staying. Plus, they had to eat, though she'd only been able to force down one slice of pizza.

She kept thinking about Tyson being a doctor. *What kind of doctor?* she wondered. Since she'd learned he was here and about his career, the anger she'd held in check all these years had risen to the surface. He'd left her to rot while he'd gone about his life. Had he ever really cared about her? Or had he been like all the other boys who told girls what they longed to hear in order to get what they wanted?

"Saffron?" Halla nudged her.

"Huh?" Saffron met her gaze.

"Kendall asked about my earrings." Halla's eyes darted to Saffron's purse and back again.

Oh, right—she'd brought a pair for Kendall. With effort, Saffron pulled herself back into the conversation. "Yeah, I made Halla's earrings. At first I started making them for friends and family, but now I design and create all sorts of one-of-a-kind pieces to sell in boutiques and online. I have a few popular items I repeat, but most are unique in some way. Part of the fun is coming up with new ideas." Saffron dug in her purse for the gift box that she'd put there clear back in Phoenix. "In fact, I made some for you. I forgot to give them to you earlier."

Kendall eagerly opened the box to reveal silver triangle bangles tipped by three square beads with the letters S I S. The tiny accent beads were a light blue and transparent. "They are so beautiful," Kendall said, taking off her earrings and slipping on the new ones.

"I have matching ones," Saffron said. "I know it's kind of hokey, but I thought—" What? That they could be like normal sisters. She cast a glance at Halla. She'd made similar ones for the original six fosters with a second tier of beads that read 1 of 6, 2 of 6, etc., depending on the order they'd come to live with Lily, and now she wondered what Halla would think of these for Kendall. Because as much as Saffron loved her foster sisters and depended on them, her childhood memories of Kendall were special too.

Halla reached for her hand under the table, squeezing it. "Saffron's very talented. I give away a piece of her jewelry on my blog every month to encourage readers to join the conversation, and my readers always respond super quick."

"So did you go to college for this?" Kendall asked.

"I took some business classes," Saffron said. "It's helped a lot with setting things up and knowing how much to charge."

"Could you show me how to make them?" Kendall took one of her earrings back off to examine it.

"Sure." Saffron grinned. "I'd love to."

"Well, I'm about finished here," Joel said, lifting up his drink. "Thanks for the meal."

"Yeah, we should all get going." Kendall put back on her earring. "I bet you're tired after your drive."

"Been a long day," Saffron admitted. Not so much for the drive but because of the roller coaster emotions she'd experienced.

"I know, right?" Kendall yawned. "Me too. And ever since I got pregnant, I'm so tired anyway."

Saffron didn't remember that kind of exhaustion until her sister spoke. An image came of herself crashing on a park bench in Phoenix after earning a meal passing out flyers. And of how she'd lain on the grass with a blanket over her face during the day, so she could stay awake at night to make sure no one stole her stuff. All of that had been so long ago. Why did it suddenly seem like yesterday?

They made their way outside, where Kendall said, "By the way, I told Tyson you were in town."

Something in Saffron's chest turned over. "What did he say?"

"Nothing, really." Kendall glanced at Joel.

"Looked to me like he saw a ghost," he said with a smirk. "You two must have been some hot item. I tell you, I like the guy, but it's weird how he stares at Kendall."

Kendall slugged him. "He does not."

"Does too. All the guys have noticed."

Kendall's blush was apparent in the darkness. "Well, it's only because I look like Saffron then."

"I thought he was engaged." Halla pulled the long strap of her tiny purse over her head and settled it near her hip.

Joel shook his head. "Not yet, but he's got a hot girlfriend."

"Hey!" Kendall protested.

Joel kissed her. "If you like older women, I mean, which I don't."

Kendall laughed. "Whatever."

Saffron hugged Kendall goodbye. "Text me when it's good for us to get together again."

"Okay, but I think I want to tell her tomorrow. My pants are already getting snug on me, and I'm eating like crazy. I think she already suspects."

"I wouldn't be surprised," Saffron said. Their mother had guessed about Saffron's pregnancy before she'd been able to confess.

Saffron started to shake hands with Joel before he hugged her instead. He smelled like sweat and sawdust and cigarettes. Did he know that second-hand smoke was bad for babies?

"I want to hate that kid," Saffron muttered as she and Halla headed to the Prius. "Or love him. But I don't."

"Me too," Halla said. "As far as nineteen-year-old guys go, Joel's pretty typical, but he's definitely not ready to be a dad. Kendall seems like she's getting a handle on it, though."

Saffron hoped so. "You mean because she's researched car seats? It's a start. I wish he were a little more mature. She needs the support. I also wish that . . ."

"What?"

Saffron pushed the button on Vaughn's key fob to unlock the car door. "Maybe if I'd stuck around, she would have learned from my mistakes. She might not be in this position at all."

"And she still might be." Halla went around to the other side of the car but didn't get in. "You know what Lily says about what ifs. You can never predict anything and God has his own plan."

"Right." Saffron climbed into the car. "Either way, she wants to tell our mom about the baby tomorrow, and I'm not looking forward to facing my mother again. You know Kendall's pregnancy is somehow going to be my fault, don't you?"

Halla laughed. "Now you're being silly. You haven't been around for eight and a half years, and Kendall didn't know why you left. Even your mother can't blame her pregnancy on you."

Saffron tried to smile, but it came out more of a grimace. Halla didn't know her mother the way she did. Or was it possible the woman had changed? Saffron would consider the possibility, if she had proof, but so far Kendall's fear of her didn't testify to any change.

"I'd like you to come with me," she told Halla. "As long as Kendall doesn't mind."

"I wouldn't miss it for the world." Halla's voice became grim. "There are only a few people I'd like to tell off as much as my father, and your mother is one of them."

Saffron knew the others included the people who had most hurt the original foster girls. People who were supposed to have protected, supported, and loved them.

"Thanks," she whispered.

In all, the day hadn't gone poorly. Kendall had forgiven her, she was still friends with Vaughn, she was prepared to face her mother, and Kendall's boyfriend wasn't the complete creeper she'd feared he might be. Plus it looked like Tyson was out of reach for good, which meant maybe she could finally go on with her life and forget him.

On their way through the lobby of the inn, she was considering the idea of visiting the hot tub for a little relaxation when a man stepped in front of her. At first, she backed up, intending to go around him, but his voice stopped her cold.

"Hi Roz."

Roz. Only one person had ever called her that. Not Rosalyn like her family or Saffron like everyone in her new life.

Her eyes lifted to a face she'd wondered if she'd ever see again. He looked the same, and yet not the same. His face still had the square jaw she'd loved, and his eyes were still dark and endless enough to lose herself in. His tanned face was topped by the same thick, dark hair. But his features had matured, and he'd grown at least two more inches. He was handsome, this older version of the boy she'd loved.

The boy who'd abandoned her.

Words clogged in her throat as she fought the urge to throw herself into his arms. "Tyson," she managed finally.

"Kendall told me you were in town."

She nodded. "I needed to see her."

"Just Kendall?"

Was he mocking her?

She felt a supporting hand on her back. Halla. She glanced toward her friend and nodded, straightening her shoulders. "How've you been?" It wasn't what she'd come to say, but maybe it was a start. "I hear you're a doctor now."

He nodded. "First year pediatric surgery resident. I'm currently at Tri-City Medical Center in Oceanside."

He seemed satisfied with the statement, and for a moment she shared his joy. "I'm happy for you."

His smile sent her back in time, cracking the barrier around her heart. Pain filled her, seeping in from the fissure, blotting out all traces of joy.

"Kendall said you changed your name?"

"Yeah." At first it had only been a nickname that a homeless woman with a love of books had given her after a self-done dye job had turned her hair decidedly orange. But within weeks, Saffron had clung to the name because it made her old life more distant and less painful, and eventually, it became a part of who she was. "I made it legal a few years ago. I'm Saffron now."

"I like it." He didn't sound sure, and she could hear the question behind the words, but the reason for her name change wasn't something she shared with everyone.

"So what have you been doing all these years?" he added. His eyes, wandering over her face, felt like a caress.

Trying to get over you, she thought. *Trying to figure out why I'm broken.*

No, she knew why she was broken. Because her family and the man she'd loved had let her down, had made losing her son inevitable, and those experiences had colored everything else in her life—all her relationships, even those with her foster sisters, who had loved her despite her inability to give as much as she was given.

Forget this, she thought. This wasn't about how much she had accomplished or suffered in the past eight and a half years. She'd come only to discover why she was still hung up on this man, why he hadn't wanted her, or if maybe there was a reason for what had happened. This last seemed unlikely now that she was facing him, but she wasn't up to having this confrontation tonight, especially in a hotel lobby. And especially not after how he'd treated her.

"You know what?" she said. "I don't feel like telling you what I've been doing. I don't think it's any of your concern. You made that clear years ago." Maybe that would put him in his place.

"*I* made it clear? You've got to be kidding!" Anger flashed in his eyes, and behind that another emotion she couldn't decipher.

Okay, so maybe they were going to do this in public. "You abandoned me," she countered. "You left me to live alone on the street. I know you were only sixteen, but so was I and—"

"Abandoned you?" He shook his head, as if to clear it. "You're the one who left."

"I didn't have a choice. Not after she found out about the baby." Saffron felt strangled now, and she wanted nothing more than to flee.

"Why couldn't you trust me?" he asked.

That was too much. Oh, how much she had trusted him! Tears started down her cheeks, and for an instant, she didn't see Tyson or the hotel lobby but saw instead the tiny face of her son. Coming back had been a mistake. Expecting him to heal her had been an even bigger one. She didn't deserve to be healed, not after she'd ruined the one good thing in her life.

Heedless of the tears, she lifted her chin and said, "I did trust you. We both did—your son and me. And you failed. Look, you've hurt me enough. Please leave. I can't talk about this tonight."

Blindly, she turned and walked away, glad to feel Halla at her side, guiding her.

How could it hurt so much?

Roz—no, he had to think of her as Saffron now—had grown from an attractive girl into a beautiful woman, one who turned heads and stole men's hearts without even trying. In a single instant, her tears had wrenched away all his fury and righteous indignation. The hurt in her face was real—he knew that as well as if they were his own feelings. Her hurt was still fresh like the pain now running through his heart. He'd wanted the best for her—always the best at whatever the cost to himself—and this moment felt like a betrayal of who he was. He'd somehow hurt her, but how? What did it mean?

He only knew that watching her leave felt like all the other times he'd had to let her go home alone, knowing he wasn't welcome, that her parents thought he wasn't good enough for her, and how he'd silently agreed with them.

He couldn't let her go like this. "Roz!"

She whirled and said through gritted teeth, "It's *Saffron*." She turned again and stalked away.

Tyson's mind raced. Something wasn't ringing true here,

and he was going to find out what. "Saffron, please. Let's talk." He started after her, but the tiny blonde with the extremely short hair jumped in front of him.

"Later. It's been a long day." Her hands pushed at his chest with surprising strength. She looked ready to defend Saffron to the death, and he was glad Saffron had a friend like her.

He lifted his hands in defeat. "Okay. But I need to know what happened."

"I'll talk to her." The blonde hurried after Saffron, and he watched until they disappeared.

Well, if he couldn't get answers from Saffron, he'd find out what he could elsewhere. He drove mindlessly back to his parents' house, hoping his mother was still up. He found her in the kitchen with a cup of coffee, waiting for him. Tears leaked from her reddened eyes.

"You've been to see her," she said quietly.

He nodded and sat in the chair across from her, clasping his hands together on top of the table. "How did you find out about the baby and that she was going to a clinic?"

"Her mother called me." The furrow on his mother's forehead deepened. "She told me she and Roz were taking care of it, but that I needed to do my part by getting you away from here. Away from Roz."

"You told me Roz had killed the baby!" *My baby.* A child like the children he treated every day at work. "Not that her mother said they were planning to. There was still time. I might have stopped her." How could his mother have done this—taken away his choices?

She sighed, her eyes pleading. "And then what? Please try to see it from my point-of-view. You were just a kid. My only child. I did what was best for you. You couldn't have supported a wife, much less a baby."

"No, you're right." He stood, propelling the chair behind him backwards with so much force that it crashed against the newly painted wall. "I couldn't have. At least not without support—which I didn't have. But it still should have been my choice."

Instead, his mother, and probably his father too, had conspired with Saffron's witch of a mother and sent him off to finish high school at the military academy his father had been pushing on him. Now he understood why his parents had changed phone plans and his number before they shipped him off. He'd barely had time to put a forwarding on the old number, hoping for a message that never came. Had his parents deleted the forwarding request? At the boarding school, he'd called and left repeated messages on Saffron's phone—only to be met with her standard message. He'd called long after her phone was disconnected, until finally one day a man who definitely wasn't Saffron answered.

He'd been such an idiot. A sixteen-year-old idiot who had blindly let others control his life. No wonder Saffron had looked at him that way tonight. No wonder she believed he'd failed her. He really had.

Now that he'd seen her again, it was so clear. No way would she have left him without interference. No way would she have destroyed their child—even if his mother had believed it.

Then where was the baby now? No, not baby. A child now, a son.

Hope sprang up inside him. Maybe it wasn't too late.

He had to see Saffron, to make her talk to him. Would she understand that he'd been lied to, that he hadn't meant to abandon her?

"I'm sorry," his mother said. "Can you forgive me?"

"I don't know." The words filled him with sadness. He turned on his heel and strode to the door.

"Tyson," his mother called.

He paused and said without looking at her, "What?"

"She called. Saffron called your phone before we changed numbers, but I erased the messages. I blocked the number." The sorrow in her voice sounded real.

"What did she say?"

The seconds stretched out between them. "That the test you bought together was positive, and that her mother knew and had taken her phone. She left a number where to reach her. But it was only for a week."

By that time, he'd been transferred to the other school. "So no mention of an abortion?"

She shook her head. "But her mother made their intentions clear, and I figured that phone number was wherever she was staying for the procedure, and that afterward, she'd be recovered enough to go away to another school."

Anger raged inside him, spilling from his mouth like a volcano after eight and a half years of holding it in. "Her mother could never be trusted. She hated me. And you know what? If you had ever made an effort to get to know the girl I loved, if you'd cared even a tiny bit for her like I did, none of this would have happened. And that grandson you've been wanting would already be here. Yes, it was a boy, and thanks to you, I have no idea what happened to him or where he is now."

Without another word, he turned from the devastation in his mother's eyes and walked out of the house.

His phone buzzed as he climbed into his silver Infiniti. He pulled it out, staring at Jana's number. For a moment, he was tempted to ignore it, but maybe hearing her voice would pull him out of this nightmare.

"Hey," he said.

"Hey, yourself." Her voice was silky, like her skin. She'd smell of flowers and taste sweeter than any dessert. "When will you be here?"

"Uh, change of plans. I'm not going to make it tonight. I'm staying over here. Tomorrow too. But I'll see you at the hospital on Monday."

"Everything okay with your dad?"

"Yeah, and we got the ramp in. He loves it."

She laughed. "Good. I can't wait to see it."

He should extend his mother's invitation now, but he didn't feel like a nice family dinner, and it wasn't fair to throw all this at Jana without warning. He'd mentioned Saffron in a conversation about former dates, but he'd never told Jana about the baby or of how in love he'd been. He wished he had now.

"We should be finished with all the repairs here by the end of Monday. After that there are just little things for me to do, like stain the ramps. I'll show you all of it soon."

"Nice. Well, I'm going to miss you tomorrow, but I guess Monday will have to do."

"Let's have lunch," he suggested.

"Okay. Give your parents my love."

"Will do."

She hesitated only a second before adding, "Love you."

"Love you too."

But it felt like a lie. Because as much as he cared about Jana, right now all he wanted was to see Saffron.

After thanking Halla for helping her back to her room, Saffron locked herself in the bathroom and took a shower, letting the scalding water wash away her tears and steal her energy until she couldn't cry anymore.

She dried off, examining her body in the foggy mirror. There were no stretch marks on her stomach from the pregnancy—she hadn't gained enough weight for that, and even when her milk had come in and she'd ached for her baby, she barely filled out her bra. No permanent signs remained to mark his existence.

She wrapped the towel around her, running over the encounter with Tyson. He'd been upset—shocked, even—at her words. Something didn't make sense about their conversation. Almost, it felt as if she'd been the one to wrong him. Was there something she wasn't seeing after all?

Or maybe it didn't matter. Maybe tomorrow, she could face her mother and be done with this town forever.

I'll ask Kendall to come home with me. Saffron didn't know if Kendall would agree, but at least she wouldn't feel abandoned by her entire family as Saffron had. Saffron wouldn't support Joel, though, so he'd have to work out a plan for himself. Lily might have some ideas about that.

Relief began to trickle through her sadness. Lily would always be there—and her foster sisters. And hopefully Kendall.

The phone on the bathroom sink buzzed with a message. Saffron wasn't sure why she felt a slight disappointment when she saw it was from Kendall. Was she expecting Tyson?

Tomorrow at two, it read. *After lunch. She's always better after she's eaten.*

Saffron couldn't help smiling at that because her mother had always been that way.

Okay, she told Kendall. *I'll text you when I get there.*

Love my earrings!

You're welcome.

How different these texts felt from the stiff ones they'd exchanged before. Whatever wounds Saffron's encounter with Tyson had reopened, the heartache was worth getting to know her sister. She had an opportunity at a real relationship, and she was not going to mess it up. Not this time.

She stared at the phone somewhat blankly for a few more minutes, but there were no more texts from her sister. She clicked into her conversations with Vaughn, scrolling through old messages. Teasing texts, planning texts, texts about how much he couldn't wait to see her.

I miss you, she typed. But she deleted the words without sending them. No way could she say it, even if it was true. She couldn't lead him on. Because as much as she did miss him, at the moment she longed more for Tyson and what might have been.

After stalking from his parents' house, Tyson found himself back at the Rodeway Inn, this time checking in as a guest. The space from his parents was welcome, given what he'd learned, and it was better than the hour-long drive to his apartment. Plus, he was still close enough in case something serious happened with his dad. His father had experienced a few episodes in the night these past months, but since the new wheelchair-accessible bathroom and the lower kitchen counters had been installed, those had mostly disappeared. His parents should be all right for the night.

Except his mother would be crying.

He sighed. Now that the initial shock was over, he realized the emotion he felt most was relief. Saffron hadn't betrayed him—at least not in the way he'd thought. Or the way he'd chosen to believe. Had he instinctively known something wasn't right all those years ago? Was that why he'd kept calling?

Maybe he hadn't wanted to know.

An uneasiness made him unable to sleep. He tossed and turned on a bed that was far more large and comfortable than the one in his old room at his parents' house. He kept seeing the betrayal in Saffron's eyes.

A son. I have a son.

He awoke at nine on Sunday morning. After a ten-minute shower and fifteen minutes of staring at himself in the bathroom mirror, working up the courage, he forced himself to leave the room and make the trek across the entire inn to Saffron's room. He stood outside her door, heart pounding, for another five minutes before he finally knocked.

No answer.

He knocked harder. Still no answer—and his anxiety cranked up. Had she already left? No, she wouldn't leave Kendall so soon. She was just out somewhere. Maybe with her sister. Unless she'd changed rooms or hotels to get away from him.

He checked the time to see that it was ten. Somewhat guiltily, he remembered that his mother liked him to help get his father ready for church at nine. Well, if his father couldn't manage with all the new improvements, his mother would find a way. She always did.

Bitterness fell over him like a thin, sticky film. So much had been lost, and all because of a few lies.

He wandered back to his room, not sure how he'd retraced his steps without paying attention. His phone rang, and expecting his mother, he answered it without checking the caller ID.

"Hello?"

"Hi there. It's me."

"Jana." He sat at the small table near the window, the upset seeping from him.

"I decided to drive down to surprise you," she said. "You

sounded tense last night, so I want to take you somewhere fun. But I'm at your parents' and your car isn't in the driveway, and no one is answering the door."

"Sorry," he said. "Actually, I stayed at a hotel last night."

"Oh." Amusement filled her voice. "Don't tell me you took my advice to make your old room into a den for your father."

"No. It's . . . I just learned something last night. It's been a bit of a shock." He'd never lied to her and he wasn't about to start. "I needed some space from them."

"Then is now a bad time?" A hint of stiffness had entered her voice. "Because I can just drive home, and we can talk tomorrow as we planned."

He wanted to tell her that might be best, but he was hesitant. He was distinctly aware, as he hadn't been years ago with Saffron, that his choices in this one moment could affect both their futures. Besides, Jana wouldn't sleep tonight not knowing what was going on, and he hated to cause her stress.

"No, let's have breakfast. I'd like to see you."

He'd like to feel normal again. But had he ever felt normal? Because now that Saffron was back, he didn't seem to feel anything like his former self. All his emotions had multiplied, as if Saffron's very presence had propelled him backward in time.

For a poignant moment, he wished it had.

But did he really? Would he give up his career and where he was in life now to find out where his relationship with Saffron might have taken him?

He wasn't sure. Did that mean his mother had taken the right path?

No. He wouldn't condone her actions.

Thoughts were still tumbling through his head when he arrived at Penfold's Café, where he planned to meet Jana. She arrived after him, and as he watched her walk across the parking lot to where he waited, a calm spread through him. She moved with sureness and grace. Her long, dark hair lifted in the light breeze, fanning out over her shoulders that were left bare by her blue sundress. He greeted her with a hug and a kiss that further settled him.

She regarded him with a furrowed brow, her dark lashes shuttering her thoughts. "Are you okay? What happened last night? Do you want a listening ear, or would you prefer to talk about something else?"

"I do need to talk to you."

"Okay, then." She took his hand, and they entered the restaurant.

Everything came out. By the time he was finished telling her about seeing Saffron, what his mother had done, and the son he never knew he had, they were seated at a relatively private table and their breakfast was sitting in front of them. Neither of them made a move to start eating.

Jana looked as stunned as he felt. "No wonder you sounded so strange last night. I'm sorry."

Her sympathy brought to his eyes the tears he hadn't yet shed. "No, I'm sorry to put this all on you."

She gave him a sad smile. "It is a lot. I don't know how to begin feeling about it, and I'm not you. But we'll get through it. You'll have to talk to her, of course."

"Of course."

They both took a bite of scrambled eggs, and for a moment they were silent. At first it was an easy silence, but it quickly became awkward. Jana set down her fork and put her hand over his. "Do you think you might still have feelings for her?"

Again, he experienced the sense that what he said could change everything. "Yes, but I don't know what those feelings are. It's been almost a decade. I-I need to know about my son."

"I know. That's huge." Jana stared down at her eggs and fruit, still touching him. "Look, this is freaking me out a little. I thought things were settled between us. I thought you—"

Loved me.

She didn't need to say the words. They hung in the air like a fog that obliterated their future.

Tyson followed the curve of her face to the mouth he wanted desperately to kiss. "I do love you, Jana. This is not the way I wanted to tell you but . . . I-I bought a ring."

A little gasp told him she was pleased.

"But I need time to deal with this," he added.

Her gaze lowered and the words came softly. "I'd be lying if I said I wasn't worried. I know you, Tyson, and you are so decisive about everything in your life—except moving forward with me. I used to think it was because you were afraid of commitment, but now . . . I wonder if it's because you still love her."

Could he after almost nine years? Yes. Saffron had changed, but he felt he knew her. Seeing her had brought him back to the days when loving her had seemed as necessary as breathing.

Jana wasn't through. "Or maybe it's because she broke your heart. We haven't been dating all that long, and I wasn't expecting a ring, but I have felt you holding back. I think this is why. But I do love you, Tyson."

"I'm sorry," he told her. "I'm sorry about all of it."

"I know."

They finished eating, and then he walked her to her car, where their passionate kiss felt more like a permanent goodbye than a "see you soon."

He forced himself to turn and jog back to his own car, so as not to see her drive away. Life was crazy. One minute he'd been sure of the direction his was heading—and now everything had changed.

9

Saffron looked up from the remains of her hamburger and french fries. She'd needed a mound of carbohydrates to find the courage to face her mother. A walk on the beach in Oceanside that morning had also helped clear her head and prepare herself.

"Aren't we cutting it short to get to your mom's?" Halla asked as they walked out to the car.

They'd stopped at a burger joint on their way out of Oceanside and it was still almost forty minutes to Saffron's old house. If they hurried, they might make their two o'clock meeting time.

"The shorter, the better," Saffron said. "So I don't change my mind."

"Right." Halla snapped her finger and pointed at her. "I forgot you're still in denial."

"And I intend to stay that way." Saffron clicked the key fob to unlock the car doors and then tossed the key to Halla. "You drive. I'm going to make a list of things I intend to say to her."

Halla's eyes brightened. "Ooh, you mean like 'why are

you such an evil witch' and 'you ruined my life' sort of stuff?"

"Exactly." Saffron waited until they were in the car before adding quietly, "She did ruin my life."

Halla didn't start the car but reached for her hand. "No, because your life is not ruined. You've made the best of a terrible situation. Yes, you made a mistake, but hers was so huge that she lost her daughter. No matter what kind of a woman she is, remember that. She has to care about you on some level. Or did at one time."

"Maybe," was all the leeway Saffron would allow. "But when I saw Tyson, I wanted to throw myself at him. You know? Like old times. I felt the same kind of connection to him. That special little thing inside that said he was mine. I've never had that with any other guy."

"Only because you didn't let yourself." Halla squeezed her hand. "It's going to be okay. I promise."

"Well, you may have to keep telling me that because I'm wondering now what might have happened if I'd done something differently back then. Why didn't I confide to a friend or teacher? My mother couldn't have made me get rid of the baby. Why didn't I go to Tyson's and sit outside his door until he came home?" Now that she was older, a myriad of alternatives seemed at hand, but eight and a half years ago, none of them had occurred to her.

"Because you were sixteen, and you didn't know everything you know now. You made the best decision you knew how."

"What I needed was Lily."

Halla laughed. "We all needed Lily. In a way, we're the lucky ones. At least we found her."

She was right. Despite everything bad Saffron had endured, finding Lily and the girls had saved her.

"But he said *I* was the one who left. And maybe he's right. In a way I did abandon him. And what if he was not only The One but The One and Only?"

"That's what you're here to find out, and if you're meant to be, that spark will still be there." Halla withdrew her hand and put the key into the ignition. "But I'm finding it hard to believe you felt any connection while you were yelling at him."

Saffron grimaced. "Yelling?"

"Yes."

"Well, let's just say I'm talented at complicating things. And whatever it was, it felt good."

"For what it's worth, I think you do need to sit down and chat with him. And sooner rather than later."

"I know." Saffron pulled up her note app and started typing. "Okay, subjects I'm going to talk to her about. How did that first thing you said go? 'Why are you such an evil witch,' I think it was."

"Oh, I can come up with more colorful adjectives, if you want. How about an immoral, cruel, nasty, revolting, horrid, sickening, wicked witch? I especially like the 'wicked' because it seems to fit so well."

Saffron laughed. "Thanks for making me feel better. I'll write down all of those. It's only the beginning."

But as Halla drove, humming along with the radio, Saffron came up with only a few more things: *Why didn't you look for me? Why couldn't you accept Tyson? How could you turn your back on your daughter?*

And the biggest of all: *Why did you let your grandson die?*

The list was small and woefully inadequate. There was more she wanted to say—like why her mother would rather have her sneaking around with Tyson than welcoming him into their home where they could be loved and taught and guided. But she could barely put that together in thoughts, much less into words.

She was relieved to receive a text from Vaughn: *Hey, what are you up to?*

Grimacing, she responded, *Going to see the evil witch.*

Do you need a bucket of water . . . or a sword?

Maybe both.

A pause, and then he wrote, *I assume the witch is your mother?*

Yes.

I'm sorry.

Thanks. Saffron hoped he'd leave it at that.

Instead, she saw the words: *I've always wanted to slay an evil witch. I think it would be something I'm good at.*

She couldn't help her smile. *Probably. You're good at everything.*

I'll never know unless I try. Do you want me to come with you? I can borrow a car and be there in a few hours.

Surprise flooded her at his willingness to drop everything when they were no longer a couple.

Well? he said when she didn't respond.

Thanks, but this is something I have to do alone. Well, Halla is with me.

Good about Halla. That makes me feel better. Call me if you need to talk. I'll keep the phone handy.

Okay.

There was nothing more, and Saffron had to stifle the

urge to continue the conversation. She needed to focus on what she'd say to her mother.

Still, she wished Vaughn could come slay her dragons. Her mother would be charmed in an instant. He had a way of talking to strangers that made him seem like a friend. It was why he was such a good teacher, even if it wasn't his life's calling. Or if her mother wasn't charmed, it wouldn't matter because Vaughn would put his arm around Saffron and she'd feel like a million bucks, even if the image of herself she saw in her mother's eyes was trash.

No, I have to stand up for myself, she thought. For so many years Lily had been her champion, followed by her long line of boyfriends. This confrontation was something Saffron needed to do on her own.

Well, not entirely alone. She had the tiny dynamo of a crutch called Halla. But Halla's strength was in such a small package that her mother didn't ever have to know how much help Halla offered.

The tires swallowed the miles to Temecula, and when the GPS directed them to turn down her mother's street, Saffron's heart started jumping around in her chest. She still hadn't added anything more to her list.

"Already?" she muttered.

"We're ten minutes late," Halla countered. "Text your sister, would you?"

"Just did."

Saffron's stomach started to ache as she waited for Kendall to emerge from the house, making the large lunch seem like a bad idea now. Kendall was probably sneaking out the back and going around, so as not to pass by her mother in the living room. Kendall wouldn't be using the garage door, either, because that would alert their mother for sure and evoke a million questions.

"I don't know if I can do this," Saffron whispered, her mouth and throat hurting with dryness.

"So let's kidnap Kendall and drive away," Halla said. "Kendall's eighteen so it's not like your mother can send the cops after us. Should I keep the engine ready?" Her voice was gently mocking.

"Okay, turn off the engine."

Halla obeyed. "Think of it this way. You've had two days to adjust to the idea of confronting her and a lifetime of thinking about what you're going to say. She, on the other hand, has no idea you're coming. That's a huge advantage right there. You have the upper hand." She glanced toward the house. "Besides, you've got someone else to protect, remember?"

Kendall was coming from around the side of the house as Saffron had predicted, moving slowly and glancing at the house every so often. It could have been Saffron sneaking out to meet Tyson nine years ago, and it tore her heart a little to see that nothing had changed.

She climbed from the car, wishing her stomach would settle, but when Kendall reached her, she was so pale that Saffron made her sit in the passenger seat. "What's wrong?"

"I just don't think I can do this."

Saffron noted that Kendall's words closely mirrored her own only a few minutes earlier, and her resolve strengthened. "Yes, you can. But when was the last time you ate?"

"This morning."

"Then you need more food. You have to eat protein more often or you'll feel sicker. And it's good for the baby."

Saffron climbed back in the car and said to Halla, "Let's get her some food."

Soon they were at a fast food drive up, ordering a grilled chicken sandwich and more fries. Afterward, Halla pulled over to the curb so Kendall could eat.

"You don't have to do this at all if you don't want to," Saffron said, watching Kendall gulp down her sandwich. "You could pack up and come home to Phoenix with me."

"But my life is here," Kendall said through a mouthful of food. "I just want to get married and be happy. I know I was stupid. We should have gotten married first and waited a few years to have a kid, but I love Joel, and we can do this. I want Mom to be excited about the baby."

Hadn't Saffron said the exact same words to her mother? "Well, you're eighteen and can move out and stay in town. She won't have any say in that."

"But Joel . . . He doesn't have a place yet. If mom would let us live with her for a year, it would really help."

Did Kendall think their mother would support them until they finished growing up and could take on the role of adults? Next, she'd be asking if Joel could come live with Saffron. An uneasiness fluttered through her mind.

"Well, what'll it be?" asked Halla. "We can pack Kendall up and head to Phoenix."

"No," Saffron and Kendall said together.

"I have to see my mother eventually," Saffron said. "But I can see her alone."

Kendall grimaced. "I'm starting to show. She's gonna find out if I don't tell her, so I'd better do it now. I want you with me—and Halla too. She won't get so mad with you two around."

"What about Joel?" Halla asked. "Shouldn't he be here to tell her with you?"

The corners of Kendall's mouth turned slightly downward. "I did ask Joel, but Mom's been really rude to him, and it'd be a huge fight, so it's probably better that he's helping his cousin move today."

"We could wait another day," Saffron said.

Kendall shook her head and didn't quite meet her eyes. Was she even telling the truth? Saffron had told lies herself as a teen—mostly about where she'd been after school. In the end, those lies had cost her Tyson and their son. Sudden grief threatened to choke her. Saffron stared out the window, struggling against the emotion, glad she was in the back so the others wouldn't notice.

Kendall ate the rest of her food as they waited. Saffron silently willed her to hurry and also to never finish. Maybe she was going crazy.

The vibrating of her phone signaled another message. It was from Vaughn. *Hey, are you still alive? Did you forget the bucket of water? And did you make sure your sword was made of pure silver in case she's really a vampire? Or is that for werewolves? I get them mixed up.*

The grief subsided. She was okay. She could do this.

"What?" Halla asked her. "You're smiling."

"Just a message from Vaughn. He thinks I should bring a silver sword in case my mother's really a vampire."

Halla grinned. "That's funny."

"Who's Vaughn?" Kendall asked, dipping another fry in too much sauce. "And isn't it werewolves who are hurt by silver bullets? Maybe we need a gun."

"It was vampires first," Halla said. "Werewolves were

only hurt by silver beginning in the early nineteenth century."

"And you know that why?" Saffron held up her hand. "Never mind. Not sure I want to know."

"Just research for a guest blog I did," Halla told her anyway.

Kendall finished her last fry and balled up the sack. "So is anyone going to tell me about this Vaughn?"

"He's a friend," Saffron said.

"A gorgeous, sexy friend, who Saffron was kissing all over the place for three months," Halla corrected. "But he broke up with her last Friday."

"He was a good kisser," Saffron admitted, warmth flushing her. "But it was just kissing."

"So why'd he break up with you?" Kendall half turned in her seat, looking at Saffron behind her.

"Because—" Saffron began.

"To prevent her from crushing his heart," Halla interrupted.

Saffron rolled her eyes. "We'd only been dating for three months."

"I fell in love with Joel after only one," Kendall said.

With Tyson it might have been less than a week, so maybe Kendall was right that time didn't matter. "Look, are you finished? Are we going to do this?"

Kendall turned around and gave a big sigh. "Okay, I'm ready. Or as ready as I'll ever be."

Halla glanced at Saffron. "You want to drive?"

"Not really."

"Good. Because Vaughn's car is sweet." Halla started the engine.

"This is Vaughn's car?" Kendall asked. "That doesn't sound like a man who thinks he's broken up."

"That's what I think," Halla said.

Ignoring them, Saffron went back to the list on her phone and began making brief notes under each of the subjects she wanted to discuss with her mother. Seconds later, she abandoned that to read another text from Vaughn.

When you get a chance, just let me know that you're okay.

Vaughn checked his phone for what must be the millionth time in the past hour, but there were no new messages. Did that mean Saffron was still with her mother? And what had happened with her family to make her end up at Lily's House? He sensed that he was on the edge of understanding more than he ever had about Saffron, but he had to stifle the frustration of not seeing the whole picture.

Of course, he had broken up with her, and none of it was his business anymore. Too bad he didn't feel broken up. He guessed what he'd really done was given her an ultimatum, and he hated it when his friends told him about their girlfriends giving them ultimatums. Ultimatums were a fast track to breaking up, in his opinion, even when the relationship was going well. Except, he'd already felt Saffron moving away from him. If leaving him was what made her happy, that was something he could endure, but she wasn't happy, not deep down, and that ate at him.

Because he loved her.

Loved her. There it was. The truth. When he held her in his arms, there was nothing better. Being with her made him happy, and she seemed happy too. It was only when the future came up, or talk of family, that she withdrew.

Maybe confronting her mother was what she needed to move on. Or maybe he'd read everything between them wrong. That was the worst—thinking that maybe he wasn't right for her and that she just needed the right man before she'd want to commit. A man who wasn't him. This other love, the man she'd loved since kindergarten. Maybe he could make her happy.

He took a breath, fighting the hurt threatening his heart. No, it wasn't over until it was over. He'd be there for her and let their relationship follow naturally. He wouldn't become another part of her life that she regretted.

Kendall led the way up to the front door of their mother's house and tried the knob, but it was locked.

"You don't have keys?" Saffron asked past the banging of her heart.

Kendall shook her head. "I always go in the garage door. We leave that open. Should we go in that way?"

"No," Saffron decided. "We don't want to surprise her like that. She'll only be more defensive. It's best to ring the doorbell." But neither she nor Kendall moved to do that.

"Oh, brother," Halla said, lifting her hand. "I'll do it."

"Well, that's why I brought you," Saffron said as the bell chimed throughout the entire house.

Halla smirked. "It's nice to be needed."

For long moments nothing happened. Saffron studied the fancy wood door, the top half featuring an iron grate covering a stained glass window—a window that didn't let her see inside the darker interior. It seemed like the same door they'd always had, but it had been so many years that she couldn't be sure.

Without warning, not even a footstep, the door opened,

and for the first time in eight and a half years, Saffron stared into her mother's face.

Veronica Brenwood had aged more than Saffron expected, though what she'd expected she couldn't say. Her mother had been twenty-eight when Saffron was born, so she had to be around fifty-three or so now. Her brow was furrowed, and her face was thinner, with tight lines gathered around her eyes. Her chestnut hair was swept up at the back of her head, the stray pieces softening her face. She was still a beautiful woman, who reminded Saffron of a grandmother she could barely recall. Confident and sure. A fighter with brilliant blue eyes that Saffron recognized as her own.

Those eyes landed on Kendall, who had moved to the side of the step, as if hoping to be overlooked. "Kendall, why are you ringing the doorbell? Who are your . . .?" Veronica's eyes pinned on Saffron, her mouth opening in a silent gasp.

"Hi, Mom," Saffron said. "Can we come in?"

Her mother flushed and emotions seemed to battle on her face. Saffron could swear one of those was pleasure but another was most certainly fear. Saffron had dressed carefully this morning in a trendy plaid skirt and a blue blouse, but now, under her mother's scrutiny, she felt rumpled after their barefooted walk along the coast.

After a tiny step in their direction, her mother seemed to take control of herself, and her emotions were tucked neatly away where Saffron couldn't even guess at them. "Please do come in." Her mother backed into the entryway, opening the door.

Stepping into the entryway was like stepping back in time. There were differences—a new painting, a vase of flowers on the mahogany wall table underneath the mirror—but the feel was exactly the same. Veronica led them into a sitting room to the left. The good room, Saffron had always called it, normally reserved for visits from the local pastor, the president of her mother's women's club, or neighbors who dropped in briefly to chat. And apparently the room for returning wayward daughters.

Not the family sitting room, but the room for strangers. That's what we are now, Saffron thought. *Next, she'll be offering tea and cookies.*

The room had been off limits to Saffron as a child, but she knew it anyway. She'd always loved the feel of the Georgian furniture, which had been re-covered at some point since she'd left. The more modern material didn't seem to fit the carved wooden legs of the sofa or chairs.

"Please sit." Her mother indicated the sofa, waiting until they were seated before taking a chair opposite them. Only Kendall didn't sit, wandering instead to the curtained window.

"It's nice to see you, Rosalyn," said her mother.

Necessary was more the word Saffron would use. "I go by Saffron now," she said.

"I see." Her mother's back grew rigid.

Of course. Saffron had been here two minutes and already she was making waves, but she felt it important to assert who she was now.

"And how have you been?" her mother asked, showing the first hesitation.

Saffron forced a smile. "Lately, I've been great."

"That's nice." Her mother gave her the fake smile she usually reserved for slow cashiers at the grocery store.

Obviously, her mother knew Saffron hadn't stopped by to see how she was doing and was waiting to learn the real reason she'd come.

Saffron glanced at Halla who made a tiny "continue-on" motion with her hand, but her mother beat her to it. "I see you and Kendall have become reacquainted." Their mother lifted her eyes to where Kendall stood before piercing Saffron again.

"On Facebook first," Kendall said, the words coming in a loud rush. "I tried to find her before, but I didn't realize she'd changed her name. So she found me."

Their mother didn't respond but continued looking at Saffron. "We thought you might come home for your dad's funeral."

Saffron stared at her. "I didn't hear about him until yesterday."

"I suppose you would have come if you had heard." The phrase wasn't a question but a definite challenge that Saffron couldn't deny.

"No, I wouldn't have." She'd been in no condition after losing her baby to do anything but take sleeping pills.

Her mother's lips pursed. "I see."

Again that insipid phrase that made Saffron want to shout at her that she didn't see anything. Saffron was having a hard time remembering why it had seemed so important to face this woman. Her mother wasn't happy to see her, and she certainly wasn't repentant. Maybe there was nothing Saffron needed to say to her after all. This woman, this place, wasn't a part of her life now and didn't deserve to be. What had Saffron hoped—that she'd appear and her mother would hug her and welcome her back, apologizing for the heartache she'd caused?

She was tempted to get up and walk out, but there was still Kendall. Besides, she'd dreamed of this day for years, and she wanted to walk away with no regrets. Except for some reason, she couldn't remember any of the points she'd wanted to make. Drawing out her phone, she turned it on, keeping it close to her leg. Just a glance should get this meeting back on track.

"Really, Rosalyn?" The coldness in her mother's voice froze something inside her. "Almost nine years since you ran away, and I can't compete with a text?"

"Since I ran away?" Saffron shook her head. "Don't you mean since you threw me out?"

"Is that how you see it?" She gave a derogatory snort. "I wanted what was best for you, and having a child then wasn't good for you—or that boy."

"Oh, you mean the boy who became a doctor?"

The widening of her mother's eyes betrayed her surprise, but her lips twisted as she said, "Not then he wasn't. And he wouldn't be one now if he'd become a father as a teen."

"Well, he did become a father anyway. And it wasn't your choice."

"Then where is this child?" Her mother's arm swept the width of the room. "I don't see him here."

Anger built inside Saffron, fueled by years of hurt—and of that horrible moment in time that was forever frozen in her memory. The instant her precious son's soft little breaths had forever stopped. Words came rushing to her mouth, hateful words that would crush her mother and push her from her life forever. Saffron felt a fierce, mad kind of glee that it would soon be over. She jumped to her feet, fists clenched, and her mother rose almost as quickly.

Kendall stepped between them. "I'm pregnant," she blurted. "I'm pregnant, and I'm having this baby, and I'm marrying Joel."

Several seconds of stunned silence filled the room as their mother took in the information. Kendall retreated, and their mother stepped toward Saffron, raising a finger to point at her. "This is *your* fault! You did this. You weren't happy leaving us alone!"

"No, Mother. Kendall's pregnancy has nothing to do with me. She only found out about my baby yesterday, but I am here to make sure she doesn't have to go through what I did."

That caught her attention. "So you didn't come to see me, but to take her side."

Saffron wanted to scream her frustration. "I was already here when she told me. But Kendall is an adult, her own person, and whatever she decides, I'll support her."

"Have you met that kid she wants to marry?" their mother retorted. "You don't know because you haven't been around. He will never amount to anything. He comes here with his greedy eyes, counting up all the stuff he'll be able to pawn when I'm not looking. He's not going to support Kendall—she'll end up supporting him. She has to stay in school. I have to protect her from him."

Saffron wasn't about to agree with her mother, regardless of how much she didn't care for Joel. "Kendall knows she made a mistake, but she loves him and wants to make it work. You can give her all the advice in the world, but in the end, it's got to be her decision."

"Not while she lives in my house."

Kendall was crying. "Please, Mom. Just let us live here for a while. We'll figure it out."

"Go upstairs *now.*" Their mother pointed to the hallway. "We'll discuss this later."

With a cry and a desperate glance at Saffron, Kendall flew across the room and disappeared into the hallway.

Saffron was tempted to tell Kendall to stop and order her out to her car, but she didn't want to be like her mother, forcing her will on her sister. Instead, she turned on her mother. "You haven't changed at all."

Her mother's gaze was mocking. "That man will ruin her life."

"You mean the way you ruined mine?"

An expression of sorrow ran over her mother's face, but in the next second her shoulders straightened and she seemed to grow two sizes. "Didn't you just say you've been doing well? I tried to help you. I tried to make you see that your mistake would change your life, make it harder for you to reach your dreams. If your life is ruined, you have no one to blame but yourself." Her cold voice pierced Saffron like a knife.

"I was sixteen. A child! I needed you."

"You never listened to me."

"Because I didn't want to kill my baby? Because I wanted to spend time with the boy I loved? It wasn't your decision." Saffron felt choked, smothered by being in the same room with this woman. At least now she knew why her mother had been able to abandon her: being right was more important to Veronica Brenwood than love.

Saffron raised her hands, cutting off what her mother was preparing to say. "That's enough. No more. We're finished here. Goodbye, Mother." She left the room, reaching the hallway and heading not toward the door but deeper into the house.

Her mother flew after her. "Where are you going?"

"To be with my sister."

"You stay out of this!"

Saffron turned and looked at her. "No, I won't. She needs me, and I'm not going to abandon her."

"You lost the right to call her sister when you left." The venom in her mother's voice shocked Saffron.

The words hurt, but Saffron knew they weren't true. "You're wrong. She will always be my sister."

"You will leave now. I mean it. I'll call the police."

"I don't think so. Unless you want the neighbors to see them dragging me out, crying."

Without waiting for her reaction, Saffron headed through the house that was both familiar and foreign to her. She passed her parents' bedroom, and her thoughts went to her father. He was gone. No chance to ask him how he'd felt about her leaving. She poked around her thoughts, testing to see what that made her feel, but mostly it was nothing. Her father had worked too much to be a part of her life.

She continued down the hallway to the other rooms, listening. The sound of crying came not from the room Kendall had used when Saffron had lived here, but from Saffron's old bedroom. A sense of inevitability struck her: the same room, the same problem, the same mother. How ironic that both daughters would face a similar situation. Saffron felt a momentary satisfaction, as if she finally had proof that she wasn't imagining the problems with her mother.

Yet it wasn't really the same. Kendall was an adult, and she wasn't alone.

Saffron turned into a room that had changed drastically. Posters of singing groups filled the walls, and only a few did she recognize. The furniture was different, from the bed to the dresser that was largely unnecessary with the walk-in closet. What had happened to Saffron's belongings? Had they been given to a charity? She didn't care too much about her childhood possessions, though she'd thought about her collection of old beads more than once over the years. Even back then she'd been fascinated with making jewelry.

Kendall sprawled stomach-down on the big bed, hugging one of four large pillows. She stiffened when Saffron entered the room, but that dissolved with a glance. "Oh, it's you." She sat up, folding her legs under her.

"It's going to be okay." Saffron sat on the bed, close enough to offer support, but far enough away that Kendall shouldn't feel crowded. "I'm here for you. You won't have to go through this alone."

"She didn't scare you off?" Kendall rubbed the tears from her cheeks and attempted a watery smile. "But she'll insist that I abort the baby, and there's no way I'm going to do that. I know it's early, but I think I can feel her moving. Like butterfly kisses inside. No way am I doing that. I want to see her. To give her real butterfly kisses."

"Well, Mom can't make you do anything. And look . . ." Saffron hesitated, wondering if, after all, maybe she didn't have the right to say what she needed to say. But because she didn't get good vibes from Joel and the supposed great love of her own life hadn't worked out, she owed it to Kendall to speak her mind. "After what happened to me, I'd be the last one to tell you to give up the baby, but Mom's choice isn't the only one, and neither is marrying Joel. You should only marry him if you want to."

"Oh, I do!" Kendall grabbed her hand. "I love him so much."

"I know. It's just . . . there's more to think about now. Where you are going to live, how to support yourself, and most of all, you have to think about the baby. Even before Joel. Your child has to come first." Did Kendall see Joel rising to the challenge of fatherhood? Saffron didn't, but she could be wrong.

Kendall nodded. "Right. And I want my baby to have both parents."

Saffron hugged her. "I'll help."

"Sorry about Mom. I can't believe she didn't even seem happy to see you."

"I never thought she'd kill the fatted calf or anything."

That brought a smile. "I'm so glad you came back."

"Me too."

But Saffron couldn't help thinking about what might have happened today if her mother had given her a hug and started crying. A show of regret wouldn't have changed the past, but it might have made things easier.

11

Halla waited in the sitting room on the couch until Saffron's mother returned from her confrontation with Saffron in the hallway. Naked agony and hopelessness marked the woman's face, which evoked the first bit of hope Halla had felt since their cool reception. Maybe there was something more to the woman than rigid control.

Even as she had the thought, Veronica glanced in her direction, visibly pulling herself together. She took in the green pants and the dressy white top that, in honor of this meeting, Halla had worn instead of her usual camo pants and black tank. She'd chosen the clothes not to impress the woman but to give Saffron one less thing to worry about in regards to her mother.

Veronica finished her appraisal and stared at Halla questioningly. Halla half expected her to call the police as she'd threatened. Instead, she sank into her chair. Halla didn't know if it was the tight stuffing or shock that made her sit so stiffly.

"I'm sorry you have to see this," Veronica said in a voice that invited commiseration.

"Actually, it was rather less than what I expected," Halla said. "If I ever see my parents again, the police probably *will* be called."

Veronica grimaced, so it was the wrong thing to say, but Halla wasn't here to please her.

"Anyway," Halla said. "I'm only here for moral support."

"And how do you know Rosalyn?"

Halla debated what to tell her. She certainly wasn't going to spill Saffron's story, but maybe a little nudge or two in the right direction would be all right. She'd be gentle, though, because the woman was still looking a little battered, despite the rigid set of her back.

"We spent time in the same foster home," Halla said. "We're both from the original girls who were with our foster mother before she was licensed and officially opened her home to teen girls. All of us became good friends. I love Saffron like a sister." Halla didn't have any biological sisters to compare, but some of the others did and they said that all the time.

"I see." Veronica relaxed marginally. "And what home was that?"

"Lily's House in Phoenix." That shouldn't be too much information to give her. Saffron had stayed on at the foster home to help Lily even after she'd turned eighteen, but she hadn't lived at Lily's House for at least four or five years.

"I see." Questions churned in the woman's eyes, but Halla guessed she was too proud to voice them. Was she relieved that Saffron had found help? Or was she angry someone had interfered with her punishment?

"She makes jewelry?"

Halla didn't remember that coming up in the conversation earlier, and Veronica had seemed surprised when they'd appeared on her doorstep, so it was doubtful Kendall had said anything. But there seemed no harm in answering. "Yes. She's really good at it too."

"She always had an eye for design. If she hadn't been so hung up on that boy, she might have done something with it."

"She did do something with it."

Veronica gave a dismissive wave. "Jewelry making is better left to the large companies."

"Not really." Halla leaned forward, resting her hands on her knees. "Indie art brings an originality that is missing in mass-produced items. Just like music and books. There is some really great work out there that would never have come to light with a big company."

"And really terrible work as well."

"Granted, but overall we have more choices, instead of having a producer or publisher or company limit the art that's released. I like choices. Of course, none of it's possible without the Internet. Thirty percent of my fifty thousand blog followers are from out of the country."

"I see." Veronica seemed to be reevaluating her. Halla held her stare, wishing Saffron would appear so they could either finish their confrontation or leave. Halla debated waiting in the car, but she might have to throw herself between Veronica and Saffron as Kendall had before dropping her little bomb.

After long moments of silence, Veronica's blue eyes fixed on her, glittering with anticipation. "Tell me about my grandchild."

Oh, no. She wasn't getting off that easily. What, did

she suddenly want to start sending birthday cards? Maybe now that Kendall was defective, she thought she might find someone else to focus on. Halla shook her head. "Look, you really need to talk to Saffron."

"I'm talking to you."

Halla stood. "And it's been a nice chat. You have a lovely home, Mrs. Brenwood."

"I want to know." Her voice compelled, demanded.

"Then talk to your daughter." Halla debated what the woman might do if she went to look for Saffron. She might decide to call the police after all.

Veronica rose from her chair and stepped toward Halla. Internally, Halla cringed, a stubborn remnant from her long-ago days living with abusive parents, but she firmed her face so nothing would show. "Mrs. Brenwood, I won't—"

"I'm glad my Rosalyn found Lily's House, and I'm glad she has a friend like you."

Okay, that was surprising.

"I am too." Halla heard footsteps in the hallway. "But if you want a relationship with your daughter, you might begin by calling her Saffron. It's her legal name now."

Saffron entered before Veronica could respond. "Come on, Halla," she said. "Let's go."

Halla wondered if Veronica would say something, but she simply stood there as they left the sitting room and made their way out of the house.

Halla fished the car key from her pocket, handing it to Saffron. She waited until they were in the car to say, "So that went well."

Saffron gave her a funny stare.

"Seriously," Halla insisted. "I expected more fireworks."

"Sorry to disappoint you. Maybe next time." Saffron sighed with resignation. "This isn't over yet."

"How's Kendall?"

"Confused. Terrified." Saffron started the engine and pulled away from the curb a little too quickly. "You know how we kind of don't like Joel? Well, I think she's worried, too, but won't say."

"It's hard to voice any worry with your mother ready to pounce."

"Exactly. But I can see her point. I don't know that either of them are ready to become parents. I think Kendall will be, though."

They were nearly at the hotel when Saffron said, "I wonder if I was ever as young as Kendall? I mean I had to be, but looking at her, I don't feel like I was."

"And?" Halla could hear there was more.

"I wonder if I saw myself and Tyson then—would I think the same thing about him as I do Joel?"

"Was he like Joel?"

"Not at all. He was going places even back then." She frowned at the road, and her sadness tore at Halla's heart. "But maybe if I'd stayed, he wouldn't be a doctor today, like my mom said. Maybe what happened was better for him."

"Ah, don't say that. His opportunities would have been different, but not necessarily worse. If you'd stayed, what would you be doing now?"

Saffron pulled into the packed parking lot at the inn. "Jewelry has always fascinated me, and even back then I wanted to design it. Well, there was a year or two after I left home that I couldn't stand to look at beads because they reminded me of all the awful things I'd been through. But if I'd stayed, I think I might have gone into interior design . . . like her."

"Your mother? Ah, that explains the cool furniture and paintings. And the awesome wallpaper."

"Yeah. Our house always looked like it was ready for a magazine photo shoot."

"I guess you inherited her ability. Or an aspect of it."

"I guess so." Saffron spied a free parking space and pulled into it.

Halla reached out to touch her arm. "You did good this afternoon. I know it was hard and that there was a lot more you needed to say to her, but it's a start."

"I don't know that anything I can say will make a difference."

"It will. It will make a difference to Kendall and to you. And I think to her too."

"She threatened to call the police."

"Yeah, but when you were out of the room, she also asked about you. She knows you make jewelry, and when I told her how good you are, she wasn't surprised. I don't know how she knew, but she did."

"Kendall wouldn't have told her." Saffron's eyes widened. "Wait. You didn't tell her about—"

"No. I told her only that we knew each other from Lily's house and for the rest, she'd have to ask you. But however she knew about the jewelry, she's had a shock today, what with you showing up and with Kendall's announcement."

"I hate it that a part of me still cares what she does."

"It's hard to help caring." Halla opened the door and waited until Saffron came around the car to say, "Look, let's go change and then get ice cream. Ice cream solves everything."

That produced a smile. "It's a date," Saffron said. "We'll have it for an early dinner."

"What would Lily say?" Halla faked horror.

"You kidding? If her kids weren't around, she'd probably join us."

Halla was feeling happy about lightening the mood, but Saffron's smile vanished as she glanced toward the inn. "Oh, no," Saffron murmured, "I think you're about to get your fireworks."

Halla followed her gaze to see Tyson emerging from the inn. He stopped when he saw them, staring. Even from this distance, Halla could see determination in the set of his shoulders. "You don't have to do this."

Saffron's eyes met hers. "It's what I came for, though, isn't it? I have to know."

"I meant you don't have to do this *now*. But I'm game if you are."

"Thanks, but I think I need to do this alone."

"You sure? Because last night when you saw him it didn't go so well."

"I was taken by surprise. But after facing my mom, I'm full of adrenalin I didn't use on her." Saffron's chuckle was convincing—or would have been if her eyes didn't look so frightened. "I'll text you if I need you."

Halla searched Saffron's face and saw that she was determined. It was just as well, because sooner or later Saffron and Tyson would need to say things that couldn't be said in front of any friend or sister, no matter how close. "Okay, but I'll keep checking my phone for messages."

"Here, take the car key in case you want to go some-where. Don't wreck Vaughn's car, though, or he'll kill me."

"No, he won't. He's in love with you, remember?"

"I'm not so sure about that. I mean, he likes me, of course, but it's creeping into friendship territory now."

Halla rolled her eyes. "In your dreams."

When Saffron didn't respond or move toward Tyson, Halla added, "Go ahead. I'll wait here for a minute just in case it doesn't go well."

Saffron hugged her. "Thank you. That means a lot."

Halla watched Saffron walk across the parking lot to where Tyson waited, hoping Saffron was ready to face these particular fireworks.

Saffron strode toward Tyson, trying to summon all the indignant anger she'd felt last night, but the words he'd spoken then made it difficult. Something happened eight and a half years ago, something that had put the betrayed expression in his eyes.

Now those eyes, dark and compelling, didn't leave her face and made her think of those days when she knew he loved her more than life. If anything, he looked better than he had last night. *Just don't smile,* she thought.

Then he did just that. Her stomach did a crazy little flip-flop as it had when she was sixteen. *Stupid.*

"I'm sorry about last night," he said. "Afterwards, I talked to my mother. She told me things . . ." He shook his head. "I had it wrong, and I should have known better. Please, can we talk?"

Her eyes couldn't help taking in his face—the defined shape of his nose, the little scar on his cheekbone that he'd earned on the football field, the dark lashes that had limited his selection of sunglasses because they were so long. And, of course, the smile.

"Well?"

Right. She should say something about now. "Sure. Let me change out of this skirt, and I'll meet you down here."

"If you don't mind, I can walk with you."

She gave a little snort. "I'm not going to run away."

His smile widened, and his eyes crinkled at the corners. "You always used to do that when you thought something was funny. I've missed that sound."

I missed your smile, your smell, your hand on mine. She shook herself a little. "Okay, you can walk with me."

They were quiet until they entered the elevator and he said, "Kendall's a nice kid."

Saffron let the door slide shut. "She's pregnant."

"What?" He shook his head. "That idiot Joel. What's she going to do?"

"They're apparently getting married. Or at least Kendall thinks so." The elevator door to her floor glided open and she stepped out. "What's he like? I mean I've met him, but how's he at work?"

Tyson's mouth twisted in a way she remembered it did when he had mixed feelings about something. "He's really skilled in woodworking. And he works really hard—as long as he's supervised. Otherwise, I'm sorry to say he's not all that dependable. I've been trying to help him develop good habits."

Saffron felt no joy at being right about Joel—and especially that her mother was right about him. But what should she do about Kendall?

"It's ironic, isn't it?" Tyson said softly.

Saffron stopped walking and faced him, surprised at the anger welling up inside her. "It's not the same as with us."

"No. I'm certainly nothing like Joel. And you were always much more capable than Kendall."

Saffron didn't know if that was a compliment or a revisiting of last night's accusations, but her anger was already flowing away. "I'll be there for her, no matter what. My mother won't force her into running away."

Tyson reached out and caught her hand. "Is that what happened?"

Warmth slid from his hand to hers, working up her entire arm. He still felt familiar. "I tried to call you."

"Your mother called mine. Told her you were getting an abortion and that she needed to keep me away from you. So my mother deleted your calls. She let me believe it was your choice."

Years of hurt and heartache filled Saffron. She blinked back tears. "You knew me better!"

His face crumpled and his jaw shook as he tried to speak. "I know. It's my fault. I'm so sorry. I should have looked for you. I knew something was off—at least I see that now. I should have confronted your mother. Somehow I should have known." His head swung back and forth, his eyes deep and hopeless. "I don't know how I can ever make it right."

He couldn't. He couldn't because their baby was dead, and that would never change. Saffron knew his pain would increase once he knew the whole truth, and she almost wished she could hide it from him. But hiding from the truth only brought more pain and loneliness. Even though she'd accepted her son's death years ago, she was still lonely.

A couple emerged from a room down the hall, and Saffron started walking, rubbing a tear from her cheek.

When she arrived at her door, she turned to Tyson, who had followed her. "I'll just be a moment."

"Okay." He leaned against the wall, his face normal now, except for the remorse in his eyes.

If only she'd known their mothers had talked. But immediately, she shook the thought away. If there was one thing Lily had taught her, it was that there was no changing the past. Only the future.

He loved me, she thought. *He didn't abandon me.* He might not have been her hero, but he hadn't meant to hurt her. Like her, he'd been sixteen—young and scared.

She changed into jean shorts and a blouse that was barely a step above a T-shirt. Pausing, she took a deep breath, staring at herself in the mirror next to the television, astonished that she didn't look as beaten and battered as she felt inside. Funny how a few words with Tyson had torn her apart much more than her confrontation with her mother.

Rubbing away a bit of smeared mascara, she started for the door. At the last second, she turned back and removed her little white jewelry box from the top drawer of the nightstand next to her bed. For a moment, she clutched it to her chest. Then she opened it and removed one of the pictures of her baby.

"He'll finally know about you," she whispered. "I'm sorry it took me so long." She kissed her finger and touched the tiny face before wrapping it inside the little blue shirt and slipping it back inside. The box wouldn't fit into her purse, so she dug out a beach bag from her suitcase, wrapping the box first in her towel for protection.

Her phone chose that moment to buzz with an unread text reminder. She clicked in to see a new message from

Vaughn. Just a question mark, which followed the previous unanswered text he'd written: *Just let me know that you're okay.*

He deserved an answer, especially now that the confrontation with her mother was over. Or at least the first battle.

I'm okay, she wrote. *A bit singed, and I think I do need a new sword, but I'm okay. The water missed.*

His answer came immediately, as if he'd been waiting. *Water is tricky that way. You have to aim it just right.*

I thought you'd never slain a witch?

Oh, but I'm an animator and have designed many witches. So I know them inside out.

Ha ha. I'll remember that. I might need lessons.

I'll bring the bucket.

Thank you. Talk later, okay? Have to finish something.

Okay. Later.

Saffron was smiling as she put away her phone, feeling stronger and happier after bantering with him. This being friends thing wasn't all that bad.

With determination, she strode toward the door.

Saffron took less than six minutes, but to Tyson it felt like an hour. His emotions ran the entire gamut, from excitement at seeing her again to anger at his mother. Underlying all his feelings was an intense curiosity about his son. What was he like? Would Saffron allow him to be a part of the boy's life?

Tyson became excited thinking about playing ball with his son, taking him to the beach, and making him pancake breakfasts. He didn't know how Saffron or Jana factored into it, but somehow he'd make things work. He'd been cheated out of so many years, and he wasn't going to waste a single moment of the future. The decision to become a pediatric surgeon now seemed like fate—something he could use to benefit his son. He'd be able to give him the best of everything.

When Saffron emerged, she looked exactly like she had in high school: long blond hair swinging free, shorts that left her sexy legs bare, and a peach blouse that showed off her curves. Only her face had matured, turning her from a teen to a beautiful woman.

He stepped toward her, one arm ready to go around her waist before jerking his thoughts back to the present reality: she was no longer his girl.

"You look really great," he said, his voice coming out rough. "Almost like the past eight or nine years didn't happen."

Her smile made her more beautiful than he saw her in his dreams. "Thank you."

They walked down the hall in comfortable silence. Where would he take her? Somewhere to eat? But he didn't relish talking in a restaurant around other people. That had been awkward enough with Jana.

"You hungry?" he asked as they reached his car.

"No. Not at all."

Then her beach tote gave him an idea. "How about a walk on the beach? By the time we get there it'll be near five and not too hot."

Again the smile that filled him with memories. "I'd like that."

On the drive, they talked about his work and her

jewelry business. About the renovations on his house and his father's health. Each of them seemed to avoid anything about their past. Tyson was aching to bring up his son, but he'd waited this long, so he might as well wait a little longer. Perhaps sharing their present lives would establish enough of a connection that they could face the past.

Despite their avoidance of topics, the conversation flowed between them with the same ease as when they were teens—an ease he'd only ever found with her and Jana. The car was filled with light, laughter, and sunshine.

Hope.

When they arrived at an unnamed beach that was difficult to get to but not popular with tourists, he threw his shoes into his car and rolled up the bottom of his jeans before following her down a rough path to the sand. There, she stowed her sandals in her bag, and the moment ignited a memory of two weeks before she'd disappeared, the day she'd told him her period was late. It had been a warm day for late March, the bright sun mitigating the cool breeze at the shoreline. She'd told him, tears running down her cheeks, and he'd held her close, wiping them away.

"We'll get married," he said. "I love you and that's all that matters."

"I love you too." Her smile broke through the tears.

That day they had walked hand-in-hand near the ocean, unmindful of the cold water that lapped at their feet. He'd felt a strength that had made him unafraid to face any future with her by his side.

Weeks later, his life had ended.

Saffron started walking toward the water, the hem of her blouse lifting up slightly in the wind, showing her smooth back, her hair whipping out behind her, as if beckoning to him. He hurried to catch up. The sand was warm but not enough to make him regret leaving his shoes in the car.

After about a half mile walking along the shoreline, he could wait no longer. He stopped and faced her. "So what happened to you? Where is our son?"

Desolation filled her face, and he understood that whatever happened, the plans he'd been building in his head for the past day would never come true.

"When you didn't return my calls, I had to leave. Find someplace to stay." She looked toward the waves, and he was relieved not to see her expression anymore. "I didn't want my mother forcing me into the clinic. She said I was underage and didn't have a choice. Of course, I know now that it was a lie, but I believed her then."

Guilt stirred in him. "My mother . . . I thought you'd made the decision to go to the clinic. That you didn't want to marry me. I called your phone so many times, but it was disconnected."

Her gaze met his again. "My mother took it from me when she found out."

Part of him itched to take her hand, to smooth the pain from her expression. The other part of him wanted to strangle her mother. "And then?"

"I traveled around. I got odd jobs. I was sick a lot at first, but after three months, I felt a little better and could work more. I eventually ended up in Phoenix. I traveled with an old woman and a couple guys who were homeless."

"They didn't hurt you?"

Her eyes burned into him. "Not them. But there are a lot of bad people out there. I learned that the hard way."

Tyson wondered what she meant but found he wasn't brave enough to ask, not yet, and she didn't volunteer more.

"There are a lot of good people too," she added, her eyes dropping to the sand. She stooped to pick up a shell, which she threw into the waves.

"And our baby?"

She stopped walking, her eyes still fixed on the ground. Tears slid down her face, and he began to fear the worst. Had she given him up for adoption? He couldn't blame her if she had.

Finally, she looked at him. If he'd thought the loss in her eyes had been apparent before, now it was an entire ocean of tears and anguish. "I didn't have healthcare. I didn't have enough food. I didn't know I could get help. I was too afraid they'd send me back to my parents and then take him away."

Her shoulders shook with sobs. His arms went around her, pulling her against the length of his body. Her hair smelled like flowers and warmth, heady and compelling, and his fingers tangled in the strands as if recognizing the path they'd traveled so many other times. They stood close together on the edge of the water until her convulsions eased.

She took a breath and arched back slightly, but he didn't let her go, and she didn't pull away. "He came three months early and lived only a few hours. I'm sorry, Tyson. Our son is dead."

Shock reverberated through him as the hope ignited inside him these past two days was abruptly snuffed out. His son was dead. Exactly as he'd thought him all these years. No. It wasn't the same. Not at all. His son hadn't needed to die. Now it was his turn to cry, to sob and have her comfort him. They clung to each other helplessly, ignoring the few passersby that witnessed their grief.

The worst was knowing he had no one but himself to blame.

At last, Saffron broke away from him and continued their walk, wading further into the water than he could with his rolled-up jeans. Her signal that she needed space. He kept pace with her, separated but still together. Gradually, their tears dried in the breeze. Cawing seagulls zoomed overhead, heedless of their turmoil.

After a time, she angled back toward him, and they walked close together. He wanted to ask more questions, but he didn't trust himself not to break down again, and he didn't want to cause her more pain.

"After . . . after he died," she said softly, "I met a college student named Lily. She took me to her dorm room. Months later we moved to an apartment and five other runaway teens joined us. Nothing official. Just her spending all her money to help us. Then she got married, became licensed with the state, and opened a foster home we call Lily's House. Remember those good people I told you about? Well, they're the good people who saved me."

"I'm glad." And he was. So very glad. Her family had deserted her, and he hadn't been there. At least she'd had someone.

"Come here. Let me show you something." She was smiling again, if a little sadly.

He followed her away from the water where she spread her towel on the sand. They sat on it together. "You came prepared. I guess I'm more predictable than I thought."

She shook her head. "The towel was only to protect

this." She drew out a small white jewelry box that she set on her lap reverently, hands resting on top.

Tyson could tell by her hesitation that whatever was inside meant a lot to her. Had she met someone else? She didn't wear a ring, but eight and a half years was plenty of time to fall in love and have more children. He'd try to be happy for her.

She opened the box and drew out a small blue bundle. A tiny shirt. Wrapped carefully inside it was a picture of a girl holding a newborn, love clearly etched on her narrow face. "It's our son," Saffron said. "I named him Tyson after you."

Only after her words did he recognize the girl as her. A very thin, young girl, who was more skin and bones than flesh. He'd seen pictures of malnutrition before in his studies, and every sharp angle of her face screamed malnutrition. "Roz—Saffron, I . . ." What could he say? The picture brought her plight into focus as her words hadn't. Tears threatened again. *What she must have endured . . .*

"He's beautiful, isn't he? They did everything they could, but finally, they just told me to hold him, and I did until he was gone." Tears made her voice heavy as she handed him another picture. "This was after." A woman there helped me get him dressed and buried. The hospital wanted me to donate his body for study, but I-I couldn't."

He understood. He'd seen parents in that very same situation. Yet how could this be his son they were talking about? He couldn't take it in. "Was anyone there with you?"

She shook her head and didn't speak. Her top teeth closed on her bottom lip, hinting that she was holding back tears. She handed him a folded birth certificate that looked almost new. He read it, and seeing his name—their names—made it more real. "Lily ordered the certificate after I went to live with her. She said I'd want it someday."

"Thank you for showing me." The pictures made him feel worse about their son's death, but he wouldn't tell her that.

"I'll make you copies if you want." She put the pictures back inside the box and set it on top of her bag.

"I would like that." Because he wouldn't let himself forget. He took her hand, rubbing it between both of his. "Saffron, I'm sorry. I'm sorry about so much. I wish I could do it all over again. I wish we could change it." He would never stop owing her for what had happened.

"I know." Her voice was stronger now. "And I should have come before. I thought I was over it. I mean, I've come to terms with his death, but sometimes I'm still angry . . ."

"At me?"

"Yes. And at my mother. At myself. At how young and stupid I was." Her eyes glittered with tears. "He didn't have to die, but he did because of all of us. None of it was his fault. I would never trade him for anything. But the timing was bad. We weren't ready, and he paid the consequences."

"So did you." Tyson was the only one who'd escaped relatively free, and he hated himself for it. He traced a vein on her hand. "I never forgot you."

She gave a little sigh, her mouth parting slightly. "I never forgot you either."

Before he knew he was going to do it, he leaned toward her. Their lips met softly at first and then with more passion as they found their way. His arms went around her, pulling her close. Her mouth opened under his. She tasted just as he remembered—felt exactly as he remembered her in his arms.

They fell back into the sand, still kissing. When at last they drew away, Tyson continued to hold her tightly. He thought of nothing but having her back in his arms and in his life. It felt right. It felt like destiny.

Saffron felt a little dazed as Tyson walked her to her door, kissing her again. More chastely than he had on the beach, but it set her quivering all the same. What was she doing? Kissing him and falling for him all over again?

Then again, why shouldn't she kiss him? She'd missed him so much, and now everything between them was falling into place, as if the horrible days after she'd left had never happened. As if their son had never died.

At that thought, a painful lump grew in her throat. She swallowed, trying to get rid of it, but it wouldn't leave.

She smiled and dug into her bag for the key card, her fingers skimming the jewelry box inside. Her heart gave a painful little beat. *It's okay,* she told herself. *Everything's okay now.* The anger and betrayal she'd felt toward Tyson was gone, and it left her feeling lighter. "I'm glad we talked."

He chuckled. "We did a lot more than talk."

"We kissed. That's all." Did he feel how right it was?

"Saffron, look, there's something I need to tell you." Tyson cleared his throat, his dark eyes grave. "I've been dating this woman, Jana Reynolds. She's an anesthesiologist where I work, and I probably should have said something before but . . . when I'm with you, it feels like before, and it's hard to think about my life right now."

Coldness entered Saffron's heart. From his expression, she could tell he cared for this woman—maybe even loved her. Had this day only been a casual trip down memory lane for him? Would he now return to his life and his new girlfriend?

Just as quickly, she pushed the thoughts aside. If there was one thing she understood about Tyson it was that he wouldn't play with her feelings. Or anyone's feelings. Not if he could help it. He'd be upfront with his intentions, whether or not it hurt. In that she trusted him. But she wasn't giving up without a fight. Not this time.

"I told her about you earlier today," he continued. "Even though you were mad at me, and I had no idea we'd still have this connection. She believes my feelings for you—or what happened between us—is why I've been hesitant to commit to her. She might be right." He took her hand. "All I do know is that I'm not letting you go. Not until we figure this out."

Saffron stepped closer, wrapped her arms around him, and kissed him thoroughly. "I'm all for getting to know each other again."

When they separated, he was smiling. "Tomorrow I have to work, but I'll be back after to finish some construction stuff at my parents' house. Can I see you before I start?"

She nodded. "Are you staying with your parents?"

"Usually, but after talking to my mom last night, I checked in here." He frowned. "I was probably too hard on her."

Saffron didn't pity Mrs. Dekker, who had been cold and unwelcoming to her as a teen. In fact, as she thought about it, she grew angry thinking about the woman's part in their son's death. Not a good sign.

"I'll see you tomorrow," she said, not responding to his comment. "Text me to let me know when you're on your way here."

"Okay. It'll be about five." He kissed her once more, lingeringly, making Saffron forget her anger at his mother.

"Goodnight." She stepped inside the room a bit dreamily, stopping to return the wave he gave her as he started down the hallway.

Halla lay on her bed, her laptop open. "Finally. I thought you got lost."

"I texted that I'd be back late."

"But you didn't give me details." Halla shut her laptop and sat up eagerly. "So what happened?"

Saffron set her bag on her own bed before sitting next to Halla, who moved over to make room. "It was horrible and wonderful and . . ."

"He kissed you, didn't he?" Halla studied her face.

Saffron's hand went to her lips. "You can tell?"

"No, I heard noise in the hall, and I peeked out the hole in the door. You two looked like you've put it all behind you. Last night you were ready to kill each other, and now you're making out like there's no tomorrow. What happened?"

"He didn't know I was trying to reach him because his mother deleted the calls. My mother told her about the baby, that she was taking me to a clinic to take care of it, and to make sure he didn't contact me. He thought I'd agreed to abort the baby."

"Your mother again." Halla's face darkened. "That reminds me. Kendall was here earlier." She pointed to a set of suitcases against the wall by the dresser. "She asked if she could stay with us tonight. Apparently, your mother isn't making life easy for her."

Saffron wasn't surprised, and that saddened her. *Poor Kendall.* "Where is she now?"

"Somewhere with her boyfriend. She said she'd be back later. But what about you and Tyson? Is it still there? The connection you had?"

Saffron gave a long, happy sigh. "Oh, yes. It's like we were made for each other. Kissing him was wonderful. I only ever felt this way with—" She broke off, confused at the thought.

"With who?" Halla's eyes widened. "You were going to say Vaughn, weren't you? So you *do* still like him."

A sliver of guilt twirled around her mind. Vaughn would be hurt if he knew what had happened with Tyson, but they were no longer a couple, and he had no say over what she did. Why did she feel she'd betrayed him?

"He's only a friend," Saffron said.

"No way. Not from his side."

"I remind you that *he* broke up with me. Anyway, Tyson has a girlfriend. Or had. But he told her about me. He wants to see where this goes." Saffron couldn't stop her smile as she grabbed Halla's hands. "I think I found what I came back for. As terrible as that meeting was with my mother today, my talk with Tyson was perfect. You should have seen him when I told him about the baby. Ever since last night he'd been hoping for a relationship with him, and he cried when I told him what happened."

Saffron paused, searching for words. "And suddenly all the resentment and hurt and anger I've been carrying around toward him was gone. I mean, I still long for my baby—and several times today it hurt even more to be with Tyson because I know for sure we could have made it—but at least I don't feel so alone anymore." Tyson still cared for her, and all the years of wondering how he could have let her face their baby's death alone no longer weighed on her.

Halla's eyes glittered with her own tears. "I'm happy for you."

"Thanks. Of course, I don't know what tomorrow will bring, but I'm hopeful. Anyway, tonight I need to focus on Kendall and how to help her. Tyson says Joel is amazingly talented but has no drive. I'm worried he's using Kendall because of my mother's wealth."

"Your mother certainly seems to think so."

"Well, she thought Tyson wouldn't amount to anything, either, so her feelings don't matter. I need to take her out of the equation altogether. Because she was wrong about us. Tyson and I would have made it." Saffron was sure about this after today. They would have struggled, but they would have made it.

Now we have a second chance.

"What do you think Kendall should do?" Halla lay back on her pillows.

Right, she needed to think about Kendall now. Saffron considered a moment. "I don't know. I don't really even know her. I think I need advice."

"Good thing you have Lily on speed dial. You call her, but first take a look at what I brought for after." Halla popped up and went to the mini refrigerator, where she'd crammed several pints of ice cream into the little freezer section.

Saffron laughed. "You brought ice cream?"

"Duh! I had no idea how late you'd be. I got it at a place called Mariposa Homemade Ice Cream, and it's not like they're open all night. Call Lily, and as soon as you're finished, we'll dig in."

Saffron rose from the bed and groped in her bag for her phone. A few grains of sand had gathered at the bottom of the bag, and it brought back the rush of being with Tyson again. If things continued for them, would they be able to make their relationship work this time around?

No, better not think too far ahead.

Lily answered on the third ring. "Hey, Saffron, how's it going?"

"I found him." Saffron paced to the door as she talked, not really caring if Halla overheard but feeling nervous to tell Lily.

"What happened?"

Saffron told her everything, from meeting her sister to seeing Tyson last night. Then the confrontation with her mother and her time with Tyson today. "You were right that there was something going on that I didn't know about. He shouldn't have believed I'd go along with my mother without talking to him, but I should have gotten help."

"You were only a kid and scared. You made the only choices you felt you had available."

Saffron sank onto her bed, tired from all her pacing. "You're right. Halla reminded me of that today. Don't worry. I'm not going back to that dark place where I held myself accountable for everything. I know I was young, and that my mother should have helped me better. But Tyson was young too. That's all I'm saying."

"Of course he was." Lily's voice was warm. "I'm so glad you're finding the closure you need."

"It might not be closure exactly."

"You think you still love him?"

Saffron thought about that, aware of Lily waiting for her answer. And of Halla, who was sitting at the table tapping at her laptop but listening all the same. "I think I never stopped. He's all I thought he'd turn out to be—and more. But he has a girlfriend, so it's complicated. And . . ." She wanted to tell Lily about the painful lump in her throat that she'd felt even while kissing Tyson, but it was too personal. It was also too soon for everything to be completely resolved between them. At least the pain she'd felt at his abandonment was gone, and maybe the rest would fade with time.

"Naturally, there are others to think about now," Lily was saying. "His family, your family, Vaughn . . ."

"I'm not sure our families work into it." *Or Vaughn.* But she didn't say this last because she knew Lily liked Vaughn and would feel sorry for him.

Lily laughed. "Honey, you've seen my struggle with my parents all these years. Family always works into it. And I can see how happy you are to have Kendall back in your life. She's your family too."

"Speaking of that, I'm not sure what to do about her. My mother won't let them live with her, and I have to admit that I understand why. I'm certainly not willing to support him. I think that's what it'd mean if they got married and stayed with me. I get the feeling . . ." Saffron searched for words, not wanting to put her sister down in Lily's eyes.

She didn't know Kendall, not really, and as much as she wanted to help her sister, she wanted to make sure it was help she was offering and not a way of enabling her to make more poor choices. "I get the feeling Kendall's waiting for someone to step in and take care of them."

"That's not too surprising," Lily said. "She's practically an only child, raised in an affluent family. She's been taken care of all her life. A lot of kids these days think the world owes them a living. It's called entitlement. They want right now what their parents worked years to obtain, but the biggest favor you can do them is not to help too much. They must learn to support themselves. And you know what? Those struggles will be special to her one day. Remember how it was for us back in that tiny apartment? And when we worked on the house?"

Those were memories Saffron held dear, and she would have never known how good it was to be able to support herself if she hadn't struggled.

"I'll tell her he can't come to live with me if she asks," Saffron said. "But I don't want to ruin things between us. And I'm afraid if she did come . . . what if he just showed up? How would I make him leave? He doesn't have a steady job, so he's basically free to go where he wants, and after what Tyson said about him, I'm not sure he'll find a job soon, wherever he lives."

"If you'd like, Kendall can come here for a few months instead," Lily said.

"I thought you're already full."

"Well, I'm two girls over the allotted ten I can have from the state, but since she's eighteen, they don't count her. I have space with the new rooms, and I can give her something to do to help out. It'd be good for her to talk with Tessa in therapy. Plus she'd be close enough for you to see often. I'm sure once Kendall figures out where she's headed, and that she's in control of her destiny, she'll be okay. They always are."

Saffron wanted to say they were okay mostly because of Lily's influence, but she was too choked up by the offer to verbalize the thought. "Thank you," she managed to whisper.

"Of course. You know that's what I built this place for, helping girls. It's just an option, if you need another one." Her voice became playful. "But if you end up staying there because of a certain doctor, having Kendall here may not work for you."

Saffron hadn't thought that far ahead. She'd never had any intention of moving from Phoenix, but Tyson's residency was here. "Well, I still plan on coming home," she said. "We're not exactly picking up where we left off, if that's what you're thinking." There were some things they could never get back, especially their son.

Lily's soft laughter came through the connection. "Okay, but remember that sometimes you've got to follow your heart. I think you'll know what to do before too long. I have faith in you, and I'm so proud of you for doing this."

Saffron blinked back tears. "That means a lot."

"Go eat your ice cream now," Lily said with another laugh. "Halla told me about it earlier, and knowing her, she's chomping at the bit after waiting so long."

Saffron looked up at Halla. "Yes, Halla is growing a little green around the mouth. Definite ice cream withdrawal. I'll go take care of her. Thanks, Lily."

Halla dove for the refrigerator. "Not if I take care of it first." She had four pints out and was dipping a plastic spoon into strawberry ice cream before Saffron had put away her phone. She pushed a pint of coconut almond fudge in Saffron's direction. "I bought us each two pints, but we can share. I wanted to try more than just one."

"You kidding? I know how you feel about strawberry ice cream. I've already risked life and limb today going to see my mother. No way am I touching your strawberry ice cream."

"Ha ha. Just because I like strawberry doesn't mean I don't love all the other flavors. Look, I got Mexican chocolate and mixed berry sorbet as well."

"Nice. I'll start on the sorbet, but I'm definitely going to have some of that coconut almond fudge after the day I've had."

They spent the next few minutes eating ice cream and debating the deliciousness of the coconut almond fudge topped with the strawberry. In fact, Halla added strawberry to all the other flavors, and Saffron barely refrained from telling her that she should give up any pretense of liking the different flavors and go straight to the strawberry.

When they'd consumed most of the pints, Halla sat back and sighed. "I know Vaughn's only taking your car in tomorrow, but what's the chance he'll make it down here before I need to get back?"

"I'm pretty sure you'll have to drive his car back to Phoenix."

"I don't like leaving you without a car. Maybe I should post and see if any of my blog readers are going to Phoenix."

"No way. If you ride with strangers, I'll tell Lily."

Halla rolled her eyes. "They aren't strangers, they're my fans."

"They're strangers, and I don't mind not having a car. I'm not going anywhere, and Kendall can give me a ride if I need one." Or Tyson could, but she didn't want to voice that aloud or start depending on him. "Besides, if you take back his car, maybe Vaughn won't feel the need to come down here."

"You sound disappointed about that."

"I do not!" Did she? But Saffron was too tired to examine her emotions in detail.

Halla laughed. "Okay, I'll drive his car home, and I can bring yours here on Friday after school. There's no way Vaughn can bring your car and get his here to drive himself back to Arizona."

"Good idea." Saffron's stress level must be high if she hadn't considered how he'd get home. Having Halla return with her car would also save her from facing Vaughn in person so soon. It was easier talking to him over text and on the phone.

Halla stood up and stretched. "Look, should I sleep with you tonight and let Kendall have my bed? I mean, I know she's your sister but . . ."

Saffron smiled. "I'd be more comfortable, but I think we might offend her. So, that's okay. I'll let her sleep in my bed, and if it's weird, I'll come over to yours."

Back in the old days, the original six foster girls had slept together like puppies wherever they fit, particularly on movie nights in front of the TV. Though it had been a long time since any of them had to pair up on mattresses on the floor, they were still a lot like a litter of puppies when they got together for their movie fests.

"Besides, she might not come back tonight," Saffron added.

"Oh, I think she probably will. Two large suitcases and a carry-on seem to say she's serious. And from listening to her, I don't think there is any room where Joel is staying."

"Sorry about her crashing our party."

"Are you kidding? She's your sister. That means she's my sister too—in a weird sort of way. I wonder how she's going to feel meeting the rest of us."

Saffron had to smile at that. "I guess we'll see. Um, so do you need to use the bathroom before I clean up? I have to shower after all the time I spent on the beach today. I swear my hair is permanently tangled."

"You go ahead." Halla grabbed the TV remote and lay on her bed. "But are you sure you want to wipe off his kisses with actual water?"

"Stop." Saffron flipped her plastic spoon at Halla.

Halla squealed and dodged the missile. "Just kidding. I'm sure you can always get more tomorrow."

Saffron gave up and stalked to the bathroom, pretending annoyance but all the time hoping Halla was right.

In the bathroom, she checked her phone, but the only messages were from Halla. They were silly, jokey things like "You kissing him yet?" And "Seriously, you're choosing a man over ice cream? What's wrong with you, girl?"

There was nothing from Tyson, which was expected, but also nothing from Vaughn, which made her feel a disappointment she didn't really understand. It was better this way, of course, especially given the strong attraction between her and Tyson.

Saffron stepped into the hot shower and thought about seeing Tyson the next day. Maybe there would be more kissing. Of course, that was after work, after he saw the woman he'd been dating. Not only did they work together, they had a past—an adult past. She couldn't fool herself into thinking there wasn't a chance their relationship was stronger than what she and Tyson had shared.

Kendall knocked on her sister's door at the inn, hoping she was still up. She hadn't meant to be out so late, but Joel had wanted to stream a movie on Netflix, and she'd fallen asleep on the couch. She hadn't meant to, but since becoming pregnant, she couldn't seem to get enough sleep. At the moment, she only wanted her comfortable bed and air-conditioned room, but she couldn't return to her mother and the brochures she'd printed about adoption. Staying with Joel in an apartment with six other guys also wasn't an option, even if they could both sleep on the couch, which was impossible. She was lucky Saffron was in town.

Maybe she could get her sister to let both her and Joel move in with her for a while in Phoenix. Getting Joel away from his friends might be the jumpstart they needed. Kendall knew he would step up when it came right down to it. He should be able to get a good job—everyone said he did beautiful work. She only wished he was a bit more excited about the baby. At first, he'd been so proud, putting his hand on her stomach possessively as he bragged about becoming a father, but lately the throwing up and nausea had put a damper on everything.

She was so tired that she didn't know how she was going to make it through school tomorrow. *Maybe I won't go,* she thought, knocking harder on the door. If she was giving school up, why bother dragging it out a few more days? She was sickest during the morning when she had her classes, and interior design had always been her mother's thing, not hers.

The door opened, and Saffron stood there in a hot pink nightshirt with matching pink and white polka-dotted shorts. She looked different somehow. Happier.

"Sorry I'm so late."

Saffron led her inside, a welcoming smile on her face. "You're just in time. Halla and I are going to watch an episode of *Charmed*."

"Never heard of it, but I'm game." Kendall tried to put excitement into her voice, which was more difficult than she thought. Who had ever expected that such a tiny baby could make her so tired?

"Good, because I have exactly the thing to perk you up." Halla, dressed in a Tweetie Bird nightshirt, was opening the little refrigerator. She pulled out two pints of ice cream.

"What, you have more? How did you get all that in there?" Saffron asked.

Halla smirked. "Very carefully. Remember, a pregnant woman always needs ice cream."

"Pregnant women and women named Halla, you mean." Saffron handed Kendall a spoon, then ushered her to the bed, where they had a laptop set up on what looked like a plastic lid belonging to a cooler.

"Aren't you guys having any?" Kendall asked.

"We already ate two," Halla said. "Two each, that is. These are for you."

Saffron rearranged the pillows. "Up you go."

Seconds later, Kendall found herself wedged between the other two, right in the middle of their conversation about ice cream and how many pints they could eat. She felt a rush of envy that they knew each other so well. It should be her and Saffron who acted like sisters, not Saffron and Halla. But their mother had stolen that from them—she couldn't blame Saffron for leaving or for not coming back sooner.

The first bite of coconut almond fudge drove all thoughts from her head. She gobbled the entire pint in pure bliss, not even paying attention to the show. But before she could dig into the second, she started sobbing.

"Oh, honey, what's wrong?" Saffron put an arm around her, motioning for Halla to take the ice cream. The sound to the show cut off as Halla paused it.

"I think I'm just tired." Kendall wiped furiously at her tears. "And a little worried. Mom wants me to dump Joel, and after Joel finishes at Tyson's parents' house, he doesn't have a job lined up. He's not even worried about it. I know he wants this baby, but sometimes I wish . . . I wish he were a little more responsible." There, she'd said it, but she needed to make them understand Joel's potential. "And don't tell me I should leave him because we love each other. I don't need anyone else telling me I'm making a big mistake. He's the father of my baby, and we're going to be a family. It's all the pressure that's making me crazy."

"Any decision you make is yours." Saffron said, her arms still around Kendall. "I'm not telling you what to do."

It felt so nice to have a big sister to turn to. Maybe two of them. Because Halla was also looking at her with concern from the refrigerator where she was stuffing the uneaten ice cream back into the little freezer.

"Meanwhile, until you figure it out," Saffron added, "you can crash here for the next few days."

Panic filled Kendall. "Is that all you're going to stay? Just a few days?"

"Well, I have to go back sometime. My life's in Phoenix, and it's really expensive for me here. But that doesn't mean I won't be there for you."

"Then did you mean it when you said I could go back to Phoenix with you?"

A guarded look came into Saffron's eyes, and her resemblance to their mother startled Kendall. "You're welcome to stay with me for a little while, but I have only one bedroom, and my apartment is filled with jewelry-making equipment. So it's not the most comfortable."

Halla snorted. "Let me tell you, her beads are everywhere. That's why she moved out of my apartment."

"Well, that and the privacy," Saffron muttered.

"We don't give her too much privacy anyway," Halla said. "We all have a key."

The jealousy Kendall had felt toward Halla returned with a vengeance. "What are you saying?" she demanded of Saffron. "You don't want me to stay with you?"

"No, that's not what I'm saying. I'm saying I don't have room for Joel. And that if you want to stay longer term, they have an opening at Lily's House. That's where I lived after . . . after I lost the baby."

"A foster home?" Kendall was aghast. "I'm not a child! I don't need anyone looking after me."

Halla returned to the bed with a box of tissues. "It's Lily's House, so not your average foster home. And believe me, Lily will put you to work. She'll probably try to get you certified by the state so she can get more girls."

"Many of us stayed after eighteen," Saffron added. "I was there until twenty. Anyway, it's just an option. I'm not sure how long I'll be staying at my apartment. Some things have happened—"

"She kissed Tyson tonight," Halla put in.

Kendall blinked. "You what? You mean . . .?" So that was why Saffron looked so happy. "I can't believe it. I thought he was almost engaged."

"Looks like we came in the nick of time." Halla's voice was sardonic, and Saffron gave her a hard stare. "Well, it's true."

"Tyson and I have a lot to work out, that's all," Saffron said. "I'm not jumping into anything, and I don't want to leave Phoenix, but that might need to change. Anyway, my love life doesn't have anything to do with what you and Joel decide to do."

Kendall pushed away from her sister and jumped from the bed. "It does when you're willing to have me stay with you but not Joel. If we were married would that make a difference? Because I can march him down to city hall tomorrow. I just don't see why it matters to you if he camps out on the couch for a few weeks."

"How long has he been at his friend's?" Saffron countered, a flush growing on her face.

Six months, but Kendall wouldn't tell her that. "It doesn't matter. It's not like it would be a burden. I could make the food, and he could fix things for you when he's not working."

"And who would *buy* the food?"

"I would!" The nerve of her. As if Kendall would want her charity. "I can get a job." She'd have to once her mother cut off her allowance.

Saffron stared at her, dismay in her eyes. "I'm sorry. He can't stay with me. I work at home, and there's not enough room. But you could come with me, and he can move to Phoenix after he finds a job there. Or you could come back here to him when he has a place ready."

That wasn't at all what Kendall wanted. "I can't be away from him!" What if he found someone else? She'd seen the way his friend's sister looked at him. Kendall knew Joel loved her, but she didn't want to leave anything to chance. "I can't believe you won't help us." She threw up her hands. "You know what? Never mind. I don't need you!" Kendall turned to leave and was surprised to find little Halla blocking her way.

"Just calm down," Halla said.

"Get out of my way!" Kendall tried to push past her, but Halla stood her ground.

"Is that really what you want? To leave? Where will you go? You have a sister here who loves you and who wants to help. As for Joel, he needs to decide what he wants to do—if he's going to man up and support your child, or if he plans to keep sleeping on someone's couch and doing odd jobs. But don't make it easy for him to do nothing."

Her words struck Kendall like a slap. Because for months

now it had been her pushing him to get a job, pushing for them to find a place to live, pushing him to be a man. She was tired of it. Bone tired. So tired she wanted to lie down on Saffron's bed and cry herself to sleep.

Somehow Saffron knew, whether by the slump of her shoulders or through sisterly intuition, it didn't really matter. Her arms went around Kendall again. "Please stay," she said. "We'll work something out. Our friend Lily has connections if Joel wants to find work. What's important is that precious baby you're carrying. I don't want you to lose her or him like I lost my baby."

Suddenly Kendall's emotions realigned. Her frustration ebbed, she felt more energy, and hope burned in her chest. The baby. Yes, she wanted everything good for this baby. That was the most important thing. More important than herself. More important than even Joel. "Okay," she whispered. "I'll stay. Thank you."

"Here, come back to the bed. We'll turn off the light and talk about unimportant stuff." Saffron cracked a grin. "Like how Halla should join Ice Cream Eaters Anonymous."

Kendall smiled despite herself. "Okay."

Saffron tucked Kendall's hair behind her ear, her concerned expression changing to one of surprise. "Nice earrings . . ."

Kendall pushed her hair farther out of the way. "Thanks. Sorry they're not the ones you gave me. They're Mom's. I borrowed them before I snuck out. I was mad at her." She shrugged. "She hates it when I borrow her things."

Halla peered at the earrings. "Hey, those look like—" She broke off at a shake from Saffron's head.

Kendall was glad. She didn't want anyone telling her

how much the earrings cost and why she shouldn't have taken them. "I'll give them back tomorrow."

Saffron's smile looked strained, though maybe Kendall was mistaken. "Well, I hope you packed pajamas," Saffron said.

Kendall nodded. "I did. But first I really need to pee." She skirted around Halla, heading for the bathroom, while the others started laughing.

There was still a sliver of anger in Kendall's heart at Halla for her interference, but she was honest enough to admit that it was most likely because she was jealous of her relationship with Saffron.

After she and Joel were married and had the baby, none of this would matter. She just needed to figure out how to make that happen. *Maybe going to Phoenix is a good idea,* she thought. Joel loved her, and if she wasn't around, it might set a fire under him to act. If it didn't, wouldn't it be better to know that now? Her heart ached at the thought.

She placed a hand on her stomach, looking in the bathroom mirror. "I promise you that I will always keep you safe. I promise."

15

"**A**re you sure they're your earrings?" Halla said as she readied to go down to the pool. "Or that you made them, rather?"

Saffron looked up from the table, where she was putting together a custom necklace for an order that had come in over the weekend. "Oh, yeah. I never posted pictures of them online either, so no one could copy them. Even if I had, I got some of those beads off a fifty-year-old purse I found at a second-hand store. There's no way anyone could have replicated them. That purse was a find I may never duplicate. I made them for a specific customer, one who obviously used a fake name to contact me."

"Well, I told you your mother knew about your jewelry." Halla pulled on a mesh coverup over her suit.

"But if she knew where I was all this time, why didn't she try to contact me?" Saffron scowled. "And why would she buy my earrings?"

"Because you're an awesome designer? Because she wanted a connection with you?"

"I think you're giving my mother too much credit." Yet

Saffron distinctly remembered the request the client had made of her before sending the required down payment, one that haunted her now.

Halla laughed. "Maybe. Maybe not. Come on. Let's get down to the pool before that gorgeous doctor comes to sweep you away."

"He won't be here for hours." Saffron followed Halla to the door, stopping for her sandals. "What if my sister comes back from school—if that's where she went."

"She'll text you. Come on."

Saffron let Halla propel her down the stairs to the pool area, where a dozen people were already enjoying the facilities. Halla threw her bag on a chair, took off her coverup, and immediately jumped into the pool and began doing laps.

Saffron removed her own coverup but stretched out on a lounge chair and closed her eyes, basking in the delicious warmth of the sun. With her thoughts of Tyson and trying not to crowd Kendall in the bed, she hadn't slept much last night. Now thoughts of her mother and the custom earrings wouldn't leave her head.

She was grateful for the distraction of her ringing phone. She squinted in the bright light to see who it was but immediately gave it up and answered. "Hey," she said.

"Hey, yourself." Vaughn's deep voice filled her ear.

"Hi, Vaughn."

"I have news about your car."

"Oh, good." Of course he was calling about the car. "What's the damage?"

"Well, it's just the brakes. No rotor damage."

"That's a relief." The last time she'd taken her car in too

late and had to replace the rotors as well as the brake pads. "They say anything about the weird noise?"

"Loose belt. Simple fix."

"That's fantastic!" Saffron had been worried about that, especially with all the money she was spending from her savings. "Will they have it ready tomorrow?"

"Yep, and I'm planning to drive it down to you this weekend—if you'll still be there." The question in his voice was unmistakable.

"I'm not sure how long I'm staying," she said. "I've got to figure something out because this hotel is costing me too much, but I'm not ready yet. I should know more in a few days. Oh, and that reminds me. Halla says she can drive back Friday, so maybe she can bring my car and save you the trip. Because I'm not sure if I'll be ready to go back even then, and I don't want you to be stranded here."

Silence met her through the phone, and for a moment Saffron wondered if she'd offended him. Then he said, "That's nice of Halla. What will you do without a car until then?"

"I don't really need to drive anywhere." She hesitated, deciding how much to share. "My sister is staying here, and she has a car, if I need something. And I have other . . . friends." It wasn't like she could tell him about Tyson. Or could she?

"So how's it going with your family anyway?"

The single question was all it took. She started explaining about Kendall and how she'd asked if Joel could stay with her, and how bad an idea that was.

"I'd offer to try to get him a job at the sports store, but from what you say, I don't think he could do the work."

"Not without constant supervision, I don't think. I wouldn't want everyone to have to deal with that."

"And your mother?"

Saffron didn't want to go too far into the subject of her mother with him. Even if she'd wanted to tell Vaughn about the baby and why she'd left, it wasn't something she could do over the phone out here in public. "I'm not sure I'll see her again. I didn't say everything I wanted to, but I don't really think she cares." Saffron tried to stifle a sigh.

"That bothers you."

"No, I'm fine with it." Saffron was beginning to feel a little hot under the sun, and she wiped her neck with her towel.

"Well something's bothering you. You sound exactly like you did when you told me about that employee stealing money from the register."

Saffron gave a wry grin, though he couldn't see her. Something *was* bugging her, and she did need to share it with someone—preferably someone who hadn't met her mother. "Okay, okay. A few months ago I had this client who requested a set of earrings. She said she was estranged from her mother and wanted something very special to show she still loved her despite everything and that she wanted her back in her life. Those weren't her exact words, but close. It was different enough that it stood out in my mind. I made some fabulous earrings with unique one-of-a-kind beads. Then last night, my sister shows up wearing the earrings."

"She ordered them?"

"No, she'd taken them from my mother's jewelry box."

"That is weird. What do you make of it? I mean, unless

you have another estranged sister who could have ordered them."

"I don't. And now I'm not sure what to think. I mean, you should have seen her yesterday. Not even a hug. If my—if I had a child, even one I'd had a falling out with, I would still give him the biggest hug ever, especially after almost nine years."

"I'm sorry," Vaughn said. "I can't imagine how that made you feel. But maybe the earrings are a good sign."

"That's what Halla thinks."

"You should talk to your mother again."

The idea made her stomach hurt. "Maybe."

"I meant what I said about coming with you, if you need someone else."

That made her weird mood lighten. "I know. Thanks. But I'm a big girl."

"Oh, of that I'm very aware." His voice was seductive, and a little thrill ran up her spine.

What was wrong with her? She and Vaughn were broken up and she'd reconnected with Tyson. *Vaughn and I are just friends now.*

"Thanks for telling me," he added. "I think I've learned more in these last two days about you than I did in the past year."

"I guess you were right about me having issues to work through." There was so much she hadn't told him—most of which she would probably never share now.

Another long pause before he spoke again. "Right now I'm wanting more than anything to ask you something, but I've got to teach a class in five minutes. Enjoy your time at the pool."

"Wait, how do you know . . ."

He laughed. "I do, that's all. Make sure to use plenty of sunscreen. You know how you burn. Talk to you later."

She wanted to ask later when—tonight? Tomorrow? But he'd already hung up. Saffron stared at her phone, feeling immensely better. She hadn't solved the problem with her mother or the weirdness of her buying the earrings, but it had helped to tell him.

What if she'd confided all of it months ago? Including about the baby? He'd wanted her to, but it had seemed too personal then. Now not confiding in him seemed odd. No wonder he'd been concerned. "Sorry, Vaughn," she murmured.

Sweat had begun running down her back. Time for a little dip in the pool. She tucked away her phone and went to join Halla in the water.

Tyson left work feeling unsettled. He'd eaten lunch with Jana today, and he'd told her he needed space to work things out with Saffron. The look in Jana's eyes had almost killed him. She hadn't cried or become upset but had stared at him sadly, as if she'd been expecting his reaction all along. For a brief moment, he wished he'd asked her to marry him last week or a month ago. What had he been waiting for?

No, he couldn't wish that because he would never have had this opportunity with Saffron, and he might never have learned the truth about his son. He had to follow his heart. Jana had a good career, and she was a capable woman who could take care of herself. He had no choice but to let her go and see where this thing with Saffron led.

At his parents' house, Joel and the other two workers Tyson had hired had already arrived to finish the back ramp, so he got them started without going inside the house. "Remember there are bonuses if we finish tonight. I'm going to grab dinner and buy some stain. After that, I'll be staining the front ramp if you have a question. If you need something before then, talk to my dad."

"Sure thing," Joel said.

Tyson waited until they were hard at work before jogging back to his car, smiling in anticipation of seeing Saffron. He didn't have long before he had to be back to check on the men, but they would finish the main job tonight, and he'd be able to take more time to be with her. More time like yesterday, which had been a complete step back in time. She was so beautiful, and every bit as fun as the girl he'd loved, only better. He wanted what they'd had—and more.

There were so many things he planned to do with her. He would show her where he attended med school in Washington DC, and take her to New York. They'd go to stores featuring name brand jewelry designs, and he'd buy her anything she wanted. He'd take care of her. He'd make all the pain of the past go away.

Somehow.

Moments later, thoughts of Jana crowded back in. He hoped she was okay. None of this was fair to her, but there didn't seem to be an option that gave everyone what they wanted or needed. After parking at the Rodeway Inn, Tyson checked his phone, thinking maybe he should text Jana something, and saw four new messages from his mother.

The first one asked why he hadn't come in after he'd gotten the men started on the back ramp. The last one read: *Please forgive me. What can I do to make things better between us?*

He didn't doubt his mother's regret, and he knew he wouldn't stay mad at her forever. Already the anger he'd felt on Saturday was fading. She couldn't have foreseen what had happened to Saffron, and he believed she wanted the best for him.

He texted back. *I'll be by later to check on the guys and to stain the front ramp. In the meantime, can you tell dad to watch them? That will keep them going. I'm going to see Roz for a while.*

He'd typed Saffron first and had to delete the name, knowing she wouldn't understand. Later he'd explain. He closed his eyes at the thought. The idea that he and Saffron could pick up where they left off was so huge that it seemed impossible. But that's exactly what he wanted to do—more than anything. Or he would if it didn't mean hurting Jana. Because without his parents' interference, he and Saffron would have succeeded. They would have made their relationship work.

His mother's reply came as he shut the car door. *I'd like to see her. I want to apologize.*

Right. He didn't think that would be happening soon. He'd recognized the look in Saffron's eyes yesterday when he'd mentioned his mother. Justified as her anger might be, how could they hope to go forward if Saffron never wanted anything to do with his parents? He couldn't abandon them, regardless of his mother's actions. He was all they had.

I don't know if she'll come, he wrote. *What happened to her after she left here was awful. I don't know if she's ready.*

And your son? she asked.

He could read hope in the sentence, and part of him wanted to leave her hanging, but a larger part didn't want to hurt her anymore. He also didn't want to tell her what had happened in person. *He came too early.* The words hurt as he clicked each letter. *He died. Because of me.*

Even the words hurt too much, and when his phone buzzed with a response from his mother, he shoved it in his pocket and didn't look at the text. Instead, he hurried inside the inn to meet Saffron.

She answered the door with only a few seconds delay, looking so good in a yellow sundress that he wanted to take her in his arms and kiss her right then. But she stepped back and motioned to someone behind her. "Hey, I know you saw her before, but I want you to officially meet Halla. She's one of my foster sisters."

Behind Saffron, the slender girl in pink camouflage pants and a pink top gave him a little wave. "Hey."

"Hi." Neither of them said anything about their first meeting, which was probably for the best. But Tyson felt Halla's eyes like a weight on him, and he found himself wanting to prove his worth to her.

Saffron turned back to him. "It's almost six, and I know you have to work tonight at your parents' house. So what's the plan?"

He shook his head. "Dinner maybe? I can take a couple hours." Tyson glanced at Halla. "Why don't you join us?"

Halla shook her head. "No, you two go ahead. I have studying to do anyway."

"I'd like you to come," he insisted. "I'd like to hear about you and all the others in Saffron's family. Saffron said that you're going back tomorrow, so who knows when we'll have another chance."

Halla glanced at Saffron, who nodded at her to accept. "Okay, sure," Halla said. "I'd love to get to know you too. I just didn't want to get in the way. You two don't have much time."

Panic surged through Tyson. "You're not going back too, are you?" he asked Saffron.

A smile played on her lips, telling him she guessed at his thoughts. "No. I'll stay at least until the weekend." She stepped forward, taking his hand.

For a brief second, he leaned over and let his head rest against hers. Her skin was so soft, her scent intoxicating. Memories tumbled through him of days long past when they couldn't stand to be apart. His hand tightened on hers. He might never let go.

Dinner was good, really good. Tyson couldn't remember laughing so much since he and Jana had visited her extended family in Washington. Saffron was smart and funny, and Halla played off her perfectly. He learned that Saffron lived alone like he had before coming to help his parents, that she supported herself with her designs, and she enjoyed hiking and river rafting. He'd never thought of her as the sporty type, but things had definitely changed. He enjoyed hiking too. Though finding time was difficult with his schedule, he and Jana had recently begun hiking twice a month.

Jana. The thought of her brought a tightening to his chest. Where was she now? Probably at her place watching Netflix or out with friends. She might even be on a date after their talk today. The idea made him uncomfortable, but he had no right asking her to wait when he wanted to be with Saffron.

"Hey, where'd you go?" Saffron asked, pulling his thoughts back to the table. "We're discussing dessert. You having any?"

"Do they have chocolate cake?" Since starting construction at his parents' house, he was always hungry for dessert.

Saffron grinned at him. "Still like it, huh?"

"Oh yeah."

"Good, so do I." Saffron signaled the server.

"So," Halla said to Tyson after they ordered. "You said you were remodeling your parents' house."

"Yeah, my father is in a wheelchair permanently now, and he couldn't do much in the house the way it was. My mother can't lift him, and it's getting harder for her to take care of him. So we lowered the counters and shelves, put a wheelchair-accessible shower in the bathtub so he can move himself to a shower chair, and on Saturday night, we put up a ramp to the front of the house so he can easily go outside alone."

"Sounds like you're nearly finished," Halla said.

"Almost. The guys I hired are finishing a ramp out the back as well, but beyond that, I'm just staining and painting. I won't need their help for that. I did want to put in a ramp from inside the garage to the house, but there's just not enough room to do it safely and park their car. So the other two ramps will have to do."

"So are you helping the workers with the back ramp tonight?" Saffron asked.

He shook his head. "They've got it covered. I'm going to stain the front ramp. I figure it'll need a couple coats over several days. I do as much as possible on my own to keep within the budget my parents set. They don't like it when I spend my money on their house." In fact, he'd taken to paying the guys bonuses under the table after each large project was finished so he could report lower official wages for his father's benefit.

His phone next to his plate buzzed for the fourth time since they'd started dinner. "Aren't you going to get that?" Halla asked. "What if it's about a patient?"

"It's not." He glanced at Saffron and her gaze compelled him to add, "It's my mother. She wants me to bring you over."

Saffron's eyes widened, and he could see her reluctance. He didn't blame her, but would she ever be able to forgive his mother? Would he have been able to in her place?

"You should go," Halla said.

"Halla, I don't think . . ." Saffron trailed off.

"She wants to apologize," Tyson added.

Saffron's gaze fixed on him. "You want me to go, don't you?"

"I'm not sure. But if we're . . . we're going to have to face her sometime. I love my parents, and for the most part, they're good people. I don't condone how my mother acted back then, not at all, but for what it's worth, I believe she was trying to look out for me."

"Well, it did work out for you." Saffron's voice was soft and hurt. "You have a great life. So she was right."

He shook his head. "It would have been better with you. With our son."

"Look, I'll be honest with you," Saffron said. "I don't know if I can forgive her."

Under the table he put his leg against hers as a show of secret support. "Well, I suspect it'll be a process, not something that will happen overnight. But it can wait. We absolutely don't have to start now."

Halla shook her head. "No, go tonight. Saffron, think of how you feel about protecting your sister. What you did to protect your son. She's a mom first. Give her a chance. I can only guess how hard it will be for you, but maybe this is one of those bandages that should be ripped off quickly before it hardens into something you can never take off."

Saffron straightened, squaring her shoulders and lifting her chin slightly as she met Tyson's gaze. "Okay. I'll come and help you with the staining. I'll have to go back to the inn and change first."

Tyson blinked twice. "It's messy. You could just watch."

"I told you how we painted all of Lily's House when we moved in, didn't I? I know about paint and staining."

"Well . . ." he started.

She smirked at him knowingly. "Oh, I get it. You're afraid I'll do it wrong. That's why you won't let the guys you hired do it."

He shrugged. "Okay, you got me. Stain's tricky, but I'd love to have your expert help—if you are an expert."

"Oh, I am. You'll see."

"Do you need me to come?" Halla asked Saffron. "Because you know I'll be there for you, if you need me."

For moral support, she meant, because of his mother. Tyson didn't miss the implication. "I'll take care of her," he said. "Don't worry. And my mother really is sorry."

"We'll drop you back at the inn so you can study," Saffron told Halla. "I'll be fine. His mom is nothing next to mine."

"With that, I have to agree," Tyson said. "She always scared me." He was relieved to see the waiter coming toward them with their desserts—slices of chocolate cake for him and Saffron, and a brownie with ice cream for Halla. Maybe they could talk about something besides his mother for a while.

They chatted as they ate, but for Tyson the cake was dry and tasteless. He still loved Saffron—there was no doubt in his mind about that—but what if she could never forgive his mother or get over the pain she'd caused them? He was having difficulty with anger toward his mother himself, but he knew he'd be able to recover the relationship because they had so many other good times to build on. But the pain in Saffron's eyes made him want to protect her, even at the expense of his relationship with his parents. She'd been through too much already.

If it came down to it, would he give up his parents for her?

At that moment, she turned in his direction and smiled, and he knew that he would.

16

Saffron could feel Tyson's nervousness on the way to his parents' house, and she wanted to make it better, but she was already wishing she hadn't agreed to come. She and Tyson barely had an idea where their relationship was heading, and his parents hadn't been any help the last time.

"Are you staying at the hotel again tonight?" she asked. "Or at your parents'?"

"Neither, I think. I'd rather head back to Oceanside. I have an early appointment tomorrow, and I don't want to risk traffic. I'll make better time tonight."

The knowledge made Saffron relax. At least there would be no awkward good-night scene or rash decision about sleeping arrangements at the inn. Because as attracted as she was to Tyson, she wasn't ready to jump into a physical relationship. At the same time, a part of her regretted not being able to spend more time alone with him. Their day at the beach had been perfect.

"So," she asked, "do your parents like Jana?"

He glanced over at her and then back to the road. "Does it matter?"

"Not really. Well, maybe a little." A lot. If his mother didn't like Jana as she hadn't liked Saffron, maybe her pushing Saffron away was standard practice.

"Uh, yeah. She and Jana get along."

Of course they did. And from his expression, it wasn't just getting along. *Great.*

When he brought the car to a stop in front of his house, she almost didn't recognize it. The trees were larger, the landscaping changed, and with the new ramp, it looked completely different.

"You think we can get it all finished tonight?" she said. "The sun's already going down. We should have eaten fast food instead of going to a restaurant."

He grinned. "If you're as good as you say you are, we'll get it done."

She slugged him, and he reacted by putting his arms around her and kissing her. All the doubts of the evening fled.

"When you hold me like this . . ." she started, but she couldn't voice the words. Hope, fear, and desire filled her—but close on the heels of these positive emotions came the pain of old hurts.

"I know," he whispered. "It'll be okay."

Something he'd always said to her, but he'd been wrong before. Oh, so wrong.

"Come on," he said, jumping from the car. She followed him out, her heart shrinking to a painful lump in her chest.

He opened the trunk and began pulling out the stain and plastic they'd purchased on their way here. "Could you lay out the plastic over the driveway where it meets the ramp? The grass doesn't matter, but I'd rather not get the stain on the driveway. While you're doing that, I'll zip around back and make sure the guys I hired aren't taking an extended break. I want to make sure they finish tonight."

"Sure, no problem." She was relieved to put off going inside to see his parents.

"I'll get the brushes and rollers when I come back. They're in the garage where I'll put a couple of these cans, since they're for the back ramp." Carrying two cans of stain, he started walking toward the garage but stopped after a few steps and added, "Unless you'd rather go around back and talk to the guys with me."

"Thanks, but no thanks. Unless my sister's there." Saffron hadn't seen Kendall since she'd left for school that morning, though she'd sent a brief text saying she'd be back at the inn later.

"She wasn't here when I talked to the guys, and I don't see her car, but she'll probably pick Joel up." He hesitated. "Everything okay between them?"

Saffron opened the plastic sheet. "I think so. Do you know something I don't?"

"Not really. One of the guys made a comment about his having to ask her permission to do things with them. I thought Joel would punch him out." He started walking again. "Hopefully, they behaved themselves while I was gone."

Saffron hoped so too—for Tyson's sake. She watched him punch in the garage code and disappear inside. She shook out the thin plastic, taking care to place it as close as she could to the ramp where it met the driveway. When she was finished, Tyson still hadn't returned, so she went to the garage to look for some tape to secure the plastic to the cement. The single-car garage didn't hold any cars at the moment—just a mishmash jumble of boards, planks, sheetrock, old appliances, and power tools. With a little snooping, she found a tote box of painting supplies and carried it out to the ramp.

She'd barely set down the box on the plastic near the end of the ramp when the front door opened and Tyson's mother stepped out. Both women froze, gazes locked. Saffron couldn't have run away if she'd tried.

Life had not been kind to Helene Dekker, and she'd aged considerably over the intervening years. Her brown hair, cut a few inches above the shoulders, was heavily streaked with gray, and her narrow face was deeply lined with wrinkles around her mouth and eyes. Her once-slender figure had blossomed, the weight mostly centered around her middle, which probably explained the gray stretch pants. She looked worn and tired and sad.

Mrs. Dekker recovered first. She moved slowly down the ramp, a tentative smile on her face. "Hello, Roz. I'm glad you came." Her eyes ran over Saffron. "You look the same. Well, not really. You've grown up some, of course. You're beautiful."

Saffron swallowed with difficulty, knowing she should thank her but also knowing she couldn't force out the words. "I came to help Tyson stain the ramp."

Mrs. Dekker reached Saffron where she stood next to the ramp. "I wanted to see you. To say"—she glanced in the direction of the garage, as if looking for help—"I know I can't make up for what happened to you, but I am sorry. I wish things were different. And I am so sorry about the baby."

Was that it? Did Mrs. Dekker expect that Saffron would forgive her for being unwelcoming to her as a teen? For deleting her calls and making Tyson think she'd abandoned him? For ultimately adding to the causes that killed her child?

Saffron gathered every ounce of strength within her, pushing past the pain that threatened to spill out in a hateful rush. "I appreciate that," she managed.

Mrs. Dekker offered a tremulous smile. "I hope we can . . . I don't know what you and Tyson plan, but I want you to know that I support whatever decision you two make. I . . . that's all."

"Thank you."

Mrs. Dekker's eyes begged for more, but the lump in Saffron's heart could offer no other response. It was easy for Mrs. Dekker to say she'd honor their wishes now, when she couldn't force Tyson off to military school to prevent him from finding her. Or mess with his phone. Tears threatened Saffron's self-control. She wished she'd gone back to the inn with Halla instead of coming here. What had possibly made her think she could face them so soon?

Without warning, Mrs. Dekker leaned forward and hugged her. "I am so, so sorry," she whispered.

Saffron couldn't react. Her heart hurt and her arms remained frozen even after Mrs. Dekker moved away. *I still hate you,* she wanted to say. But it wasn't really true. She understood why Mrs. Dekker had made her choice. For her son, for his future. For them it had worked out.

The front door opened again, and a man came out in a motorized wheelchair. Saffron hadn't seen Mr. Dekker much as a teen—she'd never even known his full name—but to her memory, his dark hair and grizzled face hadn't aged a day. Only the wheelchair was new, replacing the cane he'd used previously.

"You didn't tell me we had company," he said, gliding down the ramp.

His wife moved aside to make room for him. "I didn't know myself until a few minutes ago."

"Hey, young lady, do you like my new ramp?" Mr. Dekker asked, his face radiating pride. "My son built it. He's a doctor, you know." Either the man didn't recognize her or he didn't remember what had happened all those years ago.

"She knows, Dad." Tyson came from around the house. "She's helping me stain it. Thanks for watching those guys while I was gone."

"No problem. They just need motivation." Mr. Dekker leaned over, reaching for a gallon of stain, and squinted at the label. "You got the kind I recommended, didn't you? It's the best."

"Of course I did."

"Good. Good." Mr. Dekker set the can down with a satisfied smile.

"Would you guys like some refreshments?" Mrs. Dekker asked.

Tyson started opening the stain. "Maybe later. But probably not. We just came from dinner, and we'll only be an hour."

"I think you might be longer." Mr. Dekker started rolling toward the garage. "I have some lights somewhere, in case it gets dark before you finish."

"I already took them to the back in case the guys need

them," Tyson said. "But we can always borrow one, if we have to."

Saffron picked up a brush, anxious to get started so she could leave.

Mrs. Dekker's eyes ran down Saffron's calf-length jeans and florescent pink Lily's House T-shirt and said, "Would you like an apron or something to put over your clothes?"

"I just changed into these so I could help. I'll be careful, but they're old anyway." For a moment, Saffron was struck at the difference between her mother and Mrs. Dekker. Her mother would think Saffron's clothes were fit *only* for working in, not something to be protected.

"Well, you let me know if you change your mind. I'll be inside."

Saffron was relieved to see her go.

Tyson gave Saffron a sympathetic look and picked up another brush. "First, let's get the edges and hard-to-reach places. Then we'll bring out the rollers."

"You sure it's not going to rain?" Mr. Dekker peered at the clear sky.

"I'm sure, Dad. Shouldn't you use the ramp to go inside now? You won't be able to once we start."

"I'll go through the garage and use the back ramp when you're done. They have the floor in. Though you'll have to move the table saw in the garage. It's in front of the door to the back."

"Okay, I'll move the saw." Tyson poured stain into two smaller containers and handed one to Saffron.

Under his dad's watchful eyes, they got started. The old man was helpful, pointing out places they'd missed, and the care he took not to offend was endearing. With each request, Tyson was respectful, and it was easy to see they had a good relationship. Had they always been this way? Saffron didn't know. She knew Tyson had played football because of his father, not because he'd enjoyed the sport, and that had annoyed her back then. Maybe if Tyson's playing had given the man joy, it didn't really matter.

Saffron could tell Tyson knew what he was doing. As a teen, he'd been more likely to go see a movie or play Frisbee than to help his dad with projects around the house. He'd known little about wood stain or home renovations. All that had changed.

As they worked, he told her stories about his young patients, his love for them shining through his words. "They're so brave," he said. "Especially the littlest ones."

"Their mothers, I bet, are a mess," she commented.

He laughed. "Yes, but I do my best to cheer them up. Fortunately, most of the children do go home safely." His eyes narrowed as he spied a section of the railing they'd missed. There was no way to reach it now, not unless they trampled the bush growing next to it, because he'd already taken a roller to the ramp floor in that section to test how the finish would look on the flat surface.

"Now what?" she asked.

His eyes glinted mischievously. "Now I lift you up."

"Okay," she said, accepting his challenge. He turned his back and she climbed on.

"What on earth?" his father muttered. But he sounded amused.

Saffron stretched to reach the spot, but not before accidentally dragging her brush over Tyson's cheek. "Oops."

"Oops, I bet. Can you reach it?"

"Yes. Hold on. Don't drop me."

"Oh, but you're so heavy. It's like carrying three whole feathers. Or maybe four."

"Silly." She painted for a minute in silence. "I hate to tell you this, but I need more stain."

"Here it is." Mr. Dekker lifted a can and steered his wheelchair over.

She leaned and dipped her brush, aware of her chest brushing against Tyson's shoulder, which was even more awkward under the sharp gaze of his father. She hoped her face wasn't flushing too brightly. Careful not to dribble the stain on Tyson or the bushes, she finished the job and jumped down.

"Way better than a ladder," Mr. Dekker said, which started them all laughing.

Saffron threw Tyson a rag for his cheek. "Who knew staining could be so fun?" she said.

"You'll have to help me with the back ramp." He grinned, his eyes seemingly unable to leave her face. He looked younger staring at her like that. Wistful.

"Maybe." She returned to the section of the railing she'd been working on, near the bottom. She could almost imagine this was their house and they were working on it together. But with the thought came a rush of unexpected agony that stopped her arm in mid-motion. Why did it hurt so much? Until a few days ago, she could go months without feeling this way.

"Why'd you stop?" asked Mr. Dekker from close behind her. "Oh, the spider. I'll get him out of there." He rolled forward and brushed the insect away with his fingers. "There you go."

"Thanks." Saffron was aware of Tyson still staring at her. Let them both think it was the spider. She pushed the hurt back to a manageable size and kept staining.

All the brush work took an hour, but the rolling only another fifteen minutes. They stood back to admire their work. As if on cue, Mrs. Dekker opened the front door. "If you're done, come on in for some peach cobbler," she called.

Tyson looked at Saffron, who shrugged. At this point, what could it hurt? But the tension she'd felt when she first arrived surfaced again inside her. She cleaned up the plastic and rinsed their brushes with water from the hose while Tyson moved the table saw for his father and checked on the workers in the back. Then, after washing their hands in the bathroom, they went into a kitchen that Saffron hadn't seen enough times in the past to remember. Whatever it had been before, everything now was built for wheelchair access, except for a second sink that stood at normal height.

"So Mom doesn't have to stoop," Tyson explained. "It hurts her back."

Mrs. Dekker put her arms around him. "My boy thinks of everything."

Saffron smiled and nodded. "He's done a beautiful job."

"Sure has." Mrs. Dekker's eyes swept over him lovingly before returning to Saffron. "Come on, Roz. Let's sit down."

"Actually, I go by Saffron now," Saffron said.

"Oh, okay." But Mrs. Dekker looked confused.

As Saffron moved toward the table, her gaze snagged on a framed picture on the wall that showed the kitchen under construction. Tyson was there, his arm around a laughing, dark-haired woman, who was hefting a sledge hammer. *Jana,* she guessed.

The doctor was about Saffron's height, with dark eyes, narrow face, and olive skin. She and Tyson looked good together. Matching. He appeared happy.

Mrs. Dekker noticed her gaze. "Please have a seat," she said, indicating a chair that would put the picture out of Saffron's sight. As curious as she was about the other woman, Saffron was grateful. She sat stiffly, her hands clenched in her lap. Tyson settled next to her, casually leaning his arm over the top of her chair.

Do you love her? Saffron wanted to ask him. She bit her bottom lip to stop the words. Thankfully, no one seemed to notice her difficulty.

Her tension lessened a bit as she listened to the family talk about Tyson's work, Mr. Dekker's time in the army, and Mrs. Dekker's garden. The ease between them was comforting, though at the same time it made her feel left out. Most of that was her fault, she knew. Maybe she should have brought the pictures of her son, their grandson. But that would have only made them feel bad, she suspected, especially Mr. Dekker, who didn't seem to have a clue that Tyson had ever dated her.

"So what is it you do?" asked Mr. Dekker when they were almost finished eating.

"Oh, I design jewelry."

"Really?" Mr. Dekker nodded. "For a company?"

She laughed. "Only my own. I have a website, and I mostly sell from there. It's all custom-made. I also work at a sports store, but only part-time. I need to quit soon so I have more time to work on my own stuff, but I haven't yet because I like the people."

"I'll have to look you up." Mr. Dekker made a show of

writing down her website, while Mrs. Dekker offered more cobbler.

"No thank you," Saffron said. "It was really good, though."

"I'll pack you some to take with you." Mrs. Dekker popped up from the table. "Living at that hotel can't be very fun."

Saffron suspected this was her way of trying to make things up to her, but it made her feel worse. "No, really, it's okay. I won't be there long."

"It's no trouble. And we have so much. I'll just get it ready."

Saffron's protests died on her lips. "Okay, thanks."

Mrs. Dekker walked to the counter and turned. "In fact, depending how long you're here, we have an extra room you could stay in. Tyson would have to move out the construction stuff that's in there."

Saffron felt like a butterfly pinned to a board. She knew the woman was anxious to atone for her actions, but this was so far overboard that Saffron didn't know how to respond.

Tyson took one look at her face and intervened. "No, Mom. Saffron has a friend staying with her, and she has a sister in town. She can't stay here."

"It was nice of you to offer," Saffron mumbled.

Mrs. Dekker nodded and began dividing the cobbler into two containers. "I'll give you enough for your friend and sister too. Don't worry about returning these containers, if it's not convenient. They're disposable. I mean, I reuse them anyway, but they cost practically nothing. I take food to neighbors in them all the time so they won't have to bring them back."

"Thanks." Saffron watched her put the containers into a large paper bag, followed by paper plates and plastic forks.

"In fact," Mrs. Dekker said, "I have some cookies I made this morning . . ."

Tyson arose. "I'd better take Saffron back to the hotel now."

Saffron nearly sighed with relief. "Thanks for the cobbler."

"You're welcome," said Mrs. Dekker, who was putting something else inside the paper bag.

"We still on for tomorrow?" Mr. Dekker asked Tyson.

Tyson hesitated. "Right. Yes, of course."

Mr. Dekker said to Saffron, "Tuesdays, we go to San Diego for some new treatments. They're experimental, but"—he tapped the arm of his wheelchair—"worth it if I can get out of this thing. We meet Tyson after work in Oceanside, and he drives us down." He laughed. "We make it a family affair."

Mrs. Dekker turned from the counter, the paper bag in her hands. "We always stay overnight at my sister's. It's the only time we get to catch up these days." She chuckled, casting her son a look of pure gratitude.

Tyson gave Saffron a pained look. "Shall we go?"

"Sure." She wanted nothing more than to escape.

Tyson started for the door, and before Saffron could follow, Mrs. Dekker pushed the paper bag at Saffron. "I put some rolls and yogurt in it for tomorrow," Mrs. Dekker said. "I know girls like yogurt for breakfast. Or if the hotel has free breakfast, you can eat it for lunch."

Saffron took it by the handles, its heaviness surprising her. "Uh, thanks."

"Be sure to come back again," Mr. Dekker said. "I think you're the prettiest girl my son has ever brought around." He laughed with pleasure at his own words. "Of course, I was always partial to blondes. Not sure how I ended up married to this gorgeous brunette." He winked at his wife.

"I was the only one who'd put up with you, that's why." Mrs. Dekker placed her hands lovingly on his shoulders.

Saffron could see why Tyson cared for his parents. Deep down they were good people. Why then did she only feel pain looking at them? She was thankful the Dekkers didn't follow them out to the garage.

"Sorry about the name," Tyson whispered. "There wasn't an opportunity to tell my mom about the change."

"It's okay." He didn't need to know how that name always yanked her back to a place she didn't want to go.

Tyson didn't head out of the garage to the front but led her to the back yard, where the workers had packed up their tools and were standing around talking. Saffron didn't see her sister, but Joel lifted a hand in greeting while the other two men stared at her curiously.

"Beautiful job," Tyson said looking over the finished ramp leading down from the deck. "Looks like we're finished here." He pulled out his wallet and began passing checks out to the men. "You've done a good job. I appreciate it." The men mumbled their thanks and started across the lawn. "Hey, Joel, wait up," Tyson called.

Joel mumbled something to the others and came back to stand in front of them. "Yeah?"

"I'm thinking I'd like to build my mother a bookcase in the spare room. Do you think that would be something you'd be interested in? Just you. I know it will take longer alone, but I need your precision."

Joel grinned with the praise. "Yeah, I think so. But I can't start until next week. The boys and me are leaving town for a concert."

"Sure, text me when you get back, and we'll work it out."

"Will do," Joel said. "But I'll be gone awhile. It's in Denver."

Tyson whistled in appreciation. "That's pretty far for a concert. You must like the band."

"Yeah. John Mayer. He's awesome with the guitar." Joel thumbed over his shoulder. "Well, I'd better go, the guys are waiting."

"What about Kendall?" Saffron asked. "Have you heard from her?"

He shrugged. "She's getting some stuff from her house, I think. It's her mom's card game night. We're meeting up later." Joel gave a little wave and took off around the house.

"Why do I get the feeling he's not all that excited about building a bookshelf?" Tyson murmured, as he turned off the remaining floodlight, plunging them into darkness.

"I guess he got paid and wants to paint the town." Saffron felt sad for her sister. Unless Joel was job-hunting on the way to the concert, it wouldn't help their situation.

"Well, everyone needs a break."

"I guess." Saffron wasn't feeling as magnanimous, but then she'd had a knot in her stomach for the past hour.

Tyson stepped toward her and lifted his mother's paper

bag from her grasp, setting it on the grass. "Thank you for coming, for helping me," he said, taking her hands. "For being so good with my parents."

"They're nicer than I thought they'd be."

"People learn. They change." His arms went around her. "But I know it wasn't easy for you."

"No."

"Just no?" His voice was teasing.

She couldn't say more. She wanted to be the kind of person who could just forgive and forget, but somehow doing so felt like a betrayal to her son and the suffering he'd endured. She searched for something to change the subject, and her eyes landed on the back ramp.

"How did you learn so much about construction anyway?" she asked.

His smile was wistful, and she knew her ploy hadn't fooled him. "Some I learned from my dad, but most of it came from a roommate in college whose father built houses. I worked summers with them. It's come in handy for helping my parents. I also completely redid my condo in Oceanside. I'd love to show it to you."

"I'd love to see it."

"How about Wednesday?" he asked, his arms tightening around her. "I wish it could be tomorrow, but my dad believes in this therapy and I have to take him."

"Is it helping?"

"No, and there's absolutely no science behind it. I only take him because belief and attitude have as much to do with healing as real medicine. So I'll support it as long as he wants to go. But his nerve damage is irreversible. There's been no real change in that since he first stepped on that mine when he was in the army. But the pain's gotten worse as he ages. Which is why he's in the wheelchair now."

"I'm glad you're taking him."

"I'm thinking on Wednesday we can make a whole night of it. You could meet me at the hospital at four, we can go see my place, then have dinner." He paused but continued before she could respond. "And I've also been thinking that maybe you can stay there—if you want. Paying for a hotel room long term won't work."

Her eyes flew to his. Was he saying what she thought he was? Because guys just didn't offer their condos like that.

"No strings." His voice was hoarse and his gaze dropped to her lips.

"Oh, if I stay, there will be strings." She hadn't waited almost nine years to fall in love again only to have it go wrong a second time.

He chuckled. "Yeah, I guess you're right. But good strings."

Her heart pounded with his nearness, and all her nerves tingled in anticipation. She watched him come closer. Slowly, he kissed the right side of her mouth and then the left side. Toying, teasing, making her yearn for more.

"Okay, it's a date. I'll meet you at the hospital." If her heart pounded any more furiously, it would beat right out of her chest. "I won't actually have a car for a few days because Halla's taking ours back to Phoenix tomorrow afternoon. But I'll find a way."

"No, I'll send a car. I insist."

Saffron was a little uncomfortable not having a way back to Temecula if things didn't work out, but she found herself saying, "Okay then. It's a plan."

"Good." He placed another teasing kiss on the corner of her mouth. "Actually, I'm not sure I can wait that long to see you. What about also meeting me at the hospital for lunch tomorrow?"

His eagerness to be with her was so typically Tyson that she laughed. "You going to climb up to my window in the middle of the night if you don't see me tomorrow?"

"I might. Somehow it seems almost as important as when we were sixteen."

She understood what he meant. As if they couldn't look away because everything would vanish. "What time for lunch? I have the car until maybe two or so."

"Eleven's best, but I have some wiggle room if that doesn't work."

"It's fine."

"But we're still on for Wednesday too, right?"

"Right." The night when she'd commit to him all over again.

Maybe.

Tyson, his arms still around her, walked her backward a few steps until they hit a tree. "Remember this place?" he murmured, his low voice sending shudders through her.

Saffron hadn't until he mentioned it, but now she saw it was the same tree where he'd first told her he loved her. Tears gathered in her eyes. "Yeah."

"I still love you," he said.

"I love you too." But then, she'd never stopped loving him.

He kissed her full on the mouth, finally, but some of the magic they'd shared during their day at the beach was gone, and Saffron didn't know why or how to recapture it.

After saying goodbye to Tyson, Saffron had to push her way into the room at the inn. "What's going on here?" she asked, eyeing the additional suitcases and boxes clogging up the floor space.

Halla looked up from the table where she sat with her laptop. "Kendall's been here with more of her stuff. She apparently pulled out of school today and wanted to get all her things from her room before your mother found out."

"Smart girl. I should have done that before I left." Saffron hopped over a box and dodged a mound of folded clothes. "Speaking of Kendall, where is she?" Saffron finally made it to Halla and set Mrs. Dekker's bag on the table.

"She rushed out to meet Joel somewhere, I think." Halla shrugged. "I'm honestly hoping your mother doesn't call the police and break in here to recover this stuff. What's this?" she tapped the paper bag.

Saffron started to sink into the other chair but changed her mind and launched herself instead toward the bed, where she sprawled out with a sigh. "It's peach cobbler that Tyson's mom sent, and maybe more things. She insisted."

"Oh, nice. I'm actually hungry." Halla stood and peered into the bag. "Uh, there's a lot more than cobbler in here. Looks like bread, rolls, and . . . peanut butter?"

"Help yourself. It's for both of us."

"Sounds like it went well, then."

Saffron didn't reply.

Halla released the bag and came to sit next to her. "Uh-oh, what happened?"

"Nothing, really." Saffron blinked back tears. "It's just . . . they were super nice. His mother apologized. They adore Tyson, and he really likes them. They actually invited me to stay with them, if you can believe it. She kind of reminds me of Lily."

"Wow, that is a little weird, but it does sound like something Lily would do. Only it's not weird for Lily because she runs a foster home. But if the Dekkers are nice, what's the problem?"

Saffron sat up, pulling her knees to her chest and wrapping her arms around them. "Me. I'm the problem. I don't fit in. My heart feels like a lump of rock when I'm sitting there listening to them talk. One 'I'm sorry' doesn't change what happened."

"You don't think you can forgive her?" Halla put a hand on her back, patting gently.

Saffron thought a moment. "It's not that. I understand why she did it, and I feel better that she apologized. But it still hurts so much." The tears started to fall. "And when I think of seeing her again, and helping them, and sharing Tyson with them . . . it's hard."

"Do you think it might get easier?"

"That's what I'm guessing, but at the same time, I don't want it to. I *want* them to feel it. I want them to understand what they gave up. Because they aren't new people in my life—they were a part of what happened, and they should feel it. But they'll never understand because they weren't there those last months, and it was too long ago. I'm the only one who will ever know. Not even Tyson can know everything because he wasn't there with me."

"Oh, honey." Halla squeezed her tightly. "I don't think there's anything anyone can do about that."

Saffron nodded. "I know. It just takes time, I guess. I didn't realize I was holding so much anger inside. It'll be good to let it go." She gave Halla a watery smile. "I think."

"It is good. You'll see."

"Oh, and I saw his girlfriend. Or a picture of her, rather."

Halla blinked. "And?"

"She's beautiful. She has dark eyes and olive skin. Shiny black hair. She's slender. Definitely a product of good genes. One thing for sure is that she looks nothing like me."

"Dang those genes," Halla muttered.

Saffron flopped back on the pillows. "Why couldn't she be homely? I mean, she's a doctor already for crying out loud. How can I compete?"

"You compete plenty well, if you ask me. I saw you kissing, remember? He's into you big time."

"He did kiss me again tonight."

Halla grinned. "See? So when are you seeing him again?"

"He has to take his dad to therapy tomorrow night, but I'm meeting him for lunch at the hospital where he works. Don't worry. I'll be back before two—you can even make it to the study group for your test, if you still want to go that early. Then on Wednesday, he wants to take me to dinner and show me his condo in Oceanside." She hesitated before adding, "He invited me to stay there instead of paying for this room."

"Oooh." Halla's eyes grew impossibly wide. "Seriously?"

"He also said he loves me."

"No way! What did you say to that?"

Saffron suddenly wished she hadn't brought it up. "I've always loved him, Halla. I don't know how to stop."

"This is so exciting! I'm happy for you."

"Thanks." Saffron herself felt a bit more numb than excited. Were they moving too fast?

Halla lay down on the pillows next to Saffron, and for a long time neither of them said anything. When Saffron was about to drift off without getting ready for bed, Halla said, "If you're meeting him at the hospital, maybe it's time we check out this lady doctor and see what's what."

All Saffron's sleepiness fled. She propped her head up with her hand to look at her friend. "What are you saying?"

"Aren't you curious? Don't you want to see her in person?"

"I'm not going to stalk her."

"Okay. I'll go with you, and I'll stalk her."

"No."

Halla sighed. "All right. But can I still go?" She looked at Saffron with pleading eyes. "I promise to get lost during your romantic lunch. After, maybe we can stop at the beach again for a while before I have to leave."

"I don't know how romantic my lunch will be at a

hospital, but I guess you can come. At least you can if you push me out of this bed, so I can brush my teeth."

Halla obliged with more gusto than was needed, but at least Saffron was up and moving. Even muscles she didn't remember having were tired. She'd barely dropped back into bed when someone knocked on the door.

"I'll get it," Halla called, jumping up from the table where she was eating a peanut butter sandwich with one hand and typing with the other.

She opened the door to Kendall, who came in dragging a large box. "Sorry I'm here so late."

"You shouldn't be carrying things that big," Saffron said, climbing out of bed.

Halla was already hefting the box. "It doesn't weigh much."

"Just a few stuffed animals for the baby," Kendall said. "They were mine when I was little. Well, some were probably yours, Saffron. "You can have whatever you want. I just didn't want Mom to throw them away."

Is that what she did with my things? Saffron decided not to ask. "I hear you dropped out of school?"

"Yep." Kendall sank down on the bed with a sigh. "I did. And I'm glad. I don't want to be a designer. And at least I got back some of the tuition. That'll help me until I find a job."

Saffron studied her sister. Far from looking happy, she appeared exhausted and ready to cry. "What do you want to be?"

"I don't know," Kendall muttered.

"Are you hungry?" Saffron asked, sitting next to her.

Kendall shook her head. "I ate with Joel."

Ah, Joel. Something was up, Saffron could feel it. "I heard he's going to a concert. Are you going with him?"

"No." Her response was scarcely a whisper. "It's just for the guys."

She started crying and Saffron put an arm around her. "It's going to be okay," she murmured.

"I don't think he wants the baby anymore," Kendall said between sobs. "And maybe not me either. What am I going to do?"

"Tonight you're going to sleep," Saffron said, rubbing her back. "Tomorrow we'll figure it out."

Kendall stood. "You're right. I'm so tired I can't think straight."

Saffron gently propelled her sister in the direction of the bathroom. "Go get ready. You need rest for the baby."

Kendall grabbed one of her bags and disappeared into the bathroom.

Climbing back into bed, Saffron checked her phone and found a message from Vaughn. *Slaying any more dragons?*

Thinking of the Dekkers, she typed in a response. *Maybe one or two. You?*

There was no answer, so he was probably getting ready for bed or coming home from somewhere. She wondered if he'd told the people they normally hung out with that they were broken up. If so, he might even be on a date. She put down her phone.

"What's wrong?" Halla said.

"Nothing. Just worried about Kendall."

Twenty minutes later, Kendall had come to bed and

Saffron was nearly asleep when a return text came from Vaughn.

Why do you get all the fun? Maybe I'll come down before Halla does on Friday and bring your car. You might need more dragons slain.

He had to be joking, of course, because of his classes, but it made her smile. Her brief reply was only partially sarcastic: *My hero.*

Her last thought as she drifted off was why couldn't her sister have fallen in love with someone like Vaughn.

By the time Saffron arrived in Oceanside at the Tri-City Medical Center, she was already ten minutes late for her lunch date with Tyson. Kendall had decided at the last moment that she needed to go with them, and she was looking so down that Saffron hadn't wanted to leave her alone. Apparently, Joel hadn't changed his mind yet about not wanting her along on his trip. Saffron and Halla ended up waiting for Kendall to shower and arrange emergency pregnancy snacks for the drive.

"Not that I really wanted to go with Joel," Kendall said for the fourth time since they left Temecula. "I mean, it's not like I want to be crushed by all those fans. Or drive seventeen hours in a car with a chain-smoker. I know that's not good for the baby. But I hate that he's wasting all that money."

"And that he wants to go without you," Halla said. "That bites. But to be honest, there's a lot of places I wouldn't want to take my boyfriend, if I had one."

"Like where?" Kendall wanted to know.

"To a chick flick, a salad bar, a baby shower, shoe shopping, the hairdresser."

Kendall wrinkled her nose. "Why not a salad bar?"

Halla grinned. "Because I eat too much. It's embarrassing."

Saffron killed the engine and set the parking brake. "Okay, ladies." She tossed Halla the key to the car. "He's only got an hour, if that, so I'll meet you here in the lobby at fifteen after twelve. I'll text you if there's a change. Have fun." She looked meaningfully at Halla and then at Kendall, hoping Halla would get the message to take care of her.

"Actually, I need to use the restroom," Kendall said.

"Let's all go in then." Saffron shot off a text to tell Tyson she was here. She was supposed to meet him in the cafeteria, and she hoped he could still get away.

They took a while to find the bathroom, where Saffron freshened up her makeup and chatted with Halla until Tyson texted that he was on his way. "Now if I can just find the cafeteria," she said.

"We'll help you and then take off," Halla offered.

They wandered down a hall, following some signs, but must have missed the turn to the cafeteria. Several hospital workers passed them, and Saffron was tempted to ask directions, but Halla seemed confident of finding her way. After several more turns took them nowhere, Kendall stopped a woman in white scrubs.

The woman smiled and pointed back the way they'd come. "Just down there by that picture on the wall, take a left. Then go to the second right after that and immediately you'll see a door on your right. It's a little tricky." She peered closer at Kendall. "Don't I know you? You look familiar."

Kendall's eyes widened. "Oh right. I remember you. You look different in white and with your hair back like that.

You were dating Tyson Dekker, right? My boyfriend has been working on his parents' house."

Saffron stared. It was Jana, and she did look different in her hospital garb. She was still beautiful and slightly exotic with her dark coloring, and Saffron felt washed out in comparison. She swallowed hard, wondering if Jana might somehow guess who she was.

"Oh, right. That's it. You're the girl with all the medical questions." The woman gave them a smile that was genuine enough, but she didn't look happy.

"So weird to run into you," Kendall said, the words coming out a little forced. Saffron peeked at Halla, suspecting both she and Kendall had something to do with how they "happened" to run into Jana. No wonder they'd come in with her. She'd question them about it later.

"It's not that big of a hospital," Jana said. "I run into people I know all the time." After an awkward pause, she added, "How's the work on the Dekker's house coming along?"

"They finished last night," Kendall said. "Or at least the part my boyfriend was helping with."

"That's good. I bet the Dekkers are excited, especially Mr. Dekker. The poor man has been feeling trapped." Jana's eyes wandered over them, as if wanting to ask more, but not sure she should. "Look, I'll show you to the cafeteria. I have a few moments."

Saffron had the sense of being on a train that didn't have any brakes. Was she going to run into Tyson with Jana at her side? She made a "help me" face behind Jana's back, but Halla shrugged helplessly.

"Here we are," Jana said as they reached another hallway

that looked like all the others. "See where those people are coming in and out? That's it right there."

"Thank you," Saffron said with the others.

"By the way, I love your necklace," Jana said, indicating the chunky, double-row necklace Saffron had chosen to match her blue top.

"Thanks," Saffron said. This was the time when she would normally pull out a card and offer to make a similar one. But not this time.

Jana nodded, her smile slipping as she glanced behind them. "Well, take care." She pivoted on her heel and returned the way she'd come.

"She's really nice," Halla said.

Saffron didn't respond. She was too busy looking to see what had spooked the woman. Down the hall, Tyson was walking quickly toward them, deep in conversation with another doctor.

Saffron glanced at Halla. "I know you two somehow planned running into Jana," she said. "Thanks for the near heart attack."

Halla had the decency to look ashamed. "Sorry."

"It's good to size up the competition," Kendall added. "I knew where she worked, more or less, but the rest was fate."

"Yeah, right." Saffron bet if Jana hadn't appeared when she did, they'd still be wandering the hospital corridors.

Tyson saw Saffron and waved. The doctor with him glanced at her, said something to Tyson, and then peeled off, turning down another hallway.

In a few more strides, Tyson was with them. "So, I get the whole gang, eh? Good to see you all."

"They're just leaving," Saffron told him.

"Halla and I are going baby shopping," Kendall said. "To get an idea of what's out there and what I might need to buy. I really don't have a clue yet."

That called his attention. "You're taking prenatal vitamins, right?"

"Oh yeah. I read about that. I didn't do it before I got pregnant though, like you're supposed to." She frowned. "I hope the baby will be okay."

"I'm sure the baby will be fine. It's not too late for it to benefit."

Kendall nodded and reached over to squeeze Saffron's arm. "Have fun."

Saffron watched Halla and Kendall leave, wishing she could call them back. What had been a simple date for lunch now felt like something secret behind Jana's back. But he'd mentioned Jana knew about them, so there was nothing to hide.

Saffron straightened her back at the exact moment Tyson leaned over to kiss her. His chin hit her nose painfully.

"Sorry," he said, his grin looking a bit lopsided. "My reaction time is slow right now. It's been a long morning, and I need food. One of my little patients developed an infection, and I had to work out surgery for him this afternoon."

"Oh, no. That's sad."

"He'll be fine. I lined up the best surgeon we've got. I'll be assisting—after I fuel up."

"By all means, let's get you fed." Saffron pushed the awkwardness and her feelings about Jana aside as they hurried to the cafeteria. Tyson filled his tray with protein and plenty of carbs, while Saffron opted for protein and a few veggies.

Tyson downed three mouthfuls before he slowed enough to ask, "How was the drive?"

"Good. Fast. I'm late because of Kendall. She and Joel are fighting."

"Not good." Two more bites disappeared.

"I'm really afraid you're going to choke," she said.

He laughed. "Just making sure I have time after lunch to kiss you."

"Oh, yeah? And what makes you think I'm going to kiss you?"

He leaned over the table until their noses practically touched. "Because I can see it in your eyes."

Saffron glanced around, and although no one seemed to be watching them, she felt reluctant to kiss him here in public—and guilty somehow. "What about Jana? What if . . . isn't this awkward for you?" Had he kissed Jana here like this? And how recently?

He pulled back and ate another bite, his face thoughtful. "It's awkward if I think about it, because I don't want to hurt her. But when I'm with you, I forget about her, if that makes sense. It feels like . . ."

"Like we're kids again."

He nodded and continued eating. "This is actually good." He indicated the broiled chicken. "You going to try yours?"

Saffron cut off a piece and savored it. "It is good."

After another two minutes, Tyson's eating slowed. "Ah, that's better. I should have eaten more for breakfast."

The conversation wandered to their planned date tomorrow night, which led to a discussion about his dad's therapy and the story of his cousin, who was forty and still lived in his mom's basement playing video games all day.

Then Tyson's phone rang. He sighed, taking it out from his pocket. "Oh, no."

"What?"

"I have to go. The patient I told you about? He's getting weaker, and his mother is freaking out. I need to push his surgery up." He stood. "I'm so sorry. This doesn't usually happen. They only alert me if they absolutely need to."

"It's okay." Saffron waved his words away. "I'm glad you're putting your patient first. I guess I see why you eat so fast."

"Only when I'm working. Just in case." He leaned down to kiss her cheek. "I'll make it up to you tomorrow." His voice was low and sexy, sending shivers down her spine.

"Good. I'll expect a nice, interruption-free evening."

He winked. "It'll be better than that. Remember, your ride will be there at three to pick you up." With another kiss to her cheek, he grabbed his tray, dumping it on his way out the door.

Saffron toyed with her vegetables, her appetite gone. If she and Tyson continued their relationship, she'd have to get used to the days when he was on call. But after his residency was finished, he should have a lot more say in his schedule. They could also move from this town so he wouldn't be working with Jana. The anxiety inside her faded away with these practical thoughts, and she was finally hungry enough to eat. By the time she'd finished the rest of her food, the cafeteria was bustling with people.

A tray landed on her table. "Do you mind if I sit here?"

Saffron looked up to see Jana. Her eyes were slightly reddened and the skin around them pinched. The guilt Saffron had felt earlier returned in a rush. "Sure. I'm actually leaving to meet up with my friends."

"Slow eater, huh?" Jana jabbed her fork into a mound of rice. "Like me. My boyfriend says—" She broke off. "Never mind. Anyway, I still really like your necklace."

Maybe it was her foster mother's influence or her guilt at disrupting this woman's life, but Saffron unfastened the necklace and held it out. "You know what? I'd love you to have it."

Jana blinked and put her hand up in a stopping motion. "Oh, no. I'm sorry if you thought I was fishing for something. I have a blouse similar to the one you're wearing, and I can never figure out how to accessorize it. Now that I know, I can buy something similar."

"Not like this, you can't." Saffron set it next to Jana's plate. "I made it, and I can always make myself another one. Please, I'd like you to have it. You doctors do so much good here, and I know it can be a thankless job, especially for those doing residency."

Jana's smile was like the sun coming up after a good storm—quick and surprising. "Well, thank you. That's really nice of you. But how did you know I'm a resident?"

"Lucky guess." Saffron stood, gripping her tray. "Have a good day. I'd better go find my friends." She turned and walked quickly away.

Jana called out something, but she pretended not to hear. What was she doing, ensuring Jana would remember her so well? When Jana finally did see her with Tyson, she might be even more hurt, especially at the fact that Saffron had known who she was all along.

Saffron continued her brisk walk until she'd nearly reached the doors to the hospital, where she sank down on a bench. Why couldn't Jana be a rude, arrogant doctor with a chip on her shoulder, not someone who might have become a friend?

She was still sitting there twenty minutes later when Halla and Kendall returned. Kendall took an off-white baby outfit from a sack. "Isn't this cute? I'm pretty sure the baby will be a girl, but a boy could wear this too, don't you think? With a blue shirt."

Saffron waited for a flash of pain, a memory of her son, but all that flooded her was happiness for her sister. "Really nice. Looks expensive, though."

Kendall smirked. "It was. But I still have one of Mom's credit cards. She hasn't canceled it yet."

Saffron frowned. "You sure that's a good idea? I mean, if you're trying to do this on your own, we can find another way to get what you need."

"I don't want to do it on my own." Kendall returned the outfit to the bag. "I want Mom in my life, just not controlling it." She made a face. "But I'm sure she'll cut me off soon."

Saffron wondered why their mother hadn't cut Kendall off already. She sure had been quick to tell Saffron she needed to obey or get out. Maybe Halla was right that she'd changed.

"What happened with Tyson anyway?" Halla asked. "You look a little depressed."

"Oh, nothing happened. Well, except that he was called back to work."

Halla hooked her arm through Saffron's and pulled her to her feet. "I think what she needs is the beach. Let's go cruising for some hot guys, ladies. I mean, I'll do the looking since I'm not taken, and you two can help."

Saffron felt her spirits rise. Later, she'd tell Halla about the necklace and her second encounter with Jana, but for now she'd forget about it and revel in the beautiful day and the fact that Tyson loved her.

After a little over an hour on the beach, Saffron was ready to leave. The afternoon was too hot for enjoyment, and though she'd changed into her suit, she felt hot and sticky and sure that the little bit of sunscreen they'd applied wasn't doing a thing.

As they arrived at the inn in Temecula, Kendall's phone began ringing. "Oh," she exclaimed. "It's Joel! I'll meet you up in the room."

"Actually, I'm taking off now," Halla said. "My stuff is already in the trunk. I'm only going inside for my snacks, courtesy of Tyson's mother."

Kendall answered her phone. "Hi, Joel? Just a minute. I'm saying goodbye to Halla." She lowered the phone and said to Halla, "Mrs. Dekker was always giving food to Joel and the guys. She's a great cook. Anyway, it was so nice meeting you. I'm sure I'll see you again." She gave Halla a one-armed hug.

"I'm sure we'll see each other," Halla said. "I hope you move to Phoenix, but even if you don't, I'm always in touch with Saffron."

Kendall nodded. "We'll see. Goodbye." She turned and walked a few feet away, bringing her phone to her ear.

Halla stared after her. "Maybe Joel's changed his mind about having her go to the concert."

"That's what I'm afraid of," Saffron said.

Kendall was talking animatedly, heading toward her car. She covered the phone and yelled, "Be back later! I'm going to see him."

Of course she was. Saffron and Halla tromped inside the inn and took the elevator to their room. "So what happened at the hospital?" Halla asked, going to the refrigerator.

"I saw Jana again. She'd been crying."

Halla clicked her tongue. "Sorry about that. But really, none of this is easy. At least they weren't engaged."

"Not yet." Saffron sighed as she sat on her bed. "That's not the worst part."

"Oh? Don't tell me Tyson saw you together. Look, we did plan to run into Jana, but we didn't want that."

"I knew you guys did something. How did you do it?"

"Kendall called up pretending to be a patient to ask about her schedule and when she might be where." Halla wrinkled her nose. "She may have dropped Tyson's name. After that it was just a matter of walking up and down that hall until we ran into her. We got lucky."

"Luck doesn't seem to have had much to do with it." Saffron was too tired to be upset.

"So did she see you with Tyson. Was there a confrontation?"

"No, it was after he left. But what happened is I gave her my necklace."

"You didn't!" Halla's jaw dropped.

"I felt so bad, and she admired it, and I couldn't offer to make her one or she'd see my name and probably throw my card in my face. Well, if he's told her my name and she recognized it."

"She wouldn't have done that. She's too refined."

"Maybe."

"But it *was* stupid. It'll be awkward when she learns who you are." Halla removed the lunch she'd put together and a water bottle from the refrigerator, packing it in Lily's cooler.

"I know."

"You're not mad at me for us running into her, are you?" Halla asked.

"Not exactly. I guess I was curious about her, and I'm glad I met her. But please don't do anything like that again."

"I won't. Promise." Halla tossed her the key card. "Well, I have to leave now."

"You want help with the cooler?" Saffron rose from the bed, but Halla shook her head.

"No, it's not that big. I got it. You should get into the shower now. A cold one. I'm pretty sure you're burnt."

Saffron's skin *was* feeling kind of hot and tight. She'd take that shower and then sit in front of the air conditioner. When Kendall returned, she'd send her out for something to slather her skin with. Hopefully, she wasn't too burned. She had to be okay for her date tomorrow with Tyson. A date she'd been both looking forward to and dreading for eight and a half years.

"Okay. Give me a hug," Saffron said.

They hugged and Halla whispered, "I hope you don't plan on staying here long."

"I won't. I really can't afford it."

"I know, but don't let a lack of funds make you rush things. It would be too easy to stay here and let Tyson take care of you."

"And what's so wrong with that?" Saffron had been taking care of herself and helping Lily with other teens for so long that she didn't remember what it was like to have someone devoted only to taking care of her.

"It's not wrong—unless that's the main reason you stay."

"Point taken. You don't like Tyson very much do you?"

Halla rolled her eyes. "Of course I do. He's sweet and hot, and I wish there was one exactly like him out there for me. I think he's wonderful. As long as you're sure that's what your heart is telling you, I'll be the first one to dance at your wedding. Even if you make me wear stupid high heels and a dress."

"Thanks." Saffron hugged her again.

"Bye." Halla lifted the cooler, waved goodbye, and headed out the door.

Saffron lay back on the bed, feeling suddenly sleepy. But no, she wanted to take that cold shower, even if too much time had passed to help her skin any. Then she'd read a book until she was tired enough to take a nap.

In the bathroom, she pulled her shirt off and stood before the mirror in her swimsuit and shorts. Sure enough, the skin on her upper back and shoulders was decidedly pink. She'd definitely do what she could to soothe that before tomorrow night. At least it wasn't painful to the touch—yet—and it wasn't a deep red. Picking her shirt off the edge of the sink, she folded it over one of the towel racks. If she didn't step on it, it was clean enough to wear the rest of the day.

She was starting the water when someone knocked on the door. Kendall wouldn't be back already, so Halla must have forgotten something, though that wasn't usually her style. Most days, she was over-prepared.

"Coming," she called, leaving the water running.

She pulled the door open, a mocking smile on her face—a smile that died the instant she saw her visitor. The last person she wanted to see, and certainly the last person she'd expected: her mother.

"Where is she?" Her mother demanded. Pieces of wilted hair had escaped her customary knot, and her gray blouse was rumpled as if she'd been carrying something heavy.

"Where is who?"

"Kendall. I know she's with you. I am not in the mood for games." Her nostrils flared and her eyes resembled cubes of ice. "I had to practically threaten the workers below to give me your room number. The idiots. I even had to show my ID!"

Saffron didn't think that was typical, so her mother must have made a fuss and irritated the employees. She'd have to apologize to them later. "She's not here."

"I don't believe you."

Saffron stood back and motioned her inside. "Check for yourself. She was with me until about fifteen minutes ago. She spent the past two nights here, though, and I'm assuming she'll be back tonight."

Her mother turned on her, anger glinting from her eyes. "You need to make her leave."

Saffron folded her arms. "No, I don't."

"You're not a stupid girl anymore, Rosalyn. You must have seen what kind of man he is." Her mother's breath came more quickly with each sentence. "He's a disaster waiting to happen. He'll only hurt Kendall. She's better off without him."

"That may be so, but it's not your decision to make." Saffron passed by her mother, detouring around Kendall's belongings. She wanted to be on the other side of her mother to prevent her from coming any further into the room or staying longer than necessary.

"So it's *your* decision now?"

"No, of course not. But I'm not going to force her to do anything. It has to be Kendall's decision—or it will haunt her for the rest of her life."

"What you mean is to let her do whatever she wants. After all these years, you swoop in and play the fairy godmother and save her from her wicked mother. Is that how you raise your son?"

Fury ignited in a space of two seconds. Saffron pointed at her mother. "Don't you dare talk about my son!" With each word, she jabbed her finger closer until she was nearly touching her mother's chest. She retreated a step, and Saffron followed.

"You have no right to talk about him," Saffron went on. "Because of you, I lost the only man I've ever loved. Because of you, I nearly starved to death in the streets. I slept in alleys with strangers. I stole out of garbage cans to survive. And because of you I went into labor three months early and was all alone in a hospital crying my eyes out as I held my sweet son when his heart stopped beating. I said goodbye to my dead baby alone!" Saffron was screaming now, hands clenched into fists. "Alone! Because my mother—you— abandoned me!"

Her mother gasped, the color bleaching from her face. "I-I didn't know."

Saffron wasn't finished. It was as if all the pain in her life had concentrated into this moment, and every inhibition had disappeared. "You killed him! Every bit as if you forced me to get an abortion. So, no, I didn't go to dad's funeral. I was having a private one of my own, one that forever buried any loyalty I had for either of my parents. And then, after he was gone, there was nothing left. I had no one and nothing. I wanted to die. So I took an entire bottle of sleeping pills. Only a miracle saved me." A miracle named Lily.

Saffron paused, taking a deep shuddering breath. "How could you? How could you throw away your own daughter like that? I would give anything to have my son alive. Anything!"

Her mother stared at her, stunned into silence, her shoulders slumped. She'd aged ten years in the space of a few seconds.

"So don't tell me what I can and can't do for my sister," Saffron said. "My relationship with her is more important than forcing her down a path you want for her. It's even more important than making her do the right thing. It's her life, her choice, and the mistakes she makes are hers to overcome and learn from. You can't change her. You can only support and love and advise—and be there to hold her hand if her world comes crashing down." Saffron's hands hurt with how hard she was clenching them. But the pain was nothing compared to what was in her heart.

She took a step forward, her movements deceptively slow. "I think you should leave now. There's nothing more we have to say."

Her mother fumbled backwards a step. "I didn't mean for all that to happen. I thought you'd spend a few nights away and come back. That I could get you what you needed."

"What I needed was a mother." Saffron folded her arms again, not in defiance this time but to hold in the ache that threatened to burst forth. "I needed a family. But I don't need that anymore. Or your excuses. I have a new family now."

With that, she went into the bathroom and locked the door. She leaned against it, hoping the water she'd left running blotted out her quiet sobs. Moments later, she heard the room door click shut. She sobbed in earnest then, curled up on the floor by the tub.

She felt she was drowning, drowning, going under to that dark place that held no hope or love or light. If Halla had been there, she would have soothed her sadness. If Kendall had come back with her, they could have talked it out. But right now there was no one. Tyson was working, and Saffron didn't want to force Lily to abandon her family and foster children to come save her yet again.

She took a deep, shuddering breath. "I can do this," she whispered. "I am strong."

But she needed to talk. She needed to stop the horrible ache, and one person came to mind: Vaughn.

Veronica Brenwood opened the door and bent to lift the heavy box left outside the door during her talk with Rosalyn. All her anger had vanished with the pain in her daughter's eyes. She couldn't take that away, could never change the past, but she could leave her daughter this gift.

The box had been in the attic with all the other items Rosalyn—no, she was Saffron now—had left behind. Things Veronica hadn't been able to part with. She'd kept the box all these years, and she'd added to it as well. Today she'd hoped to use the contents to smooth the way between her and Saffron, to make her more compliant to Veronica's suggestions about Kendall. Now she only hoped to soothe her daughter's pain.

I've been such a fool. The thought didn't sit well. No one had called her that since her brother died, well before Saffron had left home. Maybe if he hadn't died, she wouldn't have messed things up so badly.

Back inside the room, Veronica pushed the heavy door closed with a loud click as she contemplated where she should put the box. She didn't want it lost in the mess of Kendall's belongings. Finally, she went to the table and set it there. With a pen from her purse, she wrote on top of the box: *For Saffron. I'm really sorry.* There was so much more she should say, but she couldn't trust that it would come out right. She didn't even dare sign the note.

Saffron was still in the bathroom, but the silence had given way to loud, heartrending sobs. Veronica hurried to the bathroom door, her hand reaching out to touch it. Her daughter was in pain. Each breath seemed a struggle, each cry that came through the door another accusation.

I caused this. The confident, beautiful, talented young woman Saffron had become had nothing to do with her but, rather, had happened in spite of her. What kind of mother was she to have forced her pregnant sixteen-year-old daughter out into the world alone?

Was she doing something similar to Kendall? The

thought made Veronica's stomach ache. Nothing she'd planned for her daughters had gone right. Two daughters, both who hated her. Both who needed love—and who had found that love outside the walls of her home.

Veronica knew she was pathetic. But one thing she understood clearly was that she had no right to knock on that bathroom door. Biting her lip to keep the tears from falling, she left the room, this time shutting the door softly behind her.

Vaughn was helping a student manipulate a drawing on the computer when a call came from Saffron. He was tempted to ignore it and call her back later, but she knew he taught during that time and wouldn't call unless something had happened. Maybe an accident in the car, but he'd already resigned himself to that possibility, so he was more worried about how she was than his car.

"Keep trying that," he told the student. "If you can't make it work, get Jodi to show you her animation. It might give you some ideas. I'll be right back."

He was already walking away and pushing the answer icon on his phone. "Hello?"

No response.

"Saffron?"

Was that a sob?

He fought his panic. "Saffron, are you okay?"

"Yes," she said faintly.

"You don't sound okay. Are you hurt? Has there been an accident? Because I don't care about the car."

"The car's fine." Her voice sounded strangled. "I-I-the dragon was here. And I told her everything, even stuff I didn't want to tell her. I wanted her to feel bad. To take responsibility."

His brave Saffron. He wished he'd been there for her. "Did it work?"

She made a sound that was a mix between a laugh and a sob. "I don't think so. I don't know. It doesn't matter. For so many years, I've practiced what to say, and I said it all. Only it didn't make me feel better. It just brought everything back. And I feel . . ." Okay, she was crying now, in earnest. No hiding it this time.

"Saffron. It's going to be okay. I promise. Look, is Halla there?"

"No, she already left."

"What about your sister?"

"She might be going to Denver."

Vaughn's concern intensified. Why was she all alone? "Tell me what happened."

A shuddering breath. "Oh, I'm sorry, Vaughn. I just realized you're probably teaching. I'm really going to be fine. I'm just sunburned, and I gave away one of my favorite necklaces to a woman who's probably going to throw it away." She took another deep, gasping breath. "And I'm hungry."

"Don't worry about my class. Whatever I teach them, I'm going to have to repeat at least five more times. I swear, it's like teaching monkeys sometimes. Half of them are too busy flirting to get anything done, and the other half are sleeping off the party they went to the night before."

That elicited a soft laugh. "That's why you shouldn't be a teacher."

"Maybe I should go to the zoo and see if they need a new zookeeper." He smiled when she gave another laugh. "Come on. Tell me what happened."

"I-I can't."

"Why not?"

"Because I never told you any of it—and it's too complicated over the phone. Part of it only Lily knew before I blurted it out today. Look, I'm feeling a lot better now. I'm sorry for interrupting your class."

She sounded lost and it made his heart ache. "The class doesn't matter."

"That's one of the things I love about you, Vaughn. You always put people first. But please go back to teaching."

"I don't need to."

"I'm really okay. We can talk later. I'm hanging up now."

"No, wait! I don't care about the class." But the emptiness on the line told him she'd already hung up. "I love you," he said anyway.

What should he do? Because she most certainly wasn't okay.

When they'd been talking the day before, with the sounds of the hotel pool around her, Vaughn had stopped himself barely in time from asking her if she'd resolved enough of her life to think about having a real relationship with him. Because he hadn't missed the fact that she'd said nothing about the man she'd gone to see, and what the omission meant, he couldn't begin to imagine. He wanted her happy, but what if she found happiness in another man's arms?

Vaughn had thought giving her space was the right thing to do, but there she was all alone, so if the guy she'd gone to see was nearby, he was either clueless or a jerk. What was Vaughn doing standing around here teaching when he could be fighting for the woman he loved? What he felt now, being in Phoenix without Saffron, wasn't living but rather some kind of odd half life where he stumbled through each day waiting to hear from her.

Enough of that. He was going to California.

Returning to his classroom, he gave a few directions and then dismissed the students fifteen minutes early. Afterward, he headed to one of his colleague's offices. Terrance was deep in conversation with a student, the door open, but Vaughn stuck his head in and interrupted. "Look, I have to take care of an emergency. Can you take over my classes the next few days? I'll take yours the next time you need me to."

"Oh, yeah?" Terrence stood and crossed to the door. "I guess I could Thursday and in the mornings tomorrow and on Friday, but not the afternoons. I'm booked solid. But I bet Chance could step in. All his classes are in the morning."

"Thanks. I'll email him." He'd have his aide pass out assignments at the Wednesday and Friday afternoon classes, if he had to. Getting fired for canceling classes might not look good on his resume, but he didn't care right now. "I'll email you my lesson plans." Vaughn started to turn, but Terrance wasn't finished.

"Will you also put in a word with Datatoon Studios for a couple of my students?"

"Sure. But you know if they aren't good enough, they won't hire them even if I recommend them."

"I know. I've got a few months to get them up to snuff."

"Thanks, man." They shook hands.

"I hope everything's okay." Terrance's comment came a little too late to make Vaughn feel he genuinely cared.

Vaughn couldn't force a smile. "I hope so too. Thanks again."

He hurried down the hall, feeling Terrance's eyes on him. His mind raced. If he spent ten minutes in his next class, he should be able to get his students started enough for his aide to supervise the rest of the hour. He'd need another five minutes to send lesson plans to Terrance and email Chance. His apartment was on the way to the freeway, so stopping there for a change of clothes would barely take any time. It was almost three now and with a little luck, he'd be on the road to California by three-thirty. He had Halla's phone number somewhere, and she'd know where he could find Saffron.

Bottom line, she needed someone, and he was going to be there.

20

Saffron hung up the phone with Vaughn, feeling like an idiot. She should have remembered he was teaching. Of course, he'd still taken the time to cheer her up. He was a good man. A good friend.

Friend. Which is exactly what she wanted him to be.

Despite what she'd said to him, she wasn't okay. She was confused about Tyson, guilty over Jana, worried about Kendall, and torn between loving and hating her mother. And she missed her baby. She missed the experiences they would never have. She missed his hand curling around her finger, his first day of school, his first . . . everything. She also missed being in control of her emotions. Because until she'd come here to face her past, she'd had a cap on these volatile feelings that now seemed intent on ripping her heart from her chest.

She laid her head on her knees, clamping her eyes shut. "I'm okay, I'm okay, I'm okay." Maybe if she said it enough, it would be true.

Pulling strength from a reservoir she didn't know existed,

she climbed to her feet and stripped before stepping into the tepid water.

She turned the water as cool as she could stand, dousing her back with it, and then inched it back to tepid. Once she wasn't shivering, she set it to cold again. When she emerged fifteen minutes later, her teeth were chattering, but her burned skin was no longer warm. It was, however, looking more red than before. Ignoring her head, which was telling her to go buy something to put on her sunburn, she slipped on her night shirt and shorts, punched up the air conditioner, and crawled between the sheets.

What about Kendall? Saffron found enough strength to check her phone. A text from Kendall had come in: *Going to Denver with Joel and the gang. See you later.*

Poor Kendall. Her mother was right about Joel, but Kendall was so in love that she couldn't see the danger signs. How could Saffron help her? And what if Saffron was wrong? Maybe Joel was Kendall's one great love, and he simply needed to grow into the role.

I've found Tyson again, Saffron told herself.

That brought more thoughts of his parents, her mother, and the baby. Tears leaked into the pillow. Saffron hugged her knees to her chest and finally slept.

A persistent banging pulled Saffron from a restless sleep. She cracked an eye open, groping for a pillow to put over her head. It couldn't be anyone she knew. Halla was back in Phoenix by now, Kendall would be halfway to Denver,

Tyson was in San Diego with his parents, and if it was her mother, there was nothing more they had to say to each other.

The banging continued. Saffron crawled out of bed, stubbing her toes on one of Kendall's boxes. Her burned back throbbed. She felt like screaming and dumping everything out the window. Or maybe jumping into her car and driving until she couldn't see anymore. Until she was too numb with exhaustion to think. Of course, she didn't have a car. Probably a good thing.

This time she used the peephole. No way was she answering if it was her mother. Or if it was Jana with an angry expression and a gun.

"Vaughn?" Saffron whispered. She yanked the door open and stepped into his arms, burrowing her face in his chest. He smelled so good and familiar. So safe. His arms went around her, and she winced when he touched her back.

"Sorry," he whispered.

Saffron didn't move away, and she barely sensed as someone passed them in the hallway. She didn't care who it was. She felt small in his arms, as if his broad chest was a barrier against the world and the pain in her heart.

"Let's get inside," Vaughn said, gently easing her back as he came forward.

He seriously smelled so good—a hint of her favorite aftershave, the outdoors, and sunshine. She breathed him in like she breathed in air. Together, they tripped, fell, and otherwise stumbled past Kendall's boxes and suitcases, the process made more difficult by the fact that Saffron refused to let him go. She knew she should back away, that she was probably sending the wrong message, but she was

incapable of stopping herself. She'd felt so alone until he
showed up.

A single tear slipped from the corner of her eye. "You're
here," she murmured.

"Of course I'm here. And I brought my sword." He
pulled away slightly, shrugged off his backpack, and reached
into one of its pockets for a bottle of aloe vera gel. "It has
analgesic in it. And I brought another remedy to use first."

The single tear became a deluge. Saffron could barely see
the consternation on his face through her tears. His arms
went around her again. Tenderly.

"It's going to be okay. I promise. Let's get your back
fixed up, and then we'll talk, okay?"

She nodded, his words soothing her turmoil.

"Can you get your suit back on so I can help you?" he
asked. "The poultice I brought is kind of messy. You can't
really do it yourself."

The thought of her suit made her wince. "I'll use a sheet."

A few minutes later, she came from the bathroom, a
sheet wrapped around her, drooping in the back to expose
the worst of her burn. Vaughn stared at her, his expression
vulnerable in a way she'd never seen before, which was
strange since she was the one not wearing a shirt. She knew
without a doubt that he wouldn't take advantage of her—
three months of dating and they hadn't slept together. He'd
never treated her with anger for not being ready.

A longing crashed over her as she returned his stare.
He was gorgeous—the blond hair partially standing on
end, the muscles showing beneath his T-shirt, the blue eyes
that reminded her of the ocean. How had she forgotten the
effect he had on her? She'd experienced it from the first time

they'd met river rafting, though she'd been dating someone else at the time, and she'd also felt it every time he'd walked into the sports store. She'd been aware of him in a way she hadn't been with other men, and that hadn't changed when they started dating. She'd told herself it was simple attraction—his kisses did something serious to her body—but how could she still be feeling that attraction now when she was in love with someone else? It didn't make sense.

Averting her gaze, she hurried to the bed and sat down.

He sat next to her. "It'd be best if you lie down on a towel. We'll let it soak for fifteen minutes and then put on the aloe. We should put on the aloe again in a few hours."

She pointed to the towel she'd discarded earlier on the floor and lay down after he spread it on the bed. He removed a plastic container from his backpack, mixed the contents with water from a bottle, and began smoothing it on. His fingers slid gently over her skin. Smooth fingers with a hint of roughness from his weekend rafting trips. Not long and slender surgeon's hands like Tyson's but every bit as careful. She'd seen Vaughn's hands work magic on keyboards, on paper, on paddles, and on her face or neck or arm when they'd been dating. But never this intimately. Each gentle touch trailed a delicious shiver that made her want to turn and kiss him.

But they were broken up, and she wasn't *that* kind of a girl. The kind of girl who kissed a man one day and made out with another the day after. Vaughn was only a friend helping another friend get over a sunburn, and why she was melting under his touch, she couldn't say. Because she was determined to see where her relationship with Tyson led, to reclaim the past that should have never been stolen from them. Yet if Tyson saw her now, she knew he'd be upset.

Saffron pushed the thoughts away. Vaughn *was* a friend, even if she was reacting like a love-starved teenager at his touch, and she needed him right now. There was no one else. What could she do, push him out the door and cling to the warmth of her sunburn instead?

Vaughn smoothed some of his mixture onto the front of her neck, the part he could reach, and Saffron stifled a moan at the relief it brought.

"Feeling better?" he asked, withdrawing his hand. His voice sounded a little rough. Sexy. It sent goose bumps rippling across her skin.

"Yeah. Thanks."

"Don't move. Just wait a bit. Let it soak in."

"Okay." Her voice sounded weird to her. Foreign.

He set the container with the mixture on the nightstand. "So what's in this stuff?" she asked.

He laughed. "Secret family recipe."

"I'm a little scared now."

"It's got oats, yarrow, calendula, lavender—among other stuff. Takes away the pain so tomorrow you won't be feeling it nearly as much."

Which would be good for her date with Tyson. The thought brought a shudder of nervousness to her stomach. Was she ready to move forward with him?

Vaughn settled next to her on the bed, his back propped against a pillow and the headboard. There were six inches between them, but it felt too close—and too far away. He didn't say anything but hummed softly under his breath.

Saffron let her eyes droop as the exhaustion crept back in. Her back did feel a lot better. Cooler somehow.

He woke her sometime later, wiping her back gently with a cool cloth. "Sorry," he said. "It's getting a little cold in here, and I want to get the aloe on so you can put something on." His voice was tense, but his hand was as gentle as before. She closed her eyes as he finished taking off the herbs and soothed on the aloe vera gel. "There."

He set the aloe next to her on the bed. "You should probably do your neck too."

She took the cue and gathered the sheet around her. She felt a little disoriented with sleep, and she was more than a little afraid she would drop the sheet and end up standing there only in her pajama shorts. Vaughn watched her with a knowing smile—with no trace of the strange vulnerability she'd seen before.

Somehow, she made it to the bathroom without flashing him. She soothed the gel on her neck and between her breasts before slipping back on her nightshirt. Ordinarily, she'd wear a bra with male company around, but there was no way that would be happening today. Her hair was slightly matted and a bit wild, but nothing Vaughn hadn't seen before during river runs. She decided to leave it.

She found Vaughn on the bed, munching on a bag of trail mix and watching something on his laptop. "I have some peach cobbler in the fridge," she told him. Her own stomach was growling.

He gave her a crooked smile. "I just ordered us a pizza. You said on the phone you were hungry, and that was six hours ago."

"What are you watching?"

"Anything you want."

"Really?" He had to be teasing her. Usually they ended up watching comedies or action shows, which they both enjoyed. She reserved the sappy romances for nights with her foster sisters, and he watched the more violent movies with his friends. "How about that remake of Cinderella?" she teased right back.

He laughed and turned the laptop screen toward her to show he'd already pulled it up. "How many times will this be?"

"Only the third." She and her foster sisters had watched it twice together. He'd bowed out of watching it with them, but he'd apparently listened to how much she'd loved it. "You don't have to," she said.

"I want to." He patted the bed beside him. "Come sit down."

She settled on the bed, relieved that her back was no longer on fire. Sitting here with him felt natural, like all the many other times they'd snuggled and watched movies together. She laid her head on his shoulder.

His hand came up to stroke her hair, but he stopped short of touching her. She tilted her head to see that his smile had faltered just a little. Was he realizing again as she was that this was not a date, and he shouldn't touch her that way? And what was wrong with her that she wanted him to?

Just habit, she told herself, lifting her head. She had to be more careful. He was too nice to hurt.

He started the movie and they were well engrossed by the time the pizza arrived. By the time they'd eaten their fill and the movie ended, Saffron had been able to push her terrible day mostly from her mind.

He closed the laptop, plunging them into darkness. "Okay, let's get more of the aloe on you."

Her heart started pounding. How could he sound so sexy just saying that? What was wrong with her? "Okay," she said faintly. But this time she wasn't hurting as bad, so she pulled her knees to her chest and lifted up the back of her nightshirt as best she could.

He switched on the light before edging toward her. Casually, he lifted the back of her shirt further and began spreading on the cool gel. A soft moan escaped her lips.

His hand paused. "Does it hurt?" he asked.

"No. It feels nice."

"Ah." His hand started moving again. Was that amusement in his voice? She didn't really care.

"So," he said after a few seconds. "Do you want to talk about what happened with your mother?"

She thought it over. "Maybe."

"What happened?"

She swallowed hard, keeping her face pointed away from him. "I had a baby."

This he apparently did not expect. His hand stilled for the space of two heartbeats. Then he picked up his rhythmic motion again. "A baby," he murmured. "When?"

"I was sixteen when I found out I was pregnant and barely seventeen when he was born. But he died."

"I'm so sorry." He finished rubbing in the gel and gently tugged the back of her shirt down. She looked at him then, arms still curled around her knees. His eyes glistened as he reached for her hand. "Tell me about it."

Before she could help herself, she was talking. Telling him how she'd felt abandoned by Tyson and about living on the street. How much hope she'd had for her son and how bitterly it had ended. She alternated between calm rushes and stretches of sobbing, but she told him everything. Even about taking the sleeping pills the week after losing her baby. About Lily finding her and rushing her to the hospital. She showed him the precious pictures in the jewelry box and told him about her reunion with Tyson.

Through it all he listened, asking a few questions, and holding and soothing her through the tears. She clung to him, grateful for his compassion. She'd always known he was a kind man, but she'd never felt so exposed before.

Of course, this confession had to change things between them, especially the part about her attempt to take her own life. Maybe that was why she hadn't yet told Tyson.

"I know it was weak," she said. "And that's why you're the only one besides Lily who knows about this. Well, and I let it slip to my mother today when I was so upset. But I don't want people to know, even those closest to me. I don't want them to think I'm weak. I haven't seriously thought about doing anything like that since . . ."

No, she had to be honest, especially since she was pretty sure he could read the almost lie in her face. "But today, the feelings I had when talking to my mother—or screaming at her, rather—reminded me of how I felt that day. I understood why I did what I did, and for the briefest second . . ." Could she really say it? "For the briefest second, I thought that if I'd succeeded, I wouldn't still be hurting now." There. Now she'd told him everything.

He tightened his one-armed hold on her, bringing her closer to his chest. His very good-smelling and safe chest. His chin came down to rest on her head, and his hand was smoothing her hair, apparently forgetting he no longer had the right to touch her that way. Or maybe her confessions had given him that right. Whatever the reason, she was glad.

"You went through a lot at far too young an age," he said so close to her ear that she could feel the warmth of his breath. "It's natural those emotions would come up again today when confronting your mom. Understanding your old self is a far cry from repeating the action." He stopped talking, and she felt him kiss her hair. "You're a good, strong woman, Saffron. I'm just sorry I didn't know any of this before. It makes things much clearer."

He had to be referring to her inability to commit, and she couldn't protest because there was a long line of wrecked relationships behind her—relationships she'd started with no intention of continuing past two months. Including hers and Vaughn's.

She pulled back enough to look into his eyes. "I thought I wanted to forget. I thought if no one knew, it would help me forget." A lump appeared in her throat, threatening to choke her. "Then I came here. Now, I want everyone to remember. I want them to feel his loss like I do." Did he hear the hardness in her voice? "Now it's them who want me to forget and go on."

Even Tyson seemed to want that. If he knew how much merely looking at his mother hurt her heart, he'd probably think her weak, unable to forgive. "It's not about forgiveness," she said, in case Vaughn had a similar feeling. "I just don't want to forget him. Ever. Or devalue his life and what we went through."

"They probably feel bad for you and think it would

be best for you to forget." The way his finger glided up her cheek and around her ear and through her hair was hypnotic. "But I don't think you'll ever forget. Or even that you should. No matter what, I think it'll always be a part of you in some way."

"I wish it didn't hurt as much when I'm with the people I knew then, or even when I'm by myself. It doesn't make sense. Coming here was supposed to make it better."

His other arm came up around her. "Does it hurt right now?" His voice was gentle like his touch.

Strangely it didn't. The memory was there, but the cavernous ache that normally filled her was missing. "I guess talking helps." Did that mean she should tell Tyson everything? Or maybe Vaughn was safe for her to confide in because he didn't hold her heart.

"You can talk about it any time you want," he said. "I'll always be here."

He couldn't mean that, of course, and if she stayed with Tyson, Vaughn would have to give up on her. But for the moment, she was going to enjoy his friendship and support.

"I should go," Vaughn whispered. "You need some sleep. I'll come back in the morning."

A surge of panic filled her. "Please stay. You can sleep in the other bed. No one else is going to be here. It's silly paying for another room when it's almost morning."

"Okay," he said. But he didn't move, and neither did she.

Saffron let herself drift, feeling comforted and for the first time in days completely content. She thought of baby Tyson, and instead of the heart-wrenching pain, she remembered the love she'd felt when she held him.

21

Vaughn awoke at the ringing of a phone. Not his. He blinked at the unfamiliar ceiling and then down to the woman sleeping in his arms. Her hair fanned out over his arm and the pillow, slightly matted as though it had dried without being brushed. Just the way it looked on river runs. Her lashes left delicate shadows on her smooth cheeks, and each curve of her face was perfect. She slept with abandon. The ends of her pink nightshirt had crept up to show matching polka-dotted shorts and a slice of her side. Her hand rested on his stomach, her cheek nestled in the crux of his shoulder. She was beautiful.

It wasn't the first time they'd fallen asleep this way watching a movie, but this morning it was bittersweet for him, knowing the only reason she was here was because the man she loved hadn't been. He'd heard the excitement in her voice last night when she'd told him about reconnecting with the father of her baby, and it was all he could do to hide his agony and prevent himself from leaving to lick his wounds in private. He wanted her happiness, after all. But how could this man give her happiness if she had to find comfort in Vaughn's arms instead?

"I won't give up," he whispered, smoothing her hair. "Not until you want me to." Because the happiness in her eyes when he'd shown up last night hadn't been fake.

The attraction they'd always shared was as strong as ever, and watching her in that sheet had nearly undone him, but he'd gotten through it somehow. Several times during the movie, it seemed as if she'd almost forgotten they were broken up and had appeared close to kissing him. He'd had to clamp down on his own self-control so he didn't read too much into it. However much he wanted Saffron, it wasn't fair to push his agenda with her now, not with what she was going through.

With her revelations, everything made sense now—everything except why she seemed so hung up on a man who hadn't fought for her. She'd excused Tyson because of his age, but Vaughn wasn't buying it. Sixteen-year-old males were some of the most obsessed, hormone-driven creatures he'd ever known. Tyson never should have believed she would leave.

Vaughn himself had no plans to back down unless she told him she wanted him to. Emotionally, he might not be able to play the role of the boyfriend she wouldn't commit to, but in reality he was still that man. He craved her touch, her smile, her laugh. He wanted to wake up every morning with her like this in his arms. He wanted to make love to her each and every day until forever. He wanted to see her smiling down at the face of their own son or daughter.

As if feeling his gaze, she moved. She sucked in a breath,

her mouth opening in a yawn at the same time her eyelids lifted. She met his gaze, blinked twice, and gave a little gasp. "Oh, sorry." She sat up, wiping her mouth with her fingertips. A mouth that was full and moist and kissable. "I didn't mean to drool on you all night."

His gaze dropped to the small wet spot on his shirt where her mouth had been. He laughed. "I didn't mind."

She raked a hand through her hair in that alluring way women had of trying to put things right. It took a renewed dose of self-control not to reach out and pull her back into his arms and kiss her senseless.

"You look beautiful." The words escaped him before he thought about how she'd take the compliment.

"Thanks," she said.

For a moment they sat there, facing each other, the sexual tension between them building. He almost felt that if he did kiss her, she'd kiss him back—and the world would stop moving. Before last Friday night, he would have done exactly that.

But that was before he'd broken up with her, and before she'd run back to the wimpy father of her child.

Child. She'd had a baby—and lost a baby. All by herself. The awfulness of what she'd gone through still shook him. It explained so much about her refusal to talk about children, to create relationships with his family, to accept his love. Seeing her so vulnerable had fired all his protective urges. He'd stayed up long after she'd gone to sleep, holding her and battling his anger against the people who'd failed her. Yet if they hadn't failed her, he would never have met and fallen in love with her. If she hadn't recovered from betrayal, she might be a completely different person from the strong-willed, determined woman who had stolen his heart. It seemed to be a paradox he couldn't resolve. He only knew he loved her, and that on some level she loved him too, even if she couldn't admit it to herself. Why else would she be looking at him the way she was right now? With an expression that ripped away all his guards and laid bare his soul.

Saffron gave a little shake of her head, accompanied by an embarrassed laugh. "Thank you for coming last night. Apparently, I needed a listening ear." She climbed from the bed and moved away, digging in a drawer for some clothes, and the tension between them eased.

"Apparently." He made his voice teasing. "Let's get ready and go out for breakfast."

"They have a pretty good breakfast downstairs. And it's free."

Another thing he loved about her. She didn't waste money—something he'd been sure she learned at Lily's House but might have also come from her time on the street. Her frugalness had certainly worked to his advantage last night when he'd suggested he leave.

"You mean the free breakfast they upped the price of the rooms to pay for?" he said, winking at her.

She chuckled. "Probably."

"Okay, we'll do lunch instead."

"I thought you were coming down to meet with Data-toon. Do you have an interview?"

He shrugged. "They don't actually know I'm here yet, though I did give them a heads up that I might be in town this week. I'll probably make the appointment for Friday." Now that he was here two days early, he wasn't sure how it would all play out. "I'll call them in a bit."

He lifted up the bottle of aloe. "So how's your back? We should probably put this on again." He told himself his reminder wasn't because he wanted to touch her.

Saffron moved her shoulders around a bit, testing her back. "It almost doesn't hurt at all. I think I might be able to put it on myself." She took the bottle from him and headed to the bathroom.

Vaughn fought his disappointment, though it was probably for the best. He was already frustrated enough as it was. "So when do I get to meet this guy, Tyson?"

She popped her head out of the bathroom. "Uh, never."

"Why not?" He had to work to make his voice light. "I mean, you and I are friends, right?" He stressed the word friends. "Why shouldn't I meet him?"

"You know why." She disappeared.

Because I'm in love with you, he thought. "I could give him some tips on sunscreen application so you don't get burned in the future."

She poked her head out again, her forehead wrinkled with a concern he would have found adorable if it didn't hurt so much to think of that other man touching her. "I won't need help with sunscreen." She hesitated. "Look, Vaughn. I know you came here to help, and I appreciate it, but that doesn't mean . . . I'm trying to get my life back."

His heart plummeted. "I know," he said, still using his teasing voice. "I won't tell him I spent the night."

She rolled her eyes and disappeared again. He heard the lock snap shut.

Sighing, he reached for his phone to call his friends at Datatoon Studios and let them know he was in town. He'd arrange for a quick visit and spend the rest of his time in California concentrating on Saffron. Except she'd told him about her date with Tyson this evening, and the way she'd talked had made it seem important. He had only a few hours to make a difference, and how could he do that when he couldn't even kiss her?

At the moment, he wanted to kiss her more than anything. Kissing her was unlike kissing any other woman. He couldn't explain it, but it was so good between them that it couldn't all be one-sided. Unless he was crazy, which maybe he was.

After setting up a meeting Friday morning with Datatoon, Vaughn stacked all the scattered boxes and suitcases neatly in a corner behind the table while debating possible plans for the day. He'd been hoping for months to take Saffron parasailing, but that wouldn't work today with her sunburn. Pulling on a wetsuit was difficult enough without inflamed skin. Maybe instead they could take a boat to Catalina Island and have a romantic lunch. It was beautiful there, and if they stayed late enough, she might have to cancel her date tonight.

At that thought, his frustration reared its ugly head again. What if nothing he did made a difference?

"Vaughn?"

He turned to see her standing there in a flared pink skirt and white top he'd never seen before that left her legs and arms bare. The top was loose and reminded him of the peasant blouses in medieval films. Her still-damp hair lay straight around her shoulders, perfectly framing a face that had come alive with subtle touches of makeup. He didn't know how women did that, but he loved her both with and without the extra paint. He knew his admiration showed in his eyes when she blushed.

"Like it?" She twirled for him. "I bought this outfit in a little store by the beach yesterday. It was insanely discounted."

"I do like it." He bowed. "Milady."

Her laughter fell over him like a gentle waterfall. "Your turn to shower," she said. "Oh, and if you brought my car, we'll need to talk about how to get you back to Phoenix. Especially if you need to leave before Halla comes on Friday."

"I did bring your car, but I'm in no hurry." He wasn't going to think about leaving her yet. "While you were in the bathroom, I made my appointment with Datatoon for Friday morning at ten."

"Oh, that's great. But how much do I owe you for my car? I'm betting they charged at least a couple hundred."

He looked away, one finger scratching a spot on his neck. "Uh, I didn't actually take it in."

"What?" She looked at him, a hand on her hip. "But you said . . . Oh, I know that look. What did you do?"

He shrugged. "It was an easy fix, and I do my own repairs when I can't get my car into a mechanic I trust. The brake parts were only fifty bucks, and the belt that was making the funny noise was ten."

"Thank you." Saffron hugged him. "You didn't have to do that."

"I wanted to." He held onto her at least two seconds

longer than necessary, but she didn't seem to mind. She smelled of lavender, aloe gel, and a hint of something else. Something that made him want to bury his face in her neck and never let go.

"I was hoping we could go parasailing during my trip," he said after retreating a step. "But that wouldn't be fun today with your sunburn. So how about we go to Catalina Island for lunch?"

Her jaw dropped in protest. "No! Let's go parasailing. My sunburn's much better today." She pulled the elastic neck of her top out to show a bit of her shoulder, but winced as her nail scraped her skin.

He moved closer to examine it. "Still red," he murmured. "The herbs and aloe gel are great, but you'd be miserable. We can do it tomorrow or Friday after my appointment instead."

Her shoulders slumped. "I know you're right, but I wish you weren't."

He touched her back over the thin material of her shirt. "You don't feel hot, at least."

"I just took a cold shower."

He gave her a slow grin. "I have that effect on women."

She started laughing, slugging him in the arm. "Yeah. Okay. I see where that's going. Get ready, or I'm going to eat without you."

Vaughn walked to the bathroom door, where he stopped for a second and stared at Saffron, who was putting away her nightclothes. He took a mental picture, hope battling against the feeling of loss in his chest. His mouth tasted like sand, and his heart pounded as if he were headed down a run of particularly rough rapids with no life preserver or paddle.

With an internal sigh, he forced himself into the bathroom and took his own cold shower.

22

Saffron surveyed the organization Vaughn had made of the room. She should have done it herself, but with all that had been going on, she hadn't even thought about it. She was accustomed to periodic chaos, having been so many years at Lily's House, but it was amazing how much better she felt without Kendall's clutter everywhere.

Her back was feeling better too, when she wasn't accidentally scratching it. She'd lathered her skin not only with the aloe, but with two layers of sunscreen to prevent further rays from sneaking in through her blouse.

The day stretched out before her with promise. Lunch at Catalina with Vaughn and then dinner with Tyson. She should let Tyson know she had a car now, so he wouldn't need to send one. Or should she? She didn't want to strand Vaughn without transportation. And the last thing she needed was for Tyson to bring her back to Temecula and find Vaughn here.

How would Vaughn feel if he was here and she didn't come back tonight? Saffron's stomach churned. *We're just friends,* she told herself. *He doesn't have a say in this.*

She hurried to her phone and saw that Tyson had been texting her since last night and had called this morning shortly before she'd woken up.

Is something wrong? His last text said. *I'm about ready to abandon my parents and come knocking on your window! But I keep telling myself you're sleeping. Or maybe you forgot to charge your phone.*

He'd sent this last text when she'd been watching the movie with Vaughn, and that brought a twinge of guilt. She should have called Tyson after her mother's visit, not Vaughn. Yet she couldn't find it in herself to regret doing so.

She texted back. *Sorry, rough night. I got sunburned yesterday and had an awful confrontation with my mom. But I'm okay. How did your dad's treatment go? I'm still planning on tonight.*

There was no reply, and she hadn't expected one. He'd be at the hospital now with patients. Well, she wasn't going to worry about him or Vaughn right now. She was going to enjoy herself at Catalina and forget everything difficult.

Her eyes landed on another text that had come in from Kendall this morning. *PLEASE CALL ME,* it said in all capital letters. Worry sliced through the contentment she'd been feeling. Hurriedly, she pushed Kendall's call icon. Three rings with no answer and then a breathless, "Hi." A slight hesitation before Kendall added, "Oh, thank you so much."

This last sounded far away and not directed at Saffron. "What's up?" Saffron said. "Your text got me worried."

"Sorry, I was paying for breakfast. But I need your help. I'm stranded in Las Vegas."

"You're what? What happened to Joel?"

"He left me here." A heavy sigh. "It's not entirely his fault. They kept smoking, and I got really car sick, even though I kept putting my head out the window. Then I started throwing up and Joel had to stop like five times. It was so embarrassing, throwing up all over the road like that. When they left this morning, Joel told me I couldn't go with them. I don't know what to do. I took out some money yesterday on my credit card, but it's not working anymore. I used the last of my cash just now on food."

Suspicion crawled through Saffron. "You got money out yesterday?'"

"Yeah, some money for the road. Everyone had to put in five hundred bucks. So I paid for a car part Joel needed to get his car working because the guy who was planning to drive bailed, and I didn't want them smoking in my car. Look, it doesn't matter. I'm glad not to be going with them."

"Joel just left you there?"

"Well, he thought you or Mom could help me."

"What a jerk," Saffron couldn't help saying.

"I know. But please let's stop talking about him. I don't want to hear even his name right now. I need help." Kendall's voice held a hint of panic. "Can you go get my car and come pick me up? I left it where Joel's been staying. You'll have to go see Mom first for the key. She has an extra. I know you don't want to see her, but I can't stay here. Please."

"Look, I'm coming, okay? Calm down. It'll take me hours to get there, though. Will you be okay until then?"

Kendall sniffed, but when she spoke, she sounded calmer. "Yeah. I asked for late check-out, and if you don't get here before two, I can hang out in the lobby. They won't care."

"Okay, I'm coming."

"I knew you would. Thank you. I'll text you Joel's friend's address, and the hotel's. And I'm sorry about having to go to Mom's."

"I won't have to. My friend drove my car down for me last night, so I have a car again."

"Really? You mean the guy who's head-over-heels in love with you?"

"He's a friend." Saffron could strangle Halla for talking too much.

"Well, I can't wait to meet him. Hurry, okay? But drive safely."

"I will. Goodbye." Saffron hung up and turned, nearly running into Vaughn. How long had he been there?

"What's wrong?" he asked, steadying her with his strong hands.

"Change of plans. I have to pick up my sister. She's stranded in Las Vegas." Saffron quickly gave him a rundown, aware of his closeness. He looked really good, muscles taut under his patterned button-up shirt and his blond hair slightly spiked. In the khaki shorts, his legs looked tanned and strong. When she dragged her eyes back to his, he seemed to be laughing at her.

"Let's go then," he said.

She blinked. "You don't have to waste your day. But I will need the car." She paused before rushing on. "Otherwise, I'll have to go get my sister's key from my mother, and she's probably at work. I'm not sure how to track her down."

Vaughn pulled her key from his pocket, tossing it to her. "Definitely take your car, but I'd like to go with, if that's okay. We'll grab some breakfast downstairs, and we'll eat lunch in Vegas instead of Catalina."

Having the company for the long drive did sound good. "Okay. But lunch is my treat."

He winked. "I don't think so. I'm the one who asked you to lunch first. Now, do you want me to drive?"

"Not on your life, mister." She always drove when they took her car, and he drove when they took his car. She hated going out with guys who expected to drive her car just because they were male.

"Good, because I have a little work on my laptop I can do."

She laughed. "When you were cleaning up, did you see my purse?"

"Over there on a box—oh, it looks like it slipped between the two boxes on top of that big suitcase."

Saffron hurried over to the bag, but the text on the nearest box called her attention: *For Saffron. I'm so sorry.*

Even after all these years, she recognized the handwriting as her mother's. She was every bit as sure that the box hadn't been here yesterday. It was about eighteen square inches and white instead of brown like Kendall's boxes that were stamped with brand logos. Instead of four flaps, the top lifted off.

Mesmerized, she grabbed the sides of the box, shaking it to pull the top free. The box was heavier than it looked, and the top fit tightly, but she finally pulled it off. A gasp escaped her lips.

"What is it?" Vaughn was at her side in an instant, his warm hand on her back near her waist.

She stared at the cellophane packages of beads. This was

the collection she'd left behind. But there were five times more beads at least, and this box wasn't the one she'd kept them in.

She dug in, picking up a handful. The new beads were all colors and designs, each one as tasteful as if she'd picked them out herself. Some were single and large, others were smaller and came in packages of a dozen. There was a gold one she was sure she could make into a necklace that would sell for a hundred bucks. Mixed in with these unfamiliar beads were beloved ones she recognized. Some she'd purchased new and others, the ones in plastic sandwich bags, were beads she'd found at vintage stores.

Vaughn picked up a few of the packages. "Did you bring these? Is something missing?"

She shook her head, letting the cellophane slip between her fingers. "I think this is my mom's strange way of giving me a hug."

"Really?"

Saffron nodded, hardly knowing how to feel. "After I left home, my beads were one of the things I regretted not taking. But many of these . . . they're new. I've never seen them before. And Kendall would have shown me if she'd brought them. My mother must have brought the box when she came yesterday."

"So the dragon has a heart after all?" He studied her with sympathy. "Does that change anything, do you think?"

"I don't know." She paused, struggling to gather her thoughts. She wavered between joy at being reunited with her collection and upset at her mother's additions. Not that the new beads weren't great, but they paled in comparison to what Saffron had suffered. "I'm not sure how they got here, actually. I didn't see her bring the box in. When she left I was in the bathroom, and I only heard the door shut once." Or maybe she wasn't remembering correctly. The whole confrontation was foggy in her mind.

"Well, I'd keep them."

"Oh, yeah. Of course." Saffron gave the beads a pat and pushed back on the lid. But did she need to say thank you? She wasn't sure she could. Unless . . .

"It might be a peace offering," Vaughn said, reading her mind. He was rubbing her back near her waist lightly as he often had after a busy shift at the sports store, obviously being careful to stick to the lower part of her back that wasn't burned. His touch felt so natural, it took her a moment to remember she should step away.

She picked up her purse and headed for the door. "Let's go. I'll figure out how to deal with my mother later."

After an hour on the road, Vaughn still hadn't taken out his laptop, and when Saffron questioned him, he admitted that he'd left it at the inn on purpose. "I decided it would be much more fun to beat you at the alphabet game," he said.

She glanced his way. "You're only beating me because I'm driving."

"Hey, a guy has to push whatever advantage he has. You know, it's genetically proven that women are better at word games."

"Really?"

"I don't know. I just made it up." His grin made her laugh.

As the city they were passing through gave way to desert, they talked about his students and his next planned river run. She also told him about her recent jewelry orders and how Lily had invited Kendall to stay with her.

"That's a great idea," he said. "This guy Joel sounds like a real loser."

"I know." Saffron frowned at the road for a long, silent moment.

"What?"

"It's just . . . how can I know that he's really a jerk? What if he acts this way because he's young? What if he's her soul mate? The one who'll make her life complete if she can wait for him to grow up a little?"

Vaughn shook his head. "Then he'd stand up and be the man she needs now. She can't wait until later."

Saffron felt him watching her, and she wondered if he suspected she was thinking of Tyson and what they'd lost. No, he couldn't even begin to imagine how it felt to lose the person you were supposed to be with forever.

"How is your sister?" she asked, wanting to change the subject.

"Good. My mom's over the moon about finally becoming a grandmother. She's going to be at the actual birth, while my dad and I hang out in the waiting room, but before that, my sister and her husband have all sorts of plans: Facebook posts from the hospital, games we're all going to play while we wait for things to progress, food we'll sneak in to my sister, and I'm under strict orders to film my dad's reaction when he first sees the baby. If you could hear all the hints my mom's sending my way about making my own babies, you'd tell me to run for the hills."

Saffron had only met his mother once at the sports store near the beginning of their dating. She'd reminded Saffron of an older Lily, but with a lot quieter house. She'd been friendly—almost too much so—and Saffron had avoided her after that meeting. Mothers tended to love her, and sometimes it was worse hurting them when she broke up with her boyfriends than it was hurting the guy. She'd made it a habit not to get close.

"I don't know," Saffron said. "You'd make a good dad." He would, too, if the way he handled the Boy Scouts during their river runs was any indication.

"I can't wait to try." His hand closed over hers, the one resting on her lap. "You'll make a good mother too."

She squeezed his hand, surprised to feel no rush of pain when she thought of her son. "Thanks." She wanted a baby, she could admit that to herself now as she hadn't before. Maybe with Tyson. Did he want children right away? She felt an odd catch in her throat, but she pushed it away.

"Let's sing." Vaughn began rifling through her CDs. "We'll pick one at random."

For the next hour, they sang along to random songs on various CDs and laughed until Saffron felt hoarse. Both of them were decidedly bad at singing, which made it that much more fun.

The next few miles passed as they chatted about Vaughn leaving the university and going back to animation full time. "I miss it," he admitted. "I loved designing game characters, but I'm not too sure about going back to Datatoon. I might want to try my hand at movie animation or maybe dip my toes into animated marketing videos."

"Well, you don't have to decide until you need to sign a new teaching contract, right?"

"I've pretty much let them know I won't be returning." He paused, and the joviality dropped away. "You know, I've been animating for ten years now, even before I left high school, and I love it, but it's not as fulfilling as it used to be. I think I might be . . . well, people my age, they're beginning to settle down. With my sister becoming a mom, and all my friends going in different directions, it's like I told you in Phoenix, I think I'm ready for something new."

The words hung between them . . . settling down . . . something new. She hadn't thought about his words in Phoenix, but she could see how it must have felt to him— that she was standing still, while he was ready to get on with living. Except now, since coming back home, settling down and finding something new was exactly what Saffron wanted. She loved her job, her foster family, and dating different men, but somewhere along the line, all of it had lost a little bit of shine. Maybe it was revisiting her past, the old wounds laid bare, but she was taking care of that. With Tyson, she'd be able to move forward.

"Why so sad?" he asked, concern in his eyes.

"I'm not. Just thinking." To her surprise, it was true. Even though she wasn't spending the day like she'd expected, it still stretched invitingly like the road before her. Waiting for her footprints.

She smiled and relaxed against the back of the seat. "Let's play name that tune. Loser pays for lunch. And no fair taking it from some killing movie I haven't seen."

"Or sappy romances."

"Agreed!"

Saffron had won seven times and Vaughn had won six when they arrived in Las Vegas, but she was certain he'd let her win the last two. It was just like him to make sure he paid for her lunch. She headed for the address of the inexpensive hotel far off the Strip where Kendall awaited them.

"We should stay the night and catch a show in Vegas," Vaughn said as Saffron searched for a parking place. "As it is, we won't be back until late, so we might as well have some fun here. I brought the aloe vera gel, if that makes a difference."

Back until late. The words slammed into her, and she gasped. "Oh, no! I forgot to tell Tyson." Their planned date, him showing her his remodeled condo—she'd completely forgotten that now she'd never be back in time. She'd planned to call him before they left, but she hadn't found a moment where she could get away from Vaughn to have a private conversation.

She glanced over to see Vaughn watching her with amusement. "You're only just figuring that out?"

"Well, I've been worried about Kendall and . . ."

"And playing song games." His face was straight but his voice mocked. "With me," he added. "Apparently, cold showers aren't the only effect I have on women. We can add forgetfulness to the list of my super powers."

"You've been playing too many video games," she retorted, bringing the car to an abrupt halt in a parking space.

What was she going to tell Tyson? The ride he was

sending was supposed to pick her up at three—and that was only an hour away. "I have to call him."

Vaughn stared at her. "So, go ahead."

"You're enjoying this, aren't you?"

"Yes, I am." He folded his arms and sat back.

She was so not making this call with him in the car. "Do you mind?"

Giving her a lazy smile, he opened the car door, but he didn't get out. Leaning over close to her, he said, "All's fair in love and war." His voice was deep and sensual, his eyes an endless ocean that seemed to wrap around her, making her senses reel.

The tension that had risen between them at the hotel was back again. She recognized it as attraction—that had never been their problem. It would be so easy to . . . "Do you mind?" she said through gritted teeth.

"Say hi to Tyson for me." He paused. "I mean . . . unless you think he'll care that I'm here with you."

She glared at him. "Go!"

With a smirk, he did as she asked. She watched him stride away from the car, heading into the hotel. He walked like a man who knew his purpose in life. She hated that she was hurting him, hated watching him use joviality to mask his emotions. Or was she reading into it only what she wanted to see?

Tyson didn't pick up when she called. "Of course," she muttered. But it was her fault. She'd put it off until too late, and she didn't want to examine why. She was ready to move on, period. She *loved* Tyson. She always had.

She texted him instead. *I am SO sorry, but I have to*

cancel. Joel abandoned Kendall in Las Vegas. and I'm picking her up. I won't be home until late. Can you please let me know if you get this? I'm really worried about your friend going to the inn and me not being here.

After five minutes, there was still no answer. Well, he'd see the message soon enough.

She climbed out of the car just as Vaughn returned with Kendall in tow. She was wearing jeans, a bright red T-shirt, and tall high heels. Her eyes were hidden by large sunglasses that covered the top half of her face. Vaughn was carrying a bright pink duffel bag that didn't diminish his manly appeal in the least. Saffron flipped the trunk lever and jumped out of the car to hug her sister.

"Nice car," Kendall said.

"Thanks."

"And he is really cute," Kendall whispered, pulling down her ridiculous glasses to eye Vaughn as he put her suitcase into the trunk. "When he came up to me where I was sitting in the lobby and asked my name, I was all flattered until he told me who he was."

Saffron ignored her. "How are you?"

Kendall shoved back on the glasses. "Great. I passed the time flirting with one of the hotel clerks."

Saffron laughed. "You get his number?"

"Of course not. I'm taken." Kendall frowned as she watched Vaughn come toward them. "At least I was."

"Joel will probably come around," Saffron said without enthusiasm. "So where are we going to eat lunch?"

Kendall gave a little squeal. "Oh, finally. I'm starved. Can we go to this Mexican restaurant I know? They serve chips right away, and I need to eat something quick."

"Are you sure your stomach can handle spicy?" Saffron asked.

"Oh, yeah, of course." Kendall waved the concern aside. "It's being in a car a long time that I can't take." She started to open the door to the back seat, but Vaughn prevented her from getting in.

"Take the front," he said. "My sister says it's better for car sickness. It's even better if you drive."

"Really?" Kendall said. "Huh. Maybe you're right. I've never felt sick when driving my own car."

"Wait, wasn't Joel driving to the concert?" Saffron asked. "Were you in the back seat?"

Kendall shrugged. "He thought putting the guys that smoked up there and me behind him would work better. It didn't."

That made no sense, and Saffron wondered why Joel hadn't prevented them from smoking at all. This was his baby too they were talking about. Stifling a sigh, she said, "You can drive on the way home, if the front seat doesn't work."

Saffron started the engine, humming as she waited for Vaughn, who ran around the car to open the door for Kendall before getting into the back seat.

"Lavender's Blue Dilly Dilly," he said, leaning forward between the two seats.

"What?" Kendall looked at him askew.

"The tune she was humming."

Saffron laughed. "I thought you said no sappy romances."

"Women aren't the only ones who can change their

minds. And we did watch *Cinderella* last night." He sat
back chuckling, as Saffron explained the game to Kendall.

Kendall wanted to try it then, so the game continued
partway through lunch, mostly driven by Kendall. But even
she paused when Vaughn told her about his first river run,
where he ended up dizzy from dehydration, which ultimately landed him in the water.

"Three days I had to stomp around in wet boots," he
finished. "But I learned my lesson about drinking water."

"So weird that you can get dehydrated with all that
water around." Kendall sat back, stretching, half her fish
tacos uneaten. "You know what? I'm going to need a doggy
bag. In two hours, I'll be starving again."

Saffron laughed. "We can get some snacks for the ride
home."

"So, no show tonight?" Vaughn asked.

Kendall's eyes opened wide. "Yes! Oh, yes! Let's stay.
They've got all kinds of cool shows here."

"I have to get back," Saffron said, lifting her cup for a
drink.

Kendall gasped. "Oh, for your date with Tyson." She
glanced at Vaughn, as if to judge how the words affected
him. Apparently finding nothing, she turned back to
Saffron and batted her eyes. "Pleeeeeease, let's stay! You can
go out with Tyson any time. This is our first sister outing."

"Sister plus one you mean. Pleeeeeease, let's stay,"
Vaughn said, copying Kendall.

He looked so funny batting his eyes that Saffron spurted
water all over her plate. That set them all laughing. "Okay,
fine," she said.

Kendall cheered, and Vaughn gave Saffron a look that ignited a slow heat in her stomach, which she decided to blame on the Mexican food.

"Let's go," she said. "I have to make a call."

23

Half an hour later, Saffron left Vaughn and Kendall in the shared sitting room of the two-bedroom hotel suite Vaughn had paid for and retreated to one of the bedrooms. The place was too much money, but he'd insisted, and Saffron was glad to have the privacy to call Tyson.

He picked up on the first ring. "Hello?"

"Hi," she said.

"Is Kendall okay?"

"Yeah, and I thought we'd be home by seven or eight, but she really wants to stay, and so does Vaughn."

A hesitation before he asked, "Vaughn?"

"I told you about him. The guy who was fixing my car. He brought it to me."

Silence on the other end of the phone. "The guy you used to date."

"Yeah."

"Do I have something to worry about here?" Direct, as was always his way.

"He's just a friend. Look, you and I have a second chance. I want to make this work between us." Why did she feel it was the teeniest bit of a lie? Maybe because if she didn't tell him about Vaughn comforting her last night, it *was* a lie. Or about the attraction she and Vaughn still shared, an attraction she thought was normal since they'd been dating for three months. She'd tell Tyson later in person.

"Okay, then," Tyson said. "I'm glad you have the company." Another pause and then, "I miss you. I know that might seem crazy, but I don't think I ever stopped missing you."

"I know. I miss you too. I wish you could be here." She did, even if he and Vaughn would both hate it.

"Let's reschedule our plans for tomorrow. I'll send someone to pick you up at three again. Will you be back by then?"

"Definitely, but I'll drive. It makes me uncomfortable to put your friend out when I have my car back." If Vaughn needed her car to go to Datatoon, she'd ask Kendall to use her car, because while Saffron wasn't sure she'd be staying at Tyson's, he'd invited her and it was a possibility. In fact, today she felt a lot less sure about taking him up on his offer to stay at his condo than she had yesterday. But was that only because Vaughn was here?

"Okay, have fun at the show. I'll try not to think of you there with your ex."

That made her smile. "I'll text you how much I'm hating it if you want." He'd taken news of Vaughn's presence with remarkable aplomb, because if the situation were reversed and he was in Vegas seeing a show with Jana, she might not be so understanding.

He laughed. "Only if you mean it." He paused and then added, "Saffron, I'm glad you came back."

"So am I."

I love you. But she hung up, leaving the words unspoken.

The popular shows were all sold out, so after walking around a few hours and having dinner at a buffet, they ended up at a concert for an unknown singer named Carly Blythe. Her energetic performance left Saffron breathless. The crowd agreed and cheered her back onstage for three encores with standing ovations before the night ended.

"Wow," Kendall said, "that was amazing. Joel will be sorry he missed it."

"Are you talking to him again?" Saffron asked.

"No, but I will."

Saffron couldn't respond because there was nothing she could say that her sister would want to hear.

"You hungry?" Vaughn asked, inserting himself between them.

Saffron and Kendall shook their heads, but Kendall added, "I still have my leftovers from lunch in case I need them."

On the way to their Vegas hotel room, Saffron and Vaughn chatted about the concert, but Kendall had sunk into silence. *She's probably exhausted,* Saffron thought. Saffron was tired too, and for the first time, she wished someone else were driving.

Once inside their suite, Saffron read a text from Tyson saying he missed her and asking if she would like to have dinner with his parents on Sunday.

A rush of trepidation squeezed her heart. He was close

to his parents, and ordinarily that wouldn't be a problem, but . . . *but what?* She loved him, and she'd been waiting eight and a half years to be with him. She'd have to suck it up and find a way to get over what had happened. Mrs. Dekker was the kind of woman who'd want friendship from her son's wife.

Wife. Saffron sat on a chair in the little kitchenette. Everything seemed all wrong, but she couldn't put her finger on why.

"You okay?"

She looked over to see Vaughn staring at her from the couch. "Yeah. I'm just . . . tired."

He gave her a smile. "Get to bed, then. If you change your mind, I'll be watching a little TV. I'd love company."

"Another time," she said, coming to her feet. But there wouldn't be another time. This was it for them.

"Goodnight."

She could feel him watching her walk to her bedroom, and it was all she could do not to turn back and curl up with him on the couch as she had so many times before. But she wasn't in crisis mode anymore, and that wouldn't be fair to him . . . or to Tyson.

As she closed the door to the room, Kendall looked up from one of the two single beds. "I know you hate him."

"Who? Vaughn? Of course I don't hate him."

Kendall sat up and swung her legs down. "No, not Vaughn. Joel. I've seen how you look at him."

"I've only met him once." Well, twice, counting Monday night at Tyson's place, but Kendall didn't know about that. "How can I be looking at him in any specific way?"

"It doesn't matter. You get that expression on your face

every time I talk about him. Just like Mom." Kendall's voice wavered and her eyes filled with tears.

"I only know what you tell me about him." Saffron dropped her purse on the other bed.

"He's a good man! He loves me!"

Saffron's patience snapped. "Then why did he leave a pregnant woman all alone with no money or car in Vegas? Why did I have to change my plans to pick up the pieces? Why is he off wasting the money he could be saving for a down payment on an apartment for his child? Why didn't he order those so-called friends of his to stop smoking in the car?"

Kendall launched to her feet, hands clenched. "Excuse me for being such a burden. I was right—you hate him."

Saffron decided she wasn't doing her sister any favors by hiding the truth. "I'm concerned, is all. You said it yourself—Joel doesn't seem to want this like you do. It's the baby who's the most important thing right now. You get that, but do you honestly think Joel does?"

"So you want me to drop him because he's unprepared?" Kendall's voice held a viciousness that reminded Saffron of their mother. "Is that what you did with Tyson? I don't even know why he's willing to take you back when you didn't care enough about him the first time to trust what kind of man he'd become."

Disbelief flooded Saffron. How could Kendall say such a thing to her? Couldn't she guess that it would hurt like a knife twisting in a wound? "You know nothing about what happened between him and me. Nothing!"

"Well, if I don't it's because you haven't told me." Kendall stomped toward the door.

Saffron blinked at her. Hadn't she told Kendall? Saffron and Halla had talked about it at length, but it was possible Kendall had missed those conversations.

"Anyway, you don't need me as a sister, not with all the make-believe sisters you have. Our blood means nothing. First you abandon me to Mom for eight years, and now you won't even tell me how you really feel about Vaughn. Anyone can see the chemistry jumping between you two. But it doesn't matter. I don't care. I don't need you. Not to rescue me, or to make me leave Joel. Excuse me. I'm going to sleep on the couch!"

Kendall dragged the door open and went through it, slamming it behind her before Saffron could recover from her shock. Her first instinct was to open the door and shout, "Good riddance, you ungrateful brat!" But the part of her who'd had to learn to live with a group of runaway teenage girls warned her she'd regret it later. So she dropped to the bed, fully dressed, and pulled the pillow over her head. She needed to take off her bra, put on some of the aloe gel, and brush her teeth with the supplies the hotel had given them, but she could do that later. Too bad they hadn't thought to bring pajamas.

Saffron heard laughter outside the door. Apparently, Kendall and Vaughn were hitting it off. She should be out there with them, but her pride wouldn't let her try to make amends. Not yet. Besides, she needed to keep space between her and Vaughn. Especially after their closeness last night.

Kendall was wrong about the chemistry between her and Vaughn, of course. They were friends and that was all. In fact, none of what Kendall had said was true. Saffron had always known that Tyson would be a success. That he'd make his way in the world. She'd known it just as she knew Vaughn would make a great father.

More laughter in the next room. Maybe he'd make a good father to a baby that wasn't even his. No, that wasn't fair. Vaughn had done nothing but treat Kendall like a younger sister.

With a frustrated growl, Saffron grabbed her earbuds from her purse and headed into their private bathroom.

Vaughn heard the girls' raised voices but couldn't hide his surprise when Kendall barreled from their bedroom. She kept her flushed face averted, going to the small refrigerator to retrieve her food.

He gave her a little time and then said, "Hey, I could use the company watching a movie, if you're not too tired. I mean, it's not as if you and I have to drive back tomorrow since it's Saffron's car, right?"

Kendall's laugh sounded a little forced. "Yeah. I'm not tired." As if to contradict the statement, her mouth widened in a yawn. "Oops," she said.

He gave a hearty laugh. "That's okay. Why don't you take my room? I'll crash here on the couch."

"That's nice of you, but I'll watch for a while." She came over with her food carton and sat on the other end of the couch, pulling her legs up under her. "What?" she said when she saw his smile.

"You remind me of Saffron. She sits like that all the time."

"You love my sister, don't you?"

His jaw clenched and unclenched. What could he say to that? Whatever spat had separated the girls would be over tomorrow, and he had no doubt everything he said would be passed on to Saffron. No matter his feelings for her, he wasn't exactly thrilled about being the topic of discussion unless it included how much Saffron cared about him too. Which he wasn't exactly sure was true.

"You don't have to say." Kendall took a bite of taco. "I can see it."

"How is she with the other guy?"

"Oh, you know about Tyson?"

He nodded. "In a way, I'm responsible for her being here."

"Yeah?" Kendall chewed on the tines of her plastic fork. "How?"

"I broke up with her."

"Oh, right. I did hear that. I guess in retrospect, it might have been a dumb thing to do."

"Maybe. But she was stuck, and I'd rather see her happy and not with me than to see . . ." It sounded too corny even to his own ears.

"Her unhappy," Kendall finished.

"Right. Something like that."

She stared at him, and he was vaguely aware of the sounds coming from the television. "I think that's the sweetest thing I've ever heard." She stabbed her fork into the taco and put the carton on the couch between them. "So what do you think of a man who would leave his pregnant girlfriend in Vegas without money or a car?"

Vaughn could sense how loaded the question was. If he told her he thought Joel was a creep who ought to be punched senseless, that might not go a long way to helping her make tough choices. "I'd think," he said slowly, "that he's blind to what he has and that if he isn't careful, he might wake up one day and find he's lost everything."

It was the right answer. Kendall blinked back tears and came to her feet. "Thank you. And I think I will take you up on the offer of your bed. If you don't mind."

"Not at all." He watched her put away the taco and disappear into his much smaller room.

The next second, she poked her head out, reminding him again of Saffron. "For what it's worth," she said. "I'm rooting for you. Tyson's nice, and I know Saffron loves him, but I think the two of you are better."

One of the sisters down, so he could be happy about that. But the most important woman wasn't letting him in. He'd made progress today. Would it be enough? Saffron would have her date tomorrow, and soon he'd be returning to Phoenix. Vaughn had the feeling that all his time was running out.

Saffron expected Kendall to be pouting and angry in the morning, but as they went down to the breakfast buffet, she acted as if their argument had never happened. "I usually don't feel this bad anymore," she moaned, her face pale and sick.

Saffron gave her a sympathetic look. "It's probably the stress."

"Sorry about last night." Kendall's words came in a rush. "I was upset because of Joel."

"I know." The words Kendall had said still stung, but Saffron would talk to her about that more later, after Vaughn had gone home.

As if knowing she was thinking about him, Vaughn turned and smiled. Saffron smiled back, feeling happier.

At the table, Kendall took out her phone to read a text. Her eyes grew impossibly wide, and Saffron held her breath. What had Joel done now?

"It's from Mom," Kendall said. "I don't believe this."

"What?" Saffron's appetite fled.

Kendall shook her head and kept reading. Finally, she

lifted her gaze to Saffron's. "She says I can stay with her and keep the baby. That she'll help me." She paused, horror seeping into her expression. "Can you imagine that? Her helping raise the baby?"

"I thought that's what you wanted."

"No, I wanted for Joel and me to stay there for a little while is all. My baby deserves a mom and a dad. But Mom's still not willing to bend on Joel staying there, and she has serious control issues."

"Well, it's a start. At least you can see Joel when he gets back. Away from the house, I mean. And she isn't pushing you to place the baby for adoption or something."

"I guess." Kendall stared down into her full plate. "I'm a little scared that I'm not strong enough . . . I don't want her to raise my child. It's too hard a life for a kid."

Saffron understood what her sister meant. After living at Lily's House and seeing the love there, that's what she wanted for her children too.

Kendall went back to reading the text. "She also says you can stay in the guest room, if you like. That there's no use staying at the inn when she has the room." Kendall met Saffron's eyes. "Wow. That's cool. I've always wanted to move in there, but she won't let me. It has an exterior door, you know. Anyway, she says she would like the chance to talk this all over with us, if we'll come to the house. She's taken the day off work."

Saffron wanted to say no, but the memory of the bead collection stopped her. She ate another bite of scrambled eggs to mask her confusion.

"You should go," Vaughn said. "Maybe you'll finally get that real hug you've been wanting."

How did he know? Saffron felt choked up, touched that he understood, and yet afraid to want something like that in the first place. When she didn't speak, he scooted closer to her on the bench seat and put his arm around her. "Don't worry. I'll come with you. Remember, I'm good with dragons." His voice soothed her and gave her the added courage she needed.

"Okay," Saffron said. "That is, if Kendall wants to."

Kendall spoke with her mouth full. "Hey, at least it gives me time to decide what I want to do."

Saffron knew the feeling. If she was staying in town, she had to find someplace more permanent to stay while she figured things out with Tyson. She'd probably take him up on his offer to stay at his place, especially after their date. Tonight would change everything between them—if she let it. Maybe then she could hold the joy she felt with him in her heart even when he wasn't with her.

Feeling Vaughn's eyes on her, she lifted her gaze, her face heated. Was that sadness in his eyes? "I'm going to grab more water," he said. "Anyone want some?" Saffron shook her head while Kendall held out her cup.

"Are you really going to be okay living with her?" Saffron asked when they were alone.

Kendall finished chewing, swallowing a bit noisily. "For a while, at least. I admit that I miss home. I miss my room, my things. I even miss Mom a little, if you can believe it."

Oh, yes, Saffron understood that—or maybe it was the idea of a mother she'd missed. "At least you have another choice."

Kendall set down her fork and reached across the table

to touch her hand. "I really am sorry about what I said last night."

Saffron held back a sigh. "I know."

"It's just," Kendall continued, "here you have two really great guys who would do anything for you, and Joel . . . he's not like they are. Sometimes I think maybe he's all I deserve."

Saffron's heart wanted to break all over again at that. "No. Don't settle. Either he gets it together and becomes the man he should be, or you have a tough decision to make. The one thing we do have is time."

Kendall snorted. "Or at least five and a half months."

Five and a half months. That was about how long it had taken for Saffron's world to come crashing down in flames. Whatever happened, she wouldn't let history repeat for her sister.

They made good time to their mother's house in Temecula, despite Kendall's frequent potty breaks. She hadn't been ill riding in the front passenger seat, but her wired-up conversation and outbursts had made a sleep-deprived Saffron nervous. Saffron had finally changed places with Vaughn to get a few winks in the back seat.

Now she was wide awake, her hair messy and her clothes feeling sticky from a second day of wearing them and sweating under the aloe vera gel and sunscreen. What was she doing here like this? They should have stopped at the inn first to change clothes. She leaned between the front seats and adjusted the rearview mirror to examine her hair. Running her hands through it tamed the beast, but she still felt awful. At least her sunburn no longer hurt.

The car was beginning to feel stifling hot without the air on. Kendall was already outside the car, glaring at the house with an air of determination. Saffron knew she should get out, but she looked again at the mirror, her stomach churning. Maybe she should touch up her mascara.

"You look beautiful," Vaughn said, as if sensing her insecurity.

She pulled the shoulder of her shirt up a bit to unstick it from her back. "Thanks. I'd rather be parasailing."

He laughed. "Maybe later."

But Saffron knew they would never go. It was already after one, and in a few hours she'd be with Tyson, making life decisions. She told herself there wasn't really any decision to make. She'd been waiting for Tyson for over eight years.

They climbed from the car, and she was glad Vaughn followed without her having to ask him to come along. Kendall wasn't much defense, and after her last run-in with her mother, Saffron's desire to flee grew with each step.

Vaughn kept close, his arm brushing hers as they approached the front of the house. The door swung open before they reached it, and there stood her mother. This time her dark hair hung loose around her neck, shorter now than Saffron remembered. Her eyes skipped over Kendall and landed on Saffron. No one spoke.

"Hi, Mrs. Brenwood." Vaughn stepped forward, offering a hand. "We haven't met. I'm Vaughn Abrams. I'm a close friend of Saffron's. I brought her car from Arizona." He stepped back again next to Saffron.

Her mother's eyes went to him and then down to where his arm touched Saffron's. Instead of displeasure, there was a need in her eyes, one Saffron didn't understand. She was glad Vaughn had explained their relationship, but now she waited for her mother to coldly excuse him. Her next words were surprising.

"It's nice to meet you," she said, stepping back and ushering them inside. "Come on in. I hope you're hungry. I made sandwiches for lunch."

"I'm starved," Kendall muttered, heading into the kitchen. Sucking in a breath, Saffron followed her.

Lunch was awkward, or would have been without Vaughn. Accustomed to dealing with strangers on a regular basis, he eased the conversation between them. When her mother learned he was teaching for the second year, she started talking about Kendall leaving school. "I know this baby changes things, but I don't want my daughter to throw her life away."

Kendall looked ready to burst, but Vaughn stepped in. "I've found that my students who have children are far better students on average and dedicate themselves more. Or at least once they discover what it is they really want to study." He turned to Kendall. "What is it you'd like to do as a career? Besides being a mother, I mean, though that's a career all on its own."

Kendall's eyes widened and went to her mother. "I . . . uh . . . I've been thinking about being a nurse."

"Really?" her mother said with a little gasp. Saffron wasn't sure if she was offended that Kendall didn't want to study interior design or excited that Kendall had a dream. But no one looked more surprised than Kendall herself.

Kendall shrugged. "I'm not sure about it or anything, but it might be interesting. I've had a few good conversations with Tyson Dekker while Joel's been working for him. He has a ton of fascinating stories about his work at the hospital."

"You should definitely look into it," Vaughn said. "You could shadow a nurse for a day, see what you think." He refocused on their mother. "A lot of my students start school and find they aren't interested in their classes. I always try to identify these students quickly so they don't waste a lot of time." He laughed. "I mean, the ultimate goal is for them to be happy, not to train for a job that will make them miserable."

Saffron sincerely doubted her mother had ever considered that, but she was nodding. "Yes, that's always been my dream for my daughters."

The food in Saffron's mouth turned to ash. Her mother wished her to be happy? This was too much, and if she didn't leave right now, she was going to throw the rest of her fancy sandwich in her mother's face, designer mustard and all. She deliberately set it down and stood. "I'm sorry, I have to go."

She made it to the hallway before her mother caught up to her. "Please don't leave."

Saffron whirled. "You never wanted my happiness. You only wanted to make me do what would make you happy. I'm sorry, but I can't have this conversation today." She needed to go back to the hotel to get ready for tonight. To begin the rest of her life—a life that didn't need to include her mother right now.

"Wait!" Her mother said, eyes wide and pleading. "I'm

sorry. I know I have a lot to make up for. I didn't know I was separating you from the only man you'd ever love. I thought he'd end up hurting you. I didn't understand anything until you told me yesterday how much you still loved him." She hesitated. "I heard you crying and I realized how awful this has been for you. Look, I know we can't go back. I know I can never make it up to you, but can we try to make this work a little for Kendall's sake?"

Saffron pushed back her anger, another lesson from Lily. "Maybe. But it's going to take time before I'll trust you." Her mother nodded, her face going blank. Saffron recognized the expression as one of her own. She used it when she tried to make things not hurt so much. That look was the only reason she forced out, "Thank you for listening to Kendall. And thank you for the beads." She nearly choked on the last words. She thumbed over her shoulder. "I'm going now."

"Thank you for coming," her mother whispered. Her face was still expressionless, but today Saffron had caught a glimpse of a person behind the mask. For now, it was enough.

As Saffron turned to leave, she looked over to the doorway of the kitchen and saw Vaughn standing there watching them, his expression one she'd never seen before. Was it resignation? Acceptance? She wasn't sure.

How much of the conversation had he heard? If he hadn't understood it before, he'd know that she loved Tyson more than anything, that there was no chance for them. Not ever. But having Vaughn's support when she needed him had meant so much. More than she could tell him, but maybe she could try.

"Vaughn," she began.

He lifted a hand. "No. It's okay." He turned to her mother. "Thank you for lunch. I'm taking off now." To Saffron, he added, "I'll get my stuff from the car."

"It was nice to meet you," her mother responded.

"A pleasure." He dipped his head in the direction of the unseen table where Kendall was presumably still sitting. "I think with support, she'll find her way. These kids some-times have the courage to make choices we never dream they can."

Saffron's mother nodded. "I appreciate that."

Vaughn passed them and Saffron hurried after him, but he was through the entryway and outside before she caught up. "Vaughn, you don't have to go. You can stay at the inn tonight, so you can go to your interview tomorrow. You said it was at ten, right?" She could make it back from Oceanside easily by then, and he could use her car.

Vaughn stopped and turned. "Wait there while you go out with the only man you'll ever love?" His voice wasn't angry or cutting, but matter-of-fact. "Oh, Saffron, you don't know me at all, if you think I'll stand in your way—or stand by and let you rip out my heart. I can see you've chosen. It's in your face, your words. I just didn't want to admit it before now." He waved his cupped hand between them. "This thing we have, it doesn't come along every day. I love you. I love you with everything inside me. No reservations. I know you love me too, but it's not enough, is it? You want him, and that means what you have with him must be stronger. I want you to be happy, so this is where we say goodbye."

Saffron's eyes filled with tears, making it hard to see his face. "Vaughn, if it wasn't for you . . ."

"We'd still be back in Arizona with me wondering why you can't love me." He closed the space between them. "Be happy, Saffron. Go for what you want. Listen to your heart. Don't worry about me. I'll be okay."

She stared up at him, tracing the familiar lines of his face. This was it. She wouldn't likely see him again, or if they did, it would be from a distance. Sadness choked her. "Vaughn, I . . ."

His eyes dipped to her lips, and the tension between them ratcheted up. Saffron's heart pounded furiously. Her mouth was dry. Why was he looking at her like that? Why couldn't she look away?

He bent and placed his lips against hers. Maybe he meant it to be a casual goodbye kiss, but the minute he touched her, Saffron's world burst into bright colors. Passion that had been building between them the past two days seeped through her limbs, infusing them with energy.

He deepened the pressure of his lips, one hand going to the back of her neck, pulling her closer. She knew she should move away, but she couldn't. She felt she could run all day, work without sleeping, kiss him for a week straight. She didn't need air, just his mouth on hers. His mouth moved more insistently, urgently parting her lips. He tasted of hunger and desire. Of yearning. Of love. The kiss continued, his mouth searching hers . . . looking for what?

He'd kissed her so many times before, but not like this. Not as if his life and soul depended on her touch. His hand kneaded the back of her neck, sending tremors through her. His other hand came up to touch her face, as if to memorize it by touch alone. He caressed her eyes, her cheek, her ear, her neck. Saffron was flying, soaring. She swayed against him, needing his strength.

Then it was over and he stepped away, leaving her mouth open and her chest heaving. Her body aching with want. "Goodbye, Saffron. Have a good life."

She watched in a daze as he strode to the back of the car, pulling out her key that was still in his pocket. He removed his backpack from the trunk and set the key on top of the car before starting down the street. He began tapping on his phone, probably texting a friend or ordering an Uber.

"Wait!" But her voice was too weak to carry more than a couple feet.

She wasn't sure how long she stood there before Kendall came to stand next to her. "Wow," she muttered. "That was like a movie kiss if I ever saw one—only way better."

"He's leaving," Saffron said. "I won't see him again." Why did that make her want to cry?

"Probably a good idea since you're in love with Tyson."

Tyson's name brought her world into focus again. "Right." She forced a shaky laugh. "I hope Vaughn will be okay."

Kendall chuckled. "Oh, he'll be okay. He's the kind of man every woman wants, and he'll find someone else. I mean, once he gets over you, of course."

That made Saffron feel terrible. She'd never given him any promises about the future, and he was no different than a hundred other guys she'd dated.

Well, maybe just a little different.

Vaughn had disappeared from view, but Saffron still stared after him. She'd been going somewhere before he'd kissed her, but she couldn't remember where.

"Can you give me a lift to my car?" Kendall said. "I'm going to move some of my things back to the house while Mom's in this weird mood. She gave me some cash a few minutes ago and made me a doctor's appointment. Mind you, I won't be staying long with her, but I'm thinking after tonight, you won't be at the inn."

Saffron started for her car, glad to have a purpose. "I've already missed checkout for today, but you may be right." She hesitated before adding, "Tyson said I could stay at his place. He said there didn't have to be strings."

"Yeah, right," Kendall said with a snort. "There are already so many strings I can barely see either of you."

Saffron stopped walking. "What do you mean?"

"I mean your past, your son, the dreams you had. Every memory you had with him. Wanting to prove to yourself and Mom that she was wrong. That you didn't make a mistake falling in love with him. I know with me those are all huge factors." Kendall tore off a bit of nail with her teeth. "Though after yesterday, I think I might be through with Joel. I'm going to let him have his fun, but when he wants to see me again, I'm going to lay down some rules."

"Tyson and I would have made it," Saffron insisted. "And I'm not getting back together with him because of the past. I love him now. He hasn't changed all that much."

"He does seem like a great guy," Kendall agreed. "If you're anything like me, you'll enjoy all the medicine talk."

Saffron didn't reply. She wasn't imagining the connection between her and Tyson. She was sure it existed—at least she was when she was with him. Her confusion had to do with Vaughn, that's all. Now *him* she was attracted to only because they'd dated.

Saffron craned her neck as she slid into the car. Still no sign of Vaughn even from the street. Well, he wasn't her concern any longer.

Some of what she was thinking must have shown in her face because Kendall put her hand on Saffron's arm. "Saying goodbye stinks, but if you really want a life with Tyson, you had to do it. From what I've seen, Vaughn isn't the kind of guy to take a back seat to anyone—or who'll stand around waiting for things to go wrong with you and Tyson. He'll find someone else. Don't worry."

That Kendall was right was apparent in the way Vaughn had broken up with her. It was what she wanted, but why did it hurt so much?

She glanced up at the house as she drove away, and was surprised to see her mother's slender figure framed in the doorway.

Tyson smiled with relief when Jana came into the room where he was talking to his very young patient and her parents. Her eyes met his, and for a moment he felt a loss he couldn't describe. Was it possible to love two women at the same time? Because he realized that his renewed feelings for Saffron hadn't changed the way he felt about Jana.

Her gaze slid past him, dark and bottomless. "Hi, Patty," she said brightly to the child. "I'm Dr. Reynolds. I'm here to make sure you're comfortable while they're fixing your hernia."

"You look like Princess Jasmin," Patty said.

Tyson grinned. Patty wasn't the first child to point that out.

Jana leaned over and whispered. "I'm under cover," she said. "I had to sneak out of the palace. But don't worry. I'm very good at what I do."

"Even for a princess," Tyson agreed.

Patty and her parents laughed, while Jana went on to describe in simple and unfrightening terms what she and her partner would be doing as anesthesiologists. The surgery was a minor one, like dozens of others Tyson had assisted with, but it was still scary for the child, and even more so for the parents, who would have to give their daughter into the care of strangers. As a resident, Jana would be working with a more experienced anesthesiologist, but she was the one who always talked to the children and parents.

"We'll take really good care of her," Jana said to them. She waved to Patty. "Your nice nurses will be taking you back in a couple minutes, and I'll meet you there."

Tyson followed her from the room. "You were perfect with her."

She smiled, her head shaking back and forth. "Princess Jasmine . . . I'm wondering if I should get a costume."

"Ooh, I'd like to . . ." Tyson closed his mouth. He didn't have any right to want to see her in any costume, not when he'd basically broken up with her because of Saffron. What he'd been going to say was more appropriate between lovers anyway, not colleagues, and that was all they were now.

Jana's smile faltered. "How are things going?"

"Good." Great, actually, but how could he say that to her? Not that it mattered. Both "good" or "great" spelled the end of their relationship. "How are you doing?"

"I miss you." Her eyes filled up then, but she blinked the tears away.

He missed her too—their conversations, the nights in San Diego with his parents, talking shop in the hospital cafeteria. But Saffron was his first love and the mother of the son he'd never know. He loved her. He had a lot to make up for.

"I'm sorry," he said to Jana, wishing he could hold her and tell her it would be all right. No way he could promise that. In fact, tonight he planned to make his intentions clear to Saffron. They'd been given a second chance, and this time he wouldn't let her down.

"I'm glad you've been honest with me," Jana said.

But he hadn't been. Not entirely. Because he still loved her.

He swallowed hard. "I'll meet you in the OR."

Walking away was hard.

A text message from Saffron eased his heart. She'd be leaving for Oceanside in about thirty minutes, and he'd see her right after he finished the hernia repair. Maybe after tonight, he could reconcile his feelings for the two women who'd stolen his heart. He couldn't wait to see her.

Before Saffron had finished getting ready for her date, packing her one suitcase and the box of beads in case she didn't return, Kendall arrived. Saffron grabbed a luggage cart from the front desk and helped her sister carry a load of her things, packing them in Kendall's car carefully to take up less room.

"No matter how you look at it, there's at least one more load," Saffron said. "But there's no hurry."

"I'll get the rest in the morning." Kendall opened her car door. "Thanks, and have fun tonight. I hope he takes you someplace romantic."

"Well, it won't be parasailing." It was meant as a joke, but it came out more as a complaint.

Kendall made a face. "Good. I was thinking more along the lines of an expensive dinner and candlelight. Text me and tell me how it goes, okay?" She started to get inside her car but stopped short, her expression grave. "Saffron . . . if . . . if Joel doesn't want to stay with me. If he doesn't want to be a dad . . . I'm thinking I'd like to go to your Lily's House—for a while at least. I want to see what it's like. I want to meet Lily and your other foster sisters. And mostly I want what I decide is best for the baby to be my choice."

"Of course." Saffron hugged her and started to back away, but Kendall clung to her.

"If I decided it was better for the baby to have a mom and a dad," she whispered in Saffron's ear, "would you hate me? Because I know you would have done anything to keep your son."

"Oh, no!" Saffron tightened her hold. "Not at all. I support you no matter what. I know how hard it is alone. I-I wish I would have talked to a counselor at school. I would rather have given him up than watch him . . ." Saffron couldn't say it. The heaviness was back, the longing for her son.

"Thank you." Kendall broke away, smiling. "Remember to text me. I expect details."

Halla had said nearly the same thing in a text. "I will."

On the drive to Oceanside, Saffron remembered that she hadn't answered Tyson about his mother's Sunday dinner invitation. They'd exchanged a few texts about her mother and Kendall and their date, but she didn't want to go on Sunday with him to his parents' house. Not this soon. They were so nice—overly nice—and it made her feel worse about not wanting to spend time with them. Maybe she could put off another visit for a few more weeks. He could go alone this weekend. She wouldn't mind.

Saffron arrived at the hospital twenty minutes before her planned meeting with Tyson at four. They'd planned for her to follow him over to the gated community where his condo was located. After a tour of his place, they'd have dinner and go from there. She was so nervous her stomach was doing flips. Maybe she needed some herbal tea to soothe her stomach. She'd seen some in the cafeteria the last time she was here.

She walked through the parking lot and was already hot and sweaty when she entered the cool hospital. Following her memory and a few signs, she attempted to find the cafeteria but had no luck. Probably because she kept going over her last moments with Vaughn and wondering how much she should tell Tyson about him.

Finally, she came across a desk and asked the woman there. As she thanked the woman, Jana appeared behind her. She smiled when she saw Saffron. "Hey, how are you?"

Saffron's stomach sank. *Of course* she'd run into Jana. Would she constantly run into her as long as Tyson worked at this hospital?

"I'm good. Thanks. But I'm looking for the cafeteria again." Saffron could see now that she'd ended up near the same place where they'd talked to Jana on Tuesday. It was almost as if Saffron had *wanted* to cross paths with her. But for what purpose—to make sure she was okay or to keep an eye on the competition?

"I seem to have a bad sense of direction when I'm inside this place," Saffron admitted.

Jana laughed. "You're not the only one. Since we're so close to it, we're always getting questions about the location. Come on. I'll show you."

"Oh, I think I can find it now."

"I'm going that way anyway." To the woman behind the desk, Jana added, "See you tomorrow."

Saffron walked with Jana to the doorway of the cafeteria, where Jana said, "I want to thank you for the other day. I was having a bit of a hard time, and while I feel funny you gave me your necklace, it cheered me up. I wore it when I went out last night."

Good, so the woman wasn't sitting around moping. "Hot date?" Saffron asked with maybe a little too much enthusiasm.

Jana shook her head. "Romance movie with the girls. We always have a sappy movie night when someone breaks up."

"Sounds like me and my sisters, only with us it usually involves a lot of something sugary and fattening." Saffron smiled, remembering the pastries Halla and Elsie had brought her. "So did it work?"

"It helps." But instead of smiling, Jana's lower lip wobbled. She bit down on it, as if searching for control.

"I'm sorry." Saffron touched her arm, feeling more terrible by the second.

"It's—I'm going to be okay. I don't know that we've broken up permanently. I mean, we still have a connection. Every time I run into him, I feel it—we both feel it. I can tell. But someone from his past came back. They have a history together, and a baby that died. I feel terrible for him, but how can I compete? That sort of relationship pulls you back, you know?" Jana shook her head, pausing as someone came out of the cafeteria.

Jana waited until they were alone to continue. "This

week was the first time in six months I didn't go with his family to his dad's weekly therapy. I love going and helping out, chatting with his mom, spending the night at his aunt's. And Helene—that's his mom—canceled our regular Thursday lunch today. I know she has to support her son's choices, but she's been like a mom to me since mine died, and I already miss her."

Saffron didn't know what to say. Here she was trying to avoid eating Sunday dinner with Tyson's family, and Jana was crying because she missed his mother.

"It's silly," Jana said, pulling herself together with a deep breath. "You hear so many stories of people who hate their mother-in-laws, but seriously, even if I didn't love him so much, I'd think about marrying him because of her."

"She sounds like a great person." The words scraped along Saffron's throat on the way out. She'd have to make a better effort to get past her aversion to the Dekkers. Mrs. Dekker was trying, and she deserved a daughter-in-law who loved her, no matter what happened in the past.

"Anyway," Jana said, "I know this is more than you ever wanted to hear about a stranger. I thought I got it all out last night, but my friends aren't willing to hear me say I still love him, and that I know he's doing the best he can with the situation. It feels good to tell someone, even if it makes me look kind of pathetic. He bought a ring, you know, but I guess now I might never see it."

A ring? Tyson hadn't mentioned that. Pressure built in Saffron's chest. "I'm so sorry," she murmured.

"Thanks." Jana gave Saffron a smile that contradicted the sadness in her eyes. "Hey, if you live around here, maybe we can go shopping sometime, or you can come to our next girls' night out and meet everyone. I'd love to see the jewelry you make and so would they."

"I'm actually from Arizona," Saffron said. "I'm here visiting family."

"That makes it tough. Well, thank you again for the necklace—and for the listening ear." She paused, taking a card from the pocket of her white jacket. "If you ever need anesthesia, let me know. I'll give you a discount."

Somehow Saffron laughed. "I'll keep that in mind."

Saffron turned into the cafeteria, not wanting to watch Jana leave. She looked so sad. As if she were in mourning like Saffron still felt she was, even after eight years. How long would it take for Jana to get over Tyson? Saffron hadn't been able to get over him or losing her son. Although maybe at last she had. Finally, she was taking control of her destiny, and yesterday in Vegas with Kendall and Vaughn, she hadn't felt sad at all. She hoped Jana recovered more quickly.

Saffron drank her tea slowly, but it did nothing for the heaviness she felt. When she finished, she realized she was late now, and she hurried through the hospital corridors to the lobby where she was supposed to meet Tyson.

There he was, looking handsome and sexy in dark dress pants and a gray button-down shirt that showed part of his neck and chest. Unlike Vaughn, his chest was smooth and hairless, so he probably waxed. A little smile crept to her face. She hadn't known that about him. The grip on her heart relaxed a little.

"Hi, beautiful," he said, his gaze running down her white pants and her sleeveless purple blouse. "You really did get a little sun." He leaned over and kissed her. It felt right, but Saffron couldn't help looking around to see if Jana was watching.

"I've been putting aloe gel on it." Speaking of which, she still had Vaughn's bottle of aloe in the car.

He grinned at her. "That's what you said over text."

"Oh, right. I've been texting with Halla too, and a few others. I've forgotten who I've told what."

He put his arm around her gently. "That doesn't hurt, does it?"

"Not at all." She leaned further into him as they started walking to the door. Okay, this was nice.

"I'll go with you to your car," he said. "Then you can drive me to mine and follow me to the condo."

"Perfect," she said.

After leaving the physician's parking lot, Saffron followed Tyson through a maze of streets to a gated condo complex where she used the code he'd given her to get inside.

"Tour now or later?" he asked as they met in his driveway.

"Whichever you prefer." She wanted to see his place but was nervous at the same time. Going inside meant being alone. It meant making decisions about where they were heading.

Tyson flashed her a grin. "I missed lunch, so if you can eat, I'd rather have an early dinner."

Saffron thought of the half-finished sandwich she'd left at her mother's. "I'm hungry too. Let's go eat first."

Taking her hand, he led her to the front passenger seat of his car. "Does Italian sound good?"

"Sounds great." She laughed. "We had Italian for our first prom. Remember?"

He grinned and opened the door. "Prom? Right, but

I suggested it more because of kindergarten when we had spaghetti for Around the World Day, or whatever it was called."

"That's right. What a mess!" How sweet that he remembered. "You always let me butt in line."

He kissed her briefly without seeming to hurry. "I was smitten even then."

Saffron smiled all the way to Dominic's at the Harbor. The restaurant wasn't busy this early on Thursday night, and they were seated immediately. She ordered the lasagna, while he opted for spaghetti and meatballs in memory of their kindergarten year. "My mom makes spaghetti all the time," he said to her. "Normally, she's a great cook, but spaghetti is not one of her better dishes. Here it's fabulous. You want to share the stuffed mushrooms for an appetizer?"

"Sounds yummy. But speaking of your mom," she said, "can we do dinner another Sunday instead? I'm not sure what I'm doing yet."

"Sure. I'll let her know."

She could tell he was disappointed that she didn't want to see his parents this weekend, but the weight on her chest wouldn't go away—a weight that felt a lot like grief. What was wrong with her?

Tyson put a hand on Saffron's. "Have you decided if you'll stay with me? I can sleep at my parents' place for a while, if that's a problem."

Saffron was saved from answering when the waiter came by with a wine list, but Tyson ordered without looking at it. How often did he come here? And how many of those times had he been with Jana? Impatient with herself, Saffron pushed the thoughts away.

"So how did your day go?" she asked.

"Great. Well, besides missing lunch. I assisted with a hernia surgery right before you came. I was worried they wouldn't get her started in time, and I'd keep you waiting."

"Was it difficult?"

"No, and I wasn't the only doctor, so we had plenty of help. They need to make sure I won't kill anyone until I finish residency." He flashed a smile that showed he was joking.

"It would make me nervous having someone checking up on me every second."

"It used to. Now I just tune it out and do my best. I love pediatric surgery. It'll take me longer to specialize, but it'll be worth it in the long run."

He continued talking, telling her about his first surgery, often lapsing into a few medical terms that had her head spinning. She'd need to get a dictionary and start learning about his life. Which she didn't mind doing. She wanted to understand what he did, what he loved. When she'd first started dating Vaughn, she made him show her some of his animations while he explained the creativity behind them. She'd even sat in on a few of his lectures. But animation was a lot closer to jewelry design than surgery.

"At least I didn't make a fool of myself and lose my lunch," Tyson said.

Had she missed the whole story? Maybe it was because her stomach was complaining. She did feel a little light-headed and disconnected, the way she did when she hadn't eaten for a while.

When the mushrooms came, she ate more than Tyson did, and her lasagna was the best she'd ever tasted. But the weirdness in her stomach didn't leave. She was content, though, to listen to Tyson talk. He told her about past patients, his plan of moving to a larger hospital, and a trip he was planning to Mexico for Christmas, which he hoped she'd join him on.

"That sounds fun," she said. "It's weird, but I've never spent Christmas anywhere but at Lily's House since I left home." She didn't want to be away this year, either, but being in a relationship meant give and take.

"I can't wait to meet this Lily."

"You'll love her."

As the conversation moved on, Tyson talked about collecting coins, the powerful telescope he'd bought, and how he'd taken up golfing.

"You know that's stereotypical, right?" she said with a laugh.

"Yeah, but I can't get any of my colleagues to come look at the stars with me. I play only to bond with the other doctors. But I happen to be rather good." He paused for a drink. "A lot better than I was at football."

Saffron began to realize she didn't know Tyson at all. She knew the boy he'd been, but while that boy had a link to the present, he wasn't the same person. He was a man now, with the dreams and experiences of a man. He had friends and hobbies and favorite foods she knew nothing about.

They had a long way to go before they really knew each other, and they'd have to make all the adjustments new couples did as they figured things out. Make compromises. Maybe have a few fights. These past few days had given her the impression they were picking up where they left off, but that wasn't exactly right. They'd both changed so much.

All too soon the meal was over and they drove back to his condo. The heaviness in Saffron's chest increased. She loved Tyson—no doubt about that—so why did she feel such dread?

26

Tyson pulled her up the walk, bursting with excitement. "I had the whole exterior restuccoed first," he said. "I didn't do that part myself." He typed in a code, and the door opened with a whirring noise.

"I like that," she said.

He grinned. "I thought you might."

So he remembered that too. One time she'd lost her house key and had been too afraid to tell her mother about it. Fortunately, they'd retraced their steps to the mall where they'd been hanging out and found her keys in the lost and found. She'd told Tyson that one day she'd have a house with a keypad.

The condo opened to a small entry that almost immediately joined a vaulted living room. A narrow staircase on the left side of the living room led upstairs. "Three bedrooms and two bathrooms are up there," Tyson said. "But let's start down here first."

Two doors off the living room revealed a small office and a bathroom, and a modest kitchen and dining area made up the rest of the main floor. "I sanded and stained the cabinets, installed the cherry baseboards, and painted all the walls," he said. "I also put new carpet in the living room. But this awesome granite countertop was already here."

"It's very nice. Cozy, yet large enough for . . ."

"For a family." He took her hand, spreading warmth through her. "See the patio? I put that in stone by stone. I even made the garden boxes. The trellises are for grapes."

"You garden?" One more thing she didn't know about him.

He blinked and stuttered. "I-uh-I-Jana does."

"Oh. They're nice."

So he'd put in the raised garden boxes and trellises for Jana. For Jana, who could still feel a connection with Tyson. What else had she contributed? Had she helped pick out his furniture like Saffron had at Vaughn's place? Helped him decide on paint color or the window shades? Maybe it was better not to know.

Next, Tyson took her upstairs and showed her two small bedrooms and a master suite. The king size bed was unmade. "Sorry about that," he said. "I was in a hurry this morning."

Did he ever make the bed? Saffron didn't know. Maybe Jana made the bed when she stayed over. Maybe she'd planned on living here. The idea of Jana and Tyson here together made Saffron's heart hurt, but she wouldn't let that ruin what she'd waited so long for. She *loved* Tyson.

"What's wrong?" Tyson stepped closer, putting his arms around her.

"Just kiss me," she said. That would do it. His touch would get Jana out of her head and help her forget this afternoon with Vaughn.

He kissed her, softly at first, but then with more assurance. His hand dropped to her waist, pulling her tightly against him. Kissing him was wonderful, familiar and new all at once. Like putting on a beautiful sweater she'd forgotten she owned.

Yet something was clearly missing—something that had been in her kiss this afternoon with Vaughn.

She wasn't giving up that easily. She kissed Tyson with more passion, putting her arms around his neck. *Make me fly,* she thought. *I need to fly.*

But her feet stayed firmly on the ground.

Her body reacted to his touch, pulling her deeper into the kiss, but mentally, she had stepped away. Because with a sudden bright, blinding realization, she knew that as good as it was kissing Tyson, she wanted to be kissing Vaughn.

Vaughn Abrams, her boyfriend turned friend. Animator, school teacher, and river guide. He made her soar with his kiss. He made her laugh and feel safe. He knew her heart.

She broke away. "Wait, I don't think . . ."

"It's okay," Tyson murmured, loosening his hold. "We've got time. Why don't we go downstairs, cuddle up, and watch a movie? Take it slow. We've waited eight and a half years. What's another few weeks or months?"

"It's not that . . . it's—" She searched his dark eyes for a way to tell him. "Don't you think . . .? It shouldn't be this hard."

"What are you saying?" He swallowed, watching her warily.

"That maybe we're trying too hard." She stood there, wrapped in his arms, not knowing exactly how to explain. "I mean, we both went on with our lives these past eight and a half years. Maybe not completely, but we did go on. We have friends, family, our careers, people we really care about."

"I still missed you." His voice was hoarse and almost pleading.

The pleading blasted through the last bits of the barrier she'd created around her heart. She welcomed the pain because with it came the realization of what had been hiding underneath—the emotions the numbness had masked too well.

"I missed you so much," she said. "Especially at first. But not every moment. I still made my goals. I helped a lot of young girls, taught myself how to design jewelry, and took classes. You became a doctor."

"Yeah. We did what we had to do to survive." The line of puzzlement between his eyes told her he didn't understand where she was leading.

"You can't tell me there haven't been times since I came back that you didn't wish you'd already asked Jana to marry you. Or wished I could be as good with your parents as she is. Or that I understood all that doctor stuff you were spouting at dinner."

"Is that what this is about?" His mouth curved into a gentle smile.

"No, that's not it." He'd know that if he knew her at all. But he didn't know her—he only knew the girl she had been.

"Of course we'll have to learn about each other," he continued. "That's only natural. But you know it'll work between us." He leaned over and kissed the tip of her nose. "I'm crazy attracted to you, and I love you."

Saffron nodded. "Me too, but there are more lives involved than just our own. How can we forget that? There are your parents, there's Jana . . ."

"And Vaughn." He spoke the name with a hint of anger.

She inclined her head in acknowledgement. She'd be a liar if she didn't because Vaughn had never been far from her mind since leaving Phoenix. "I love being with you, Tyson, but besides feeling like I'm ruining everyone's lives, I'm also experiencing this huge sense of loss." She brought her hand up between them, pressing it into her heart. "I can forgive, but I don't really want to forget, and being with you, with your parents, is like reliving the past every day."

"That'll change. Fade with time. We only have to make it through this first hard part." But he didn't say it with the same conviction he'd used when he said he missed her. It seemed they both had the same doubts. Maybe it would never be okay. Maybe they'd missed their chance.

Tears started down her cheeks. "Is it hard with Jana?"

He shook his head once, almost sharply as if he regretted doing so. Maybe if he'd added that he didn't care how hard it was with Saffron, his answer wouldn't matter. Maybe if he kissed her again they would still be able to make this thing work.

He didn't.

"I know if I'd stayed all those years ago," she said, "or if you'd gotten my call, that we would still be together. We would have been one of the few who made it, but now . . . I think we're trying too hard."

The next words would be the hardest, but Kendall's talk of trying to prove something to her mother and Jana's obvious belief that Tyson couldn't let Saffron go because of their son's death made them necessary. "Today I feel . . . I wonder if maybe we want to be together more to make up for the past than because we love each other now."

He didn't say anything for a long moment. He simply stared, his eyes brimming with unshed tears. Then he said, "Why do I feel this way about you? Why did I feel when you came back that my life suddenly made sense again?"

She understood exactly what he meant. "I think"—her voice dropped to a whisper—"we needed to say goodbye."

Tyson leaned into her, tightened his arms around her body, and buried his face in her neck. For long moments, they stood there holding each other as if they'd never let go. "I still love you," he whispered.

"I love you too. I suspect a part of me always will. But you're *in love* with Jana." *And I'm in love with Vaughn.*

He didn't lift his head, and she felt the wetness of his tears against her skin. "We could still make it," he whispered.

"I know. But we don't need to anymore." She pulled back, seeking his eyes. "I know you're okay. You know I'm okay. We also know deep down that we're both in love with someone else."

Tyson didn't deny it. "Is he good to you?" his voice grated like gravel under their feet.

Saffron nodded, the tears still falling, though she felt lighter than she had in days. "As good as you are to me."

"I'm glad. Or else I'm not sure I could let you go. There's so much I need to make up for."

"No, you don't. It's enough for me to know the truth of what happened when I left."

"I'm trying to believe that."

"Believe it." She stepped away at the same time his grasp

loosened. "Thanks," she murmured. "For everything. I'm going back to Temecula now, okay?"

He said nothing, his face fighting for composure. Finally, he grabbed her hand and took her downstairs, leading her outside to her car. He gave her a last kiss on her cheek and another hug. Then he let her go.

Safely in the car, Saffron rolled down her window. "Call Jana," she said. "Call her right now. Tell her we decided we're better off as friends."

He put a hand on the window frame. "I am your friend. If you ever need me for anything, I'll be there."

"I'll hold you to it. Call her. Promise?"

He grimaced. "I don't know. I've hurt her pretty badly."

"But you chose her in the end. That means something. Please promise me? You don't want to spend another eight and a half years regretting losing her." She needed to know he'd be looked after. That someone would love him past this decision, one that forever separated him from atoning for their lost son.

"Okay. I promise."

He stayed there watching as she drove away.

She cleared the gates before the tears came again. She cried hard then, but not at losing Tyson or because she missed her son. Seeing Tyson again had healed the hurts of the past. No, she cried with relief at losing the heavy burden that had encased her heart for far too long. The numbing shield that had nearly caused her to throw away the light and love and laughter she shared with Vaughn. It was a cleansing cry, the kind that took away the bad so the good could spread and fill up more room in her heart.

She understood as she hadn't before that the heaviness

she'd felt all day—no, that she'd felt since leaving Phoenix—was because of her relationship with Vaughn. Missing him and wanting him and mourning his loss.

Lily's words came back to her: *Sometimes you've got to follow your heart.*

Saffron finally understood what her heart wanted, but how could she follow her heart now? She had no idea where Vaughn was, or if he'd want to see her. Calling him wasn't enough—not after he'd said his goodbyes and let her go. She had to see him in person so she could make him understand it wasn't Tyson she loved.

Her mind raced as she ran through possibilities. With a sigh of relief, it came to her. She didn't know where he was now, but she did know where he'd be tomorrow at ten—at his Datatoon interview.

Please don't let it be too late.

A loud *clunk* dragged Saffron from a deep sleep, the best she'd had in eight years. Groggily, she opened her eyes to see Kendall standing next to the bed in her room at the Rodeway Inn.

"Sorry," Kendall said in a whisper that could probably be heard in the lobby. "I was trying to get the rest of my things before you checked out. But I didn't think you'd be here. Didn't you take all your stuff yesterday? Why aren't you at Tyson's?"

Memories of last night came rushing back. Saffron sat up abruptly, panic pushing away the sleepiness. "Oh, no. What time is it?" She'd set her alarm. Why hadn't it gone off?

"Almost nine thirty. Don't worry. There's plenty of time before checkout."

"It's not that!" Saffron jumped from the bed, ripping off her nightshirt and digging for clothes that were in her open suitcase.

"Then what?"

"I have to get to Winchester before Vaughn. I searched Datatoon last night on the Internet and there are two parking lots. What if I miss him when he gets there?"

"Slow down. You can just call him."

"No! I have to explain in person." Saffron finished with her bra and yanked a T-shirt over her head. It wasn't how she planned on looking when she went to see Vaughn, but it would have to do.

Kendall placed her hands on both of Saffron's upper arms, shaking her the tiniest bit. "Saffron! What are you talking about?"

"I love him." Saffron said. "I realized last night that you were right. I love Tyson, partly for the boy he was but mostly because of the past. Because I wanted to validate everything I went through—running away, losing my son. But Tyson's a different person now. I'm a different person. And while I know we could make it work, my heart's not really in it. I want Vaughn! I have to tell him before he goes back to Arizona."

"I knew it!" Kendall squealed, bouncing a little in her excitement. "I knew he was the one. It was that kiss yesterday, wasn't it?"

"Not just the kiss." But Saffron couldn't imagine living without kisses like those every day. She fished two sandals from her suitcase and tossed them over near the door. "Can you put anything you see of mine inside this suitcase and shut it for me? I need to brush my teeth. I have only two chances to find him—when he leaves and when he arrives, because I don't know what car he's driving. And it takes thirty minutes to get there. I have to hurry!" Without waiting for an answer, she ran into the bathroom, where she found her errant phone. No wonder she hadn't heard the alarm.

Her mouth was full of toothpaste when Kendall appeared in the doorway. "All done. But leave your suitcase, okay? I'll keep it in my car. You've still got the toiletries to pack. Are you going to put on makeup?"

Still vigorously scrubbing her teeth, Saffron eyed her makeup bag and shook her head. "No time."

"Then leave it all to me." Kendall pulled a granola bar from her purse. "Eat this on the way, okay? I don't want you passing out from lack of food. They don't taste great—I think they're too healthy for that—but they always make me feel less nauseated." She laughed, patting the tiny baby bump on her lower abdomen.

Saffron spat out the toothpaste, rinsed her mouth, and hugged her sister. "Thank you."

"Don't worry about anything. I'll make sure I get it all packed."

"It should mostly be in the suitcase already," Saffron said, stuffing her phone into her purse. "And I told them I was checking out today, but be sure to turn in your key card."

"I will." They hugged again.

"Okay, I'm off." Saffron hurried past her and opened the door. At the last minute, she remembered to shove her feet into the sandals she'd thrown from her suitcase.

"Good luck!" Kendall called.

Saffron sprinted to the elevator, mentally screaming at the couple who held the door for their two children coming at a snail's pace toward them from down the hall. Of all the days for children to be slow. The parents nodded at her, and she smiled, all the while thinking, *Hurry, hurry, hurry.*

Wait, the stairs. She didn't have her suitcase with her, so the stairs were a better option. She left the elevator at a run. Despite her annoyance, she was practically cruising on air. She was going to see Vaughn! What would he say? What if she'd hurt him too badly for him to forgive her blindness?

No, she wouldn't dwell on that. She'd make it up to him somehow.

She munched Kendall's granola bar on the freeway. Her sister had been right that it wasn't very good, but she swallowed the dry bits down with a bottle of water she had left over from their trip to Vegas. The cars around her seemed to amble slowly, getting repeatedly in her way. So much for the idea of Californians being speed demons.

Would she make it in time?

Finally, she spied the exit for Winchester. She steered off the freeway and followed the directions her phone called out in a mechanical voice. Twice she made the wrong turn, which she blamed on Google. They were going to hear feedback from her, that was for sure.

When the Datatoon building appeared, she almost missed the turn. She drove up to the main entrance and parked in a visitor stall at two minutes before ten. There were a dozen other cars, but she couldn't begin to guess if one might be a rental belonging to Vaughn.

She waited two minutes before driving around to the back of the two-story building, which took longer than expected because it was deceptively larger than it appeared from the front. She parked and watched a few employees enter the building, using a key card to get in. Vaughn wouldn't have one of those, so back around to the front it was. He must have arrived before she had, which seemed likely since he'd want to make a good impression. Should she go inside and ask? Maybe leave a message for him? She wouldn't want to endanger his job prospects by interrupting.

She was halfway to the door when she glanced down and saw that her sandals, one pink and one yellow, weren't matching. Even worse, she was still in her pink polka-dotted pajama shorts. At least her maroon D-backs tee was clean. But had she brushed her hair? She hurried back to the car to rake her fingers through her hair and wipe off any smudged mascara.

Her phone rang, jolting her from her efforts. Halla. She grabbed it. "Oh, Halla! I'm a mess. You should see me."

"It's going to be okay. Did you find him yet?"

"I got here too late. Wait. How did you know?"

"Kendall and I bonded that day we went to the beach. She's as good as one of us now. And since you didn't bother to call me, I had to get the scoop from her."

"I've been a little occupied." She'd meant to call Halla last night, but after researching Datatoon, she'd been too tired to rehash what had happened between her and Tyson.

"That's okay. What do you mean, you're a mess?"

"I was in such a hurry to get out here that I'm all mismatching, and I didn't comb my hair."

Halla laughed. "Yes, but you did brush your teeth."

"Can't believe she told you that."

"She did. And apparently Vaughn has magical kissing abilities you didn't tell me about—and I know you've kissed him plenty before."

"It was him all along," Saffron said. "And I have to make it up to him. But I don't know if he rented a car, took a bus—do they even have buses in Winchester?—or if a friend dropped him off. Maybe he rescheduled. He could be back in Arizona for all I know."

"Well, you can either wait out there for a few hours and see if he shows up, or go inside and ask for him." Halla paused before adding, "Or you could ask your incredibly talented blogger friend who just happened to receive a text from him a few minutes ago."

"What? Really? You did?"

"Yeah. After Kendall told me where you'd gone, I texted him and asked when he was coming to get his car. He said he was heading into a job interview, so he hadn't finalized his plans, but he'd let me know for sure after he talked to the friend he was staying with."

Saffron's gaze rose to the building, a rush of anticipation setting her heart pounding. Vaughn was in there some-where. "I don't want to interrupt his interview," she said. "But what if the friend works here? What if they leave out the back door?"

"You'll have to go in. Don't worry about what you look like. I've seen you in the mornings, and you're beautiful. Besides, he loves you no matter what. Now go get him! And this time call me after it's over. Don't make me get things second-hand."

"Okay. Thanks."

Halla's peptalk giving her courage, Saffron threw her phone into the passenger seat and went back to setting order to her hair. She'd slept on it wrong, and there was a weird cowlick on one side, but a little water tamed it down a bit. Well, if you closed your eyes halfway and looked at it sideways. At least the mascara came off with a little bit of the petroleum jelly she kept in her purse for impromptu hiking trips with Vaughn. She found a lip gloss as well and pinched some color back into her cheeks—not that she'd need color if she was going inside dressed like this. Her face would likely be red with embarrassment.

And the shoes. Did she go barefooted or with the mismatching sandals? She finally opted for bare feet. Saying she ran off without shoes was better than admitting she was so distracted that she couldn't match her own shoes.

Or maybe there were some in her trunk. She got out to look and found a pair of old blue tennis shoes she'd tossed inside over a month ago because the sole of one had torn almost completely off. But they matched! She put them on and flapped up to the building, the loose sole catching with every step.

"May I help you?" A receptionist asked, looking up from her computer screen. She was one of those women who were handsome and on the muscular side rather than slender and beautiful. Her long dark hair was pulled back into a ponytail, and she wore no makeup on her square face. Her T-shirt had Datatoon stamped across the front. If they were that casual here, maybe Saffron wouldn't end up too embarrassed.

Saffron tried not to flap too loudly as she moved up to the desk. "I'm looking for a friend of mine, and he's here for an interview, so I don't want to interrupt, but I wanted to wait here for him. Maybe you could let him know after the interview?"

"Oh, you must mean Vaughn." The woman's smile

widened. "He's here. But it's hardly an interview. We all know Vaughn and would take him back in a heartbeat. He's basically here to see our new computer upgrades. We're hoping to convince him to abandon academia."

"I don't think that'll be too hard. It's his cousin's river rafting business that keeps taking him back to Arizona, not teaching."

"I know, right? I never figured him as a teacher."

"He's actually really great, but his first love will always be animation."

The receptionist picked up a phone. "What did you say your name was? I'll let him know he has a visitor."

"Oh, no!" Saffron hurried to say. "I can wait. As long as he comes out this way."

"If they're playing the new game, that could be forever."

"Um . . . I kind of want to surprise him." Because he might not want to see her otherwise. "Please could I just wait?"

The woman's face turned thoughtful. "I think I'm getting it now. From what he's said, I gather it's not teaching or the rivers keeping him in Arizona, but a woman. Are you her?"

Saffron knew her face was turning red. "Uh, yeah. I don't know. I mean, I might have been for a few months, but we had a . . . thing yesterday, and I made a stupid choice."

"Was there lots of yelling?"

The eager question invited confidence. "Not really. But there was this kiss . . ." Saffron paused and leaned on the counter. "A really amazing kiss and . . . please, I need to talk to him. I can sit here all day, as long as he comes out this way."

"Are you kidding? You can't wait to see him when you've shared an amazing kiss." The woman's eyes sparkled. "This is the most exciting thing that's happened here since Sandra in accounting was proposed to through an animation hidden in one of our games. As if she would have ever found the animated ring they put inside an ancient jewelry box. Dumb programmers. She's never played a game in her life. If I hadn't given her the heads up, those too wouldn't be married now." She pulled the phone to her ear, her fingers dancing over the buttons. "Let me ask what they're doing. Because like I said, if they're testing the new game, it's better that we interrupt."

"No, really I—"

She held up a finger, signaling Saffron to wait. "Hey, you guys busy? You have Vaughn there, right? Yeah, I thought as much. Look could you send . . . oh, never mind, I'll bring her down. You don't need to know who. Just be ready for a visitor."

She set the phone down and came out from behind the desk. Her eyes traveled down Saffron's clothes. "Cute shorts. I keep telling them we should be allowed to wear shorts on casual Fridays, but no, they say jeans and T-shirts are casual enough for office staff. Not really fair when the designers and programmers can wear jeans anytime." She rolled her eyes. "Come on."

Saffron tried to walk naturally, but the flapping of the shoe was obvious. "Sorry," she said. "Looks like my shoe has a problem."

The receptionist gave a nod. "Tough day, huh? I'm Belladonna, by the way."

"Nice to meet you," Saffron said mechanically. At least

the unusual name wouldn't be hard to remember. "I'm Saffron."

The corridor seemed to stretch out forever, and by the time they paused at a door, Saffron's insides were in an epic battle. Anticipation was beating out nervousness, but not by much. Belladonna opened the door with a flourish and propelled Saffron inside a dimly-lit room where four men and a woman sat with eyes glued to two different monitors. Saffron didn't recognize the men sitting in front of the nearest monitor, but one of the men staring at the second was Vaughn. No one looked in her direction or appeared to notice her entrance.

"Better act quick," the first man said, his laugh more a cackle than anything else. "Or I'm going to smash you."

"Oh, yeah? Well watch this bit of—" Whatever Vaughn was going to say was lost as he glanced up and saw Saffron. Immediately, he stood, his game forgotten. "Saffron? What are you doing here?"

"I'm-I'm-I'm . . ." Saffron's voice wobbled embarrassingly. Here she was about ready to cry in a roomful of strangers.

Vaughn sprinted across the room, his arms going around her. "What happened?" His voice was tense and a little angry. "Did he hurt you?" His eyes held hers as he touched her face, as if searching for damage.

"No." She shook her head. "It's not that. It's . . ."

All eyes in the room were fixed on them. Someone mumbled something about his avatar burning in a pit of fire, but Vaughn didn't seem to care.

"Saffron?" He gently tucked a messy lock of hair behind her ear, his eyes straying down her body, still searching for signs of distress.

"I love you," she said in a near whisper, bringing his attention back to her face.

His anger vanished. "You . . . what?"

With more strength, she added, "I love you with all that I am, Vaughn Abrams. I love you with everything inside me. No reservations." Would he recognize the words he'd said to her yesterday? "This thing between us? There's nothing stronger."

Passion flared in his eyes. He kissed her then—to the whooping of the Datatoon employees. He kissed her eyes, her cheeks, her ears, and her mouth in succession before starting over again, creating a firestorm that threatened to consume her.

"Uh, let's give these two a little privacy, huh?" Belladonna's voice came from far away.

Saffron was vaguely aware of people filtering past them, a few making catcalls while others grumbled good-naturedly. Vaughn didn't seem to notice. He ran his hands through her hair and down her back, all the while kissing her until she didn't know which way was up. She was flying, tumbling through endless space where all that mattered was the touch of his lips against her skin.

"I'm sorry," she muttered.

He put a finger over her mouth. "It doesn't matter. Today, we start over." She couldn't help nipping his finger with her teeth. He groaned and bent his head to hers, urgently seeking her mouth.

"One more thing," she said between his kisses. "Do you think you could take me parasailing today?"

Vaughn threw back his head and laughed. "I think you'll need better shoes than the ones you broke on the river last month. And I'm positive pajamas shorts aren't the best thing to wear under your wetsuit."

She bit her lip. "You noticed, huh?"

"I noticed. Especially the shorts. So did every man in here, and every last one of them wanted to be in my place." Vaughn pulled her to him, nearly pushing the breath from her lungs as he sought her lips again. "Parasailing, sure. Whatever you want."

"I want you," she said. "Only you."

He kissed her again. "It's about time."

❤❤ EPILOGUE ❤❤

Saffron stood on the porch at Lily's House as Vaughn and Lily's husband, Mario, brought in Kendall's belongings. At five months along, Kendall was showing enough to be obviously pregnant but not big enough to be uncomfortable. When Joel had continued his irresponsible ways, she had decided to take Lily up on her offer of coming to Lily's House.

She would be helping out by driving the girls and making dinner, though Saffron knew for a fact that Kendall could barely make ramen noodles. It didn't matter—Lily would teach her.

"I'm so thrilled you're going to be close," Saffron said, hugging her. Saffron had talked to her on the phone almost every day since her visit to Temecula, but they had only been together once in the past six weeks.

"I know. Me too!" Kendall looked past Saffron to where their mother stood awkwardly next to Lily. "Thanks for coming with me, Mom."

"Well, I couldn't very well let you pull that trailer all the way here alone, now could I?" Their mother's voice held a hint of sharpness, but her face was relaxed. With her hair in an elegant twist and her blue pantsuit unwrinkled, she looked too perfect for having driven in a car for five hours. To Saffron, she added. "I plan to stay a few days to make sure Kendall's settled. I'd like to have dinner with you, if you can spare the time."

Before Saffron could answer, Lily said to Kendall, "How about we leave these two to talk while I show you up to your room? Don't worry. I made sure it wasn't one of the rooms with the bunkbeds. I don't want you climbing around."

Kendall laughed. "Sure, I'd love to see it." She started to leave but stopped short and pulled an envelope from her purse. She handed it to Saffron. "Oh, I almost forgot. Tyson stopped by last week and asked me to give you this."

Saffron ripped open the envelope, already knowing what to expect. Sure enough, it was a wedding announcement for Tyson and Jana. He'd included a picture as well, and their happiness radiated from the page.

"So he finally proposed. Good." She knew he'd made up with Jana from a few texts they'd exchanged, but seeing this made it more real. She didn't have to worry about him anymore.

"I know, right?" Kendall said. She winked at Saffron and left with Lily, looking back once to mouth, "Be nice to Mom."

Saffron turned to her mother. After long seconds of awkward silence, Saffron said, "I see you're wearing the earrings I made. So how long did you know where I was?"

Her mother's mouth twisted into something between a smile and a grimace. "Two months before you showed up in Temecula. Kendall left her Facebook up one day on our computer, and I saw you two were in contact, so I hired a private investigator to research where you were. He found the public records of your name change, but it listed this address"—she lifted a hand to indicate Lily's House—"and you weren't living here anymore. He gave me the URL to your online store."

Saffron's stomach ached, but she wasn't sure exactly why.

"I just wanted to know you were okay." Her mother paused, sighing heavily. "I hope that's all right. I-I didn't feel I could ask. I ordered the earrings because I wanted to have a part of you."

Could her mother's need be like the little jewelry box with the pictures Saffron kept of her son? She didn't think it was exactly the same, but having that piece of her child helped her understand her mother's motivation. Maybe there was a chance for them. In time. They'd never be best friends—and that was okay. Saffron had her sisters, Lily, and Vaughn's mother, whose love and acceptance had already made her feel a part of his family.

"I'm borrowing Kendall's car while I'm in town," her mother said. "I'll be here for three days."

"I have time for dinner tomorrow," Saffron said.

Her mother dipped her head graciously. "You pick the restaurant and let me know what time. You have my number." She started down the stairs but paused at the bottom, turning to say, "Thank you for helping your sister. She's begun talking about placing the baby for adoption. I know it would be the best thing, but I admit I've grown attached to the idea of having a grandbaby."

Saffron stood there mutely, pondering her mother's words. She half expected the old hurts to take control of her heart, the longing for her son to bring tears, but all she felt was regret for the past and hope for Kendall's future. No matter what had happened, the past made her who she was today—and she liked herself.

Vaughn came out the front door, his arm slipping around her waist. "All finished unloading." He smiled and nodded at her mother before adding to Saffron, "Hey, the girls want to see that new game we're testing for Datatoon. You should come see if you can pick out the one animation I did for it."

He'd decided to take the job Datatoon was offering after the school year ended, but only if he could work from Arizona, commuting monthly for a week at a time as needed. Saffron knew that was for her, but maybe someday she'd be ready to go farther away from Lily's House.

"Well, I'll see you tomorrow," her mother said. "I'm glad to see you two happy."

They watched her go down the walk to the car parked in the driveway. "She's so different, and yet still so . . ."

"Dragonlike?" Vaughn ventured.

She slugged him. "No . . . well, yes." She paused. "It feels good to let the past go."

"I'm glad." He nibbled at her ear, his warm breath tickling her, and she couldn't help rotating to kiss him. "Well?" he said between kisses. "How about my illustration? I'll even show you the room where it's hidden."

"Let's do it."

She let herself be led inside to the newly added game room off the kitchen, where Kendall, Halla, Lily, Mario, Zoey, Ruth, Bianca, Elsie, and at least a dozen other current and former foster girls had gathered. Saffron settled on the couch, wedged between Vaughn and Halla. Someone put a controller into her hands.

"This is a super awesome game," Halla said.

Saffron's rather sexy female character was wearing pink polka-dotted shorts. "Is your animation the shorts?" she asked.

Vaughn smirked. "No. That was one of the guys at Datatoon."

"Right." He'd told her they hadn't stopped teasing him about her appearance there.

"Follow my character," Vaughn said. "I'll show you the room where it is."

Saffron followed him to a dragon cave where piles of coins littered the floor.

"Watch out for the dragon!" Halla warned, nearly too late.

Saffron wielded her sword, battling the dragon, and Vaughn joined her. Soon the dragon flew away, licking its wounds.

All the animations were excellent. From the stalactites on the ceiling to the realistic coins and jewels scattered under her feet. "Hmm, that shield up on top of the treasure pile?"

"Nope," Vaughn said. "That's part of the real game. My animation was put in only for those of us who know."

Something in the way he said it reminded Saffron of her visit to Datatoon and her conversation with Belladonna about the programmer who had proposed to the woman in accounting. Saffron didn't play games much either, but Vaughn really wanted her to see this. Could he have made it just for her?

Heart pounding and anticipation making her clumsy,

she searched the room, touching objects, lifting or hacking them open with her sword. Nothing. She moved her character deeper, into an inner chamber, sweeping the area with an animated magic flame. All the girls seemed to hold their breaths. It was in this room then, and they all knew about it.

Vaughn grinned encouragingly. The press of his leg against hers was both distracting and compelling.

Where could it be?

There. On the ledge, sitting inconspicuously next to richer-looking goblets, was a short silver cup that resembled one Vaughn used in his apartment to toss his extra change. She moved her character next to it, reaching up high for the cup. She couldn't quite grab it, so she scooted over a gold chest from the corner and stepped up on it. The moment she placed a hand on the silver finish, the cup disappeared and a huge diamond ring rose in a flurry of magic light.

Blinking words flashed across the screen: Saffron, will you marry me?

She turned to Vaughn, who was holding out a ring, the exact one she and the oh-so-sneaky Halla had been admiring last week at the mall.

"Well?" he asked. "Will you?"

She nodded. "Yes. Oh, yes, I will."

Rachel Branton has worked in publishing for over twenty years. She loves writing women's fiction and traveling, and she hopes to write and travel a lot more. As a mother of seven, it's not easy to find time to write, but the semi-ordered chaos gives her a constant source of writing material. She's been known to wear pajamas all day when working on a deadline, and is often distracted enough to burn dinner. (Okay, pretty much 90% of the time.) A sign on her office door reads: Danger. Enter at Your Own Risk. Writer at Work. Under the name Rachel Branton, she writes romance, romantic suspense, and women's fiction. Rachel also writes urban fantasy, paranormal romance, and science fiction under the name Teyla Branton. For more information and to download a free Lily's House novella, please visit www.RachelBranton.com.